TUNNEL VISION

A COLDWATER CHRONICLES THRILLER

D. R. YOUNG

DRYWRITES.COM

First edition

ISBN: 979-8-9931410-0-8

Ebook ISBN: 979-8-9931410-1-5

CONTENTS

"Choice, not chance,
determines your destiny."

- Aristotle

1

A DIFFERENT KIND OF MONDAY

Through the streaked glass of his 1972 Dodge Dart, John Chance drew a deep breath and squinted into Coldwater's morning sun. The red brick of the county courthouse across the street beckoned to him. One week into his new role as a prosecutor, and Coldwater already felt like a cage.

He'd been forced to return home after seven years of college and law school. Like it or not, he was now serving a six-month employment sentence before he could escape.

He had plans—big ones—and they didn't unfold in this sleepy town in southeastern Missouri. Ninety minutes north, St. Louis' skyline and a better prosecutor's job beckoned, promising a future far from Coldwater's quiet and boring streets. He received last-minute word that the position wouldn't be ready until the New Year, which meant he'd have to hole up here, confident that nothing in this town could derail his long-held plans.

Except for the first time he saw Annaleigh Stanton.

It was late May, and more than just the weather was starting to heat up. Merely being in her orbit stirred a dangerous temptation to stay.

Each morning, he timed his arrival at 8:15 sharp, his heart quickening as her car pulled into the parking lot. Their walk across the tree-lined street circling the courthouse became a cherished ritual. Five extra minutes of easy laughter and small talk, and her face beamed with every word. After holding the heavy door for her, he'd catch her warm smile and usher her inside with a chivalrous act they both appreciated.

With every unconscious flick of her hand, tucking rogue brunette strands behind her ear, he fell further into trouble. The kind that could make a man forget his St. Louis dreams and chain himself to this backwater town only to be nearer to her.

She was the entire package. Short brown hair that danced in the spring breeze. Long, thin legs stretched her to an impressive five-foot-ten, allowing her to look most opposing counsels eye to eye. It also brought her to only three inches shy of John's height, except for the days when she chose wedges.

She also wielded a mind sharper than his, though he'd only admit that one when alone. John prided himself on being the smartest. Throughout high school, college, law school, and even at his graduation a month ago, he was top of his class. Yet here, in Coldwater, Annaleigh easily outshone him. It was the first time he didn't hate coming in second to a peer.

The morning's rising heat threatened to plaster his suit to his back as he waited in his usual spot. At 8:22, her cherry red Chevy Cavalier purred into the lot, tires squeaking. He stepped out, catching lavender perfume through her open window.

"Morning, Annaleigh," he said, same as every day. She smirked, slinging a satchel over her shoulder.

"Waiting for me again?" Her repeated tease carried a playful edge that made his pulse jump.

"Nope, just got here." Every morning, the same white lie.

She wasn't his boss. "I'm just your mentor," she'd insisted all week. The orders she barked suggested otherwise. Six months in Coldwater? With her? There were certainly worse fates.

While he mused, she surged ahead and reached the door first. He had glanced away for only a moment, but lost her in the shadowy rings plaguing his peripheral vision.

Damn these eyes, John thought.

With a purposeful tug of the handle, the door creaked open under her pull.

"Lawyers who haven't passed the bar exam go first."

He squared his shoulders, chin raised. "Next testing slot is coming up soon. I bet I'll break 300. Not many people do, I hear."

Her laugh was warm, but her eyes flicked past him, toward the courthouse's shadowed entrance. "You better. I got 309. Now, in you go." Her free hand waved him forward as her satchel swayed in the air.

They climbed the stairs, her trendy, slim-fitting pant suit rustling, his steps heavier than he meant. At the top, the musty scent of old paper hit hard and drew him in. He savored it, but wished the scent also came with a view of the Arch.

Standing guard over the entrance to the bullpen stood the tastefully decorated desk of Eugenia Johnson. Though no one dared to call her that.

Her official name plate sat covered with sticky notes that articulated her *real* name in handwritten, blue ink—Genie Glitter. Despite her repeated requests, her boss, Coldwater County Prosecutor Doyal Gamble, refused to spend money on a new nameplate for a self-given nickname.

John learned a quick lesson within three minutes of arriving on his first day after he peeked under the sticky notes.

"Now, sugar," she had said, in the smoothest Southern drawl he'd ever heard, "what's under them notes is of no consequence. What you see is what you get, and I'm all glitter." She modeled her larger-than-life platinum blonde hair, waving her hands around its volume. He had tried to apologize, but her honey twang wouldn't allow it. "No need for sorries, darling. Life's a stage, and I treat everything like opening night. Once you say something, it's out there. But we all know you're trying your best. Stick with me and I'll teach you how to shine!"

Ever since, she'd provided some of the brightest parts of his days. Literally. Her outfits could have her headlining at the Grand Ole Opry. Twice, in one week, he'd seen her sport a white jacket with rhinestones swirling around each shoulder over a light blue buttoned-up shirt that, from most angles, looked to be made completely of multi-colored sequins. The bright parts of his day, indeed.

Her desk sat unusually empty, with her chair tucked into its hollow. Annaleigh frowned, circling it.

"Genie's never late."

"Agreed, although I can only confirm for the past five days. Without that shimmer and hearing her trademark jingle, I'm not sure I can echolocate where I sit," John said, trying to contain a grin. "She's like a lighthouse, guiding me to my notepads and pens."

Annaleigh's frown curled upward. "Well, it's been nine months for me, and she's never missed. But, I'm with you. She's my favorite disco ball, too."

"She told me once she hadn't taken a sick day since Reagan. I didn't realize we were supposed to keep time via an election cycle." He set his case on his desk and looked around. "She's not in the conference room."

"That woman's a tank. Perhaps Mr. Johnson kept her, if you get my drift." She stifled a giggle, caught herself, and straightened her posture.

John's head snapped to her. "Ew. Now that you've brought it up, though, are we supposed to call him Mr. Johnson? Or, maybe Mr. Glitter? She hasn't said, and I was a little afraid to ask."

Annaleigh shrugged as she glided towards her office. "Same here. Dealer's choice, I guess—"

John and Annaleigh flinched in unison as Doyal Gamble's office banged open and Coldwater's mayor, Cameron Raith, stepped out. He shut it fast behind him and straightened the jacket of his tailored suit and adjusted the wide curl of his cowboy hat.

"Wasn't expectin' company so early," he drawled, slow and syrupy.

"Mr. Mayor," Annaleigh said, surprise threading her tone. "Surprised to see you as well, sir. What brings you here this morning?"

John's gut tightened. Last week's initial meeting with the mayor didn't go quite as desired. At least, this time, Raith was alone and not toting around his hulking sidekick. Gamble seemed stressed after every meeting with the man. John braced for frost, hoped for jovial. Raith strode over, boots thudding on warped boards, trailing a faint tang of chewing tobacco and leather. Their hands clasped, and Raith's iron-hard grip numbed John's knuckles.

"We can shake this time, young man," he said, chest puffing, chin high.

I guess it's frost.

"Appreciate it, mayor," John said, matching the stare. "No bodyguard today?"

"No need for him right now. That is, unless you're a threat?" Raith's chin climbed, peering down his nose, jerking John close.

John's jaw bit down, his cheeks reddening. He realized the true meaning of Gamble's warning to always watch your words around Raith.

"Not at all, sir," he said, voice low, eyes unflinching. "It was just a casual remark—"

Raith threw John's hand mid-thought and spun to Annaleigh. "Y'all must be wonderin' why I'm here."

Annaleigh's brows dropped as mental dominoes fell. "Genie!" she blurted. "Where is she? Is she okay?"

"Sent your secretary home. She's fine, by the way," Raith said, waving it off. "No need to fret."

"It's Gamble, then..." John muttered.

Raith's emotionless glare swiveled to meet his. "There's been a tragedy. Sit down." He pointed to the bullpen chairs.

John eased into his chair, leaned back, and rubbed his chin. Annaleigh perched on the edge of hers, arms crossed.

Raith feigned sitting but instead slid a nearby chair under a desk. He remained towering above them.

"There's no sugar coatin' this. Doyal Gamble is dead."

Annaleigh gasped, hand to mouth, eyes watering.

John clenched his gut. He kept his eyes dry as shame flared within. Two disgraceful thoughts materialized. His first thought was to grab her hand. The second, if he'd still have a job. He swallowed both.

"Dead?" She shot up, voice cracking. "What happened?"

"Somethin' not natural, I reckon," Raith said, yanking his hat off, gray hair mussed. "Least not from what I saw. Unusual, twisted, like he pissed somebody off real good." His chuckle slithered out, mirthless, chilling the room. "I guess lawyers can't argue their way out of everythin', eh?"

John shivered.

How could he be so flippant at a time like this?

"Unusual, how?" he asked, rising. He held his voice firm, despite the forming knot in his throat.

"That's all for now," Raith said, gesturing to the stairs. "Crime scene's waitin'. They need you to ID what's left of him, Ms. Stanton. I already did, but the Sheriff asked for you. As if the mayor's word ain't strong enough."

Annaleigh's jaw tightened as Coldwater's mayor laid a thick hand on her shoulder. She stared into the void below her feet.

"There's no preparin' you for what you're gonna see, by the way. It's not pretty," he added. "Not tryin' to sound callous. Doyal was a friend. We all deal with tragedy in different ways."

John grabbed his keys, slid his arm around her shoulders, and eased her away.

"I'll drive."

She didn't resist being led away. They trailed Raith out of the building, each footstep hitting sharply on the stairs. His black Chevrolet Blazer gleamed around the corner, hood scratched just right and carrying the right amount of dirt on the grill, a Coldwater trademark of pushing fallen branches off the road after a spring storm.

"I'll lead," Raith called out.

John guided Annaleigh across the street, returning to the scene of hopeful smiles and teases mere moments earlier. He opened the Dart's passenger door, and Annaleigh slipped in, silent.

Closing the door, he scanned the town square, Ozark plateau dust swirling lazily in the early day sun. A distant pickup rumbled, muffler coughing, as crows cawed from the distant hills. It was before nine and most shops were still shuttered, yet to open. The sidewalks, eerily hushed, begged for foot traffic.

John grew up here. These kinds of tragic events don't happen in this town.

A lot changed while I was gone. And, not for the better.

The car door slammed shut behind him as he glanced at his passenger. Her eyes were no longer wet. Rage had evaporated the tears, leaving only red singe marks painting her sclera. She buckled hard, belt snapping taut.

"Drive," she commanded.

John turned the key and pointed the car at his first crime scene.

2

DUBIOUS FIRST IMPRESSION

John hated to drive.

Not because of idiot drivers who drove too slowly or those who forgot to follow simple instructions, such as the one that indicated a complete stop at those pesky red, octagonal signs. He winced and shuddered when he witnessed those and sometimes pictured violent thoughts—like wishing he could deflate their tires with a flick of his hand.

He didn't hate to drive due to the Dart's uncomfortable vinyl seats and how they squeaked with every movement. It wasn't the glitches in the AM/FM radio dial, slipping with every bump and losing the signal.

Nor was it the pull handle of the headlights, designed in such a way that it would deactivate when pulling the door handle.

It wasn't even because of the Dart's oddest design, the floor-mounted button that toggled the high beams.

No, he hated driving because it was mentally draining.

The only saving grace on the drive to the crime scene was that it unfolded in daylight. He found driving at night far worse.

Botched eye surgeries had scarred his vision, trapping his periphery in a ring of shadows. Seeing objects or people meant looking at them directly. Once something moved to the side, it became lost in the haze.

Simple tasks now demanded focused effort, exhausting him. Reading the menu at a fast-food joint strained his eyes. Walking took even more dedication lest he bump into something, or someone, that teleported into view from the edge.

Driving took hardened vigilance. His eyes darted left and right, protecting the journey, but generating headaches. His head constantly pivoted, making him look like an animatronic. All for the noble purpose of building a one-hundred-eighty-degree field of vision. A field of vision that everyone else claimed for free.

At least this drive was different. It had a purpose, even if it meant his role was chauffeur. He did it for Annaleigh. And, for the memory of Doyal Gamble.

The vintage road to the crime scene stretched ahead, two lanes of chipped asphalt that glistened in the morning light. Needles from the flanking pines shone with dew, adding to the other stimuli catching his attention.

His eyes ached from the glare, but he didn't dare blink. Not yet. Not with Annaleigh beside him, sharing his silent dread and imagining the horror they were about to witness.

Unusual. Twisted. What were they about to walk into?

Flashes of red and blue clawed across his rearview mirror.

Not again. Not today, damn it.

He flicked his gaze up, catching the cruiser's silhouette drawing closer, its siren a crescendo slicking through the Coldwater stillness. His jaw clenched, and blood rushed to his cheeks as the memory hit.

One week ago, day one, almost this exact time, when similar lights sank their first bite into him.

He had just left the confines of his childhood home, heading to his first day of work in this same Dart. He had only made a few turns before hitting the narrow street that wound its way to the courthouse and Coldwater's infamous town square. The unstriped, two-lane road had been empty, only him and the hum of its 6-cylinder engine, until those American cherries had splayed across his rearview. The siren's sudden wail had been the perfect frequency to make his arm hair stand on end.

John cursed under his breath, eased the gas, and drifted the car onto the shoulder. The tires crunched to a stop on the gravel. A small cloud of dust rose and floated forward in the breeze. It didn't want to be here, either.

The sun-baked dashboard radiated under his twitching fingers as the man in uniform approached, his shimmering badge joining the pine needles. He leaned in through the rolled-down window, close enough for John to smell his wafting aftershave—cheap, with a hint of cedar.

"Did I do something wrong, Officer?" he said, biting his tongue, refusing to name-drop himself.

"It's Sheriff, John. Sheriff Dane Parnell. Welcome back to Coldwater."

John remembered the feeling of shock and inadequacy, always having prided himself on being the most knowledgeable in any debate. One day in Coldwater, and he'd already lost his footing.

As the two men exchanged wry remarks, Sheriff Parnell's eyes danced with amusement, already privy to copious bits of information about John's life and return to Coldwater. John surmised that his mother was the source of Parnell's knowledge, due to her extreme fondness for sharing family updates with anyone and everyone. The exchange left him slightly off-balance, as if he were navigating a game of verbal chess with an old pro.

"Well, I know sometimes I run to my mom for info. I guess I didn't expect law enforcement to do the same."

"Information can be true, John, no matter where it comes from," Parnell rasped, his country voice low and slow. "I've known Bonnie quite a while now. I trust her. I've only known you for three minutes. Feel free to interpret that however you wish."

"Wow, great tip, sir. Truly sage advice. I'm so glad the opportunity arose that you could share it with me."

In John's memory, his line exited his mouth without any hint of sarcasm. Based on Parnell's reaction, memories can be a fickle thing.

"Oh, you want advice? Fine, here's what I got, young man. Many in this town will have your best interests at heart. They won't be ashamed to let you know it, either—good people, most of 'em. There are also a few who don't care about you or your interests, only how you can help them advance theirs. You'd be wise to tell the two apart and align yourself on the right side."

"Sheriff, we *are* on the same side. At least, I thought we were."

Parnell tapped the Dart door and forced a smile that caused his thin mustache to wrinkle. "Keep your eyes open, son. Good choices are out there. It's up to you to find them."

Then, he walked away. No salutation, no handshake. A simple pat of the car door and a casual, country stroll back to his black cruiser as his boots squished through the gravel. John had driven away, Parnell's red and blue lights shrinking in the mirror while the cryptic warning had stuck in his mind.

Now, those familiar lights yanked him back. The oncoming cruiser, white and menacing, roared closer, unrelenting. John's pulse raced, sweat beading on his neck.

Was Parnell tailing him again? Testing him?

The cruiser blew past and continued ahead.

Someone else's problem now.

His focus continued to follow it, glossing over the decreasing speed of the mayor's SUV. He squinted, still locked onto the flashing lights.

"John! Turn—now!" Annaleigh's shout cracked the haze, as sharp as a gavel strike. Her hand jabbed the air, suit jacket sleeve rustling.

Jolted, he snapped his head around, catching her with wide eyes, red-rimmed and fierce. No time to argue. His foot jammed the brake as the tires kissed the road's edge, kicking up rocks and pinging the undercarriage. He yanked the wheel hard, lurching to the right down an unpaved road, dust swirling in their wake.

"Sorry," he said, frowning. "All good. Paying better attention, starting now."

The crime scene sprawled ahead, a jagged clearing leading into the pines, yellow tape flapping in the breeze like a wounded bird. The air thickened, heavy with the scent of scorched wood and something sour.

John killed the engine, keys jangling as he shoved them in his pocket. His loafers hit the dirt as he made his way around to get her door. Annaleigh slipped out, her slim-fitting pant suit whispering against her legs, her scent a fleeting lifeline in the stench.

She didn't look at him. She couldn't. Her gaze locked onto the chaos beyond the tape. Deputies milled about, a tarp fluttered, the excited buzz of flies permeated the air, and amidst it all, stood Parnell.

There he was, on the far side of the tape, hands on his hips, silhouette slicing the sun into shards. His hat covered his eyes, and yet John felt the weight of that stare once again, heavy as a judge's verdict. No drawl, no cryptic quip. Only silence, thick and waiting, like the moment before a storm breaks.

John squared his shoulders, chin lifting as he strode forward. Annaleigh kept pace, her breath shallow but steady, her wedges sinking slightly into the soft earth.

Up close, the scene sharpened. The tarp's edges whipped in the breeze to reveal momentary glints of sunlight reflecting off a pair of black dress shoes. A whiff of singed flesh hit his nose like a punch. He swallowed hard, tasting bile, his stomach flipping again.

Unusual. Twisted.

Mayor Raith's words thumped in John's chest. He could feel them now, beating inside him like a drum.

We need you to ID what's left of him.

Last week's warning from Parnell echoed in his skull, louder now, as the Sheriff's shadow stretched toward him. The man John had aligned with was now dead.

Did I choose the wrong side?

Whatever came next, whether it was words, a glare, or a test, it wouldn't be gentle.

Not with Parnell.

3

FALLING INTO PIECES

T all pines shrouded the crime scene, sprawled at the far edge of a dewed clearing. Their sap scent cut the morning chill and mixed with the murmurs of deputies beyond the yellow tape. John squinted, shadows dancing on the edges—*these damn eyes*—unnervingly focusing on what waited.

The tree trunks and leafy bushes served as natural boundary markers. Luckily, for Detective Hollis Mumber, it meant he didn't have to drag out the metal stakes from the trunk of his brown Caprice. In typical Mumber fashion, he miscalculated the strength of the bushes on the far corner. The branch had since snapped, leaving one side of the lopsided polygon to flap in the occasional breeze.

The same wind that toyed with the tape lifted sections of the tarp, releasing into the air a burnt tag that stung John's nose.

Shadows from the grove drenched most of the scene, although a few focused beams of sunlight snuck through the canopy, as if trying to highlight the unspeakable acts that had taken place here.

Annaleigh joined John at the edge of the tarp, leaving Raith far behind up on the road. Staccato breaths betrayed her firm exterior. Like John, she was doing everything possible to hold it together.

Mumber waddled over to them and nudged a thick chunk of wood from the corner of the tarp, keeping his foot in place to keep it from prematurely uncovering.

"Normally... we'd reveal the face of the victim to ask for identification." He compressed his wrinkled hands together. "In this case... it wouldn't help. So we'll show you the entire body. Are you ready?"

They exchanged confused glances, then replied to Mumber with a series of uncertain nods. A final warning from the detective landed hard.

"If you need to vomit... please don't do it on the body."

Mumber raised his chin to a nearby deputy, who removed a rock at the other end of the tarp. They worked in unison to peel it away.

John's stomach flipped, sweat prickling his neck as he choked back bile. He slammed the back of his fingers against his mouth, and his knees wavered, the ground tilting under him. Annaleigh's inhale rasped beside him. Her hand dug into his arm. Her eyes darted to the sky. Like him, she tried everything, as if she could unsee it.

A lifeless husk lay where they expected to see their boss. Doyal Gamble was dressed in the fitted navy suit that he wore every day. Dirt matted on his pants, around his shins, as if he'd fallen. Across his torso, blood stains had turned his white shirt a deep shade of crimson.

His naturally high hairline of brown and gray speckled hair was intact, but below that, to his chin, there was nothing.

No face.

No shape.

No distinguishable features of any kind.

What remained was a concave crater filled with crusting red goo and pink tissue.

Skin drooped off the side, flapping over his ears.

Everything was melted away, like the remnant of a long-burning candle. The grotesque sight reminded John of a failed clay figure, misshapen by a lingering sun.

John's throat tightened, but he was unable to look away from the inhuman sight. His eyes drifted downward from Gamble's missing face and encountered another anomaly.

Beyond their feet, the man's left arm ended in a scorched stump just below the shoulder. Cauterized muscle tissue and skin receded enough to expose a rounded end of bone, dotted with crimson ash.

Annaleigh drooped her head. Her other hand clutched her chest, wincing with empathetic pain. With shaking fingers, she pointed to the monogrammed pocket square, its silk blackened at the edges.

"D.G.," she muttered. "That's him."

Gamble's right hand, still intact and lying palm down in the grass, caught John's gaze. Staring at the blood-streaked ring gleaming on his pinky, his hand rose, squeezing the air, feigning a handshake as he disappeared into a memory.

"John, nice to finally meet you. I'm Doyal Gamble, Prosecutor of Coldwater County." His voice, much like his slender frame, had possessed a delicate quality that seemed to waver on the brink of being whisked away by the slightest breeze.

"Same to you, sir." They had shaken hands, surprisingly violent, with Gamble raising and lowering John's hand further than anyone ever had. It came off as passionate, not controlling, but still a jolt. John did his best to hide a wince as the man's large pinky ring gouged into John's fingers.

"Come on in and have a seat." Gamble ushered John into his office, strode around, and sat down in an ornate, leather high-back chair. John chose the only available spot, an unassuming seat with paisley upholstery facing his new boss. His shoes scuffed the worn rug, his gaze snagging on an obnoxious number of photos on the wall.

Gamble with the Governor.

Gamble with the state's Attorney General.

Gamble with some blonde guy in a suit.

In fact, every photo included him with another well-coiffed man, grinning like old frat brothers.

Noticing John looking at his ego wall, he launched into a myriad of tales, outlining in exquisite detail backstage introductions, late-night deals, courtroom wins, and a senator's cigar-fueled rant. John nodded, jaw aching from forced smiles, wondering how this peacock had time to serve justice to an entire county.

"Mr. Gamble, this is all very impressive." He had remembered advice from his mother, Bonnie, who taught him that a little grease goes a long way.

"First, call me Gamble. You can drop the 'mister'. And, yes. Yes, it is impressive, I agree," he replied with a broad, toothy smile.

John attempted to change the subject. "I noticed that the office is pretty quiet this morning. In fact, the only person I saw out there was your secretary, who, by the way, has the most unusual name I've ever heard. Quite the character. Are the other associates due in later? The ones I'll be working with?"

Gamble rubbed his pointy chin. "We call them staff attorneys around here, but an astute observation, young man. The answer is no, they will not be in later."

John sported a quizzical look.

"We're used to running a lean ship here, but it's been a little leaner, as of late." Gamble unfurled both of his hands. "Seated in your chair are all the staff attorneys I employ."

"I didn't realize that, sir." He gulped. "Not quite what I expected. Doesn't matter to me, I'm up for the challenge."

"That's what I like to hear. We're going to get along fine." Gamble's practiced, toothy smile returned. John's eyes drifted upward, and he realized it matched all the photographs.

"There *is* another lawyer here, though, just not at the same level as you. My assistant prosecutor is downstairs in court. You'll meet her a bit later. Smart as a tack that one. Most likely you'll end up learning more from her than from me." He chuckled, stood up, and stretched out his hand again. "Welcome to the law."

"Mr. Chance?" Detective Mumber cleared his throat. "Mr. Chance?" Mumber's voice and repeated snaps cut through the fog and brought John out of the past. "I said... would you like to provide a secondary ID?"

John's chest was heavy with grief. Gamble's laugh still echoed in his mind. "Yeah, that's his ring. It's him. It's Gamble."

At the mention of his name, Annaleigh stifled a sob.

Mumber and the deputy folded the tarp over and returned the small wood stumps to their respective corners. The detective fumbled the tree chunk, nearly dropping it, and muttered to himself.

"That'll be all for now, thanks," he said. "I'll expect you two to come by the station to give your formal statements." He paused, fishing for words, then added with a hesitant tone that undercut the command, "And, uh... don't talk to nobody about this, not yet. Sheriff's orders."

Parnell lingered by the tape, boots rooted, never crossing close to the tarp. John caught him gesturing deputies to keep clear, voice low—like a conductor dodging the stage.

Why stay all the way back here?

John's gut twisted. Parnell knew more than he let on, same as that traffic stop. His stare bore deep. "See you at the station later. Be ready with your alibis."

"You think one of us did this?" John said, incredulously. "Are you serious?" Annaleigh's arms halted John's movement, bracing across his chest.

"Not now," she said, gaining her composure. She eyed the Sheriff and offered her best "thank you" smile.

Parnell raised the yellow tape and gestured for them to exit. "My condolences, Ms. Stanton," he drawled.

John followed Annaleigh and ducked under the tape. With each step, pine sap fought hard to overtake the stench floating in the air. He glanced at her, searching for the words. Her flushed cheeks, red-rimmed eyes, and clenched jaw told a deeper story of what she was holding back.

"This isn't right," he muttered, out of Parnell's earshot. "I know you keep defending that guy, but he's had it out for me ever since I came back. I'm still ticked at his little traffic stop stunt."

Squished footsteps turned crunchy as they passed from the grass clearing to the gravel shoulder.

"You have to see it from his perspective," Annaleigh said. "Trust is earned, not given. You may be from here, but you haven't lived here for seven years. It's a fresh slate now, and you're a completely different person. Some advice, respect the position, if not the man."

They froze mid-step, the wail of sirens and shouts of first responders drowning out the frenzy. No thudding boots this time. No warning barge from the shadows of Gamble's office, like earlier.

Mayor Raith appeared as a flicker from between the parked sedans, hat brim low, coating his darkened eyes. He inserted himself squarely in their path. His hand clamped Annaleigh's shoulder, heavy and deliberate. Her flinch jolted John's pulse. Raith's eyes flicked to him, daring a move, then his focus settled back on her.

"Ms. Stanton," he drawled, viscous and thick. "We need to have an uncomfortable conversation."

4

UPWARD MOBILITY

Annaleigh Stanton planted her wedges in the gravel, its bite sharp through her soles. The air still held captive faint traces of scorched flesh, but she masked her nausea.

Coldwater's mayor, Cameron Raith, had sprang out of nowhere, providing her and John yet another fright. The middle-aged man had closed in, much quicker than she expected. Closer, too.

His hand clamped her shoulder with a hot, heavy grip exuding hints of aftershave that wafted from his cuff. The touch lingered too long. Words exited his mouth as a monotonous, unrecognizable buzz. She'd felt a hand like this before. Her skin crawled, a memory of stale cologne and a locked office door.

She exhaled, suppressing the shudder.

She shifted her weight, allowing the subtle movement to dislodge his hand. She stepped backwards and stood next to John.

"Sorry, Mayor. What did you say?"

"I said we need to have an uncomfortable conversation, young lady. In light of what you saw down there." He motioned across the clearing and toward the tarp. She swallowed hard.

"Of course, sir. I completely understand. If I were in your

situation, I'd do the same thing. Bringing in a seasoned prosecutor from a different jurisdiction is the right move—"

"Bring a stranger into our town?" He side-eyed John. "No offense, son. You're a boomerang, so I'm compelled to count you as a familiar."

In her peripheral vision, she noticed John's head cock. She offered him a reassuring glance and a head shake with an intent for him to let it go. His shoulders relaxed.

"No ma'am," Raith said, his focus shifted back on her. "I'm not goin' to do that. Sounds like you don't have a lot of confidence in yourself. Gonna have to fix that if you're to become a lady prosecutor."

It was as if she were in court and the opposing lawyer had objected. A reasoned retort erupted.

"Mayor, if you know me at all, you'll realize a lack of confidence is not in my inventory of skills. The best litigator in this town *is* a lady prosecutor." Her eyes drifted to the tape, a flicker of regret she buried. She squared her shoulders, voice steady.

"There it is. The kind of fire I like to see." He stuck out his hand. "That's why I'm appointin' you to the role of Interim County Prosecutor. What do you think about that?"

She couldn't think of anything except Gamble's melted face. The stench of charred flesh clung to her suit jacket, the stump of his arm's moist reflection replaying in her mind. She'd scrub it out later, alone. It may not ever come out.

Her chin lifted, a practiced nod signaling acceptance. This was not expected, but duty demanded precision, not sentiment.

"I can't fill his shoes, but I'll do my best to try. However, the County Prosecutor is an elected position. Does a mayor have the power to—"

"Damn right a mayor does. In the event of an unforeseen tragedy, such as this one, I can appoint anyone to do anythin'." A big, broad smile stretched across his face. "At least, until we gather the funds up for a special election, of course." He winked. She silenced another shudder growing up her spine.

"Understood. I appreciate the opportunity, though it's certainly not how I wanted it to happen." She motioned to John. "He started last week but hasn't passed the bar exam yet—it's not until July—so he can't legally represent us in court. I already handle most of the open cases, but there are other duties I'll need to take on. It's going to be a lot, sir. We might need another—"

"Spare the legalese, Counselor. For now, I need you to clear the deck. Move 'em, close 'em, I don't care. I've got a job for the two of you that takes priority." This time, it was her head that cocked to the side as Raith continued. "The Sheriff's Office will be startin' an investigation with their *prized* detective. I want you to start a different one. For me," he said with a finger point. "I want you to dig through any case Gamble ever touched and look for clues, evidence, whatever *fancy* term lawyers have. Somethin' that might identify who could have done this. You talk to every lunatic in this town and get some answers." The mayor leaned in and dipped his head, staring at her through his brows. "And, if you find anythin', you come and tell me *first*."

They stood motionless, trying to absorb Raith's unorthodox request. John rubbed his chin.

"You mean if we discover the identity of a murderer, you don't want us to take that straight to law enforcement?"

A feeling of pride welled up inside Annaleigh, knowing of John's thoughts of Parnell. Her comment about respecting the Sheriff's position had apparently resonated with him.

Raith noticed a younger deputy loitering nearby and waved him away. Once alone with the two prosecutors, his boasty drawl turned deeper and softer.

"I'm gonna to share somethin' with you, but this is confidential, so it can't leave this spot." He again looked over his shoulder. "For a while now, your boss and I have been worried about the Sheriff and his little 'special investigation division'. We weren't sure they've been actin' on the up and up, if you get my drift. Truth be told, City Hall has lost some trust with the Sheriff's whole department." He pointed again at the crime scene. "With poor Doyal lying in pieces over there, I believe there's been an attack on this town and its leadership."

She exchanged a worrisome glance with John.

"Until we know what we're dealin' with here," Raith said, "we need to keep it in the family. The last thing I want is for that *goddamn Mumber* to fuck everythin' up."

Every prosecutor she'd ever worked with cussed like a sailor, but it was the first time she'd heard the mayor use the words.

"Is that understood?" Raith asked, with force.

Annaleigh shook her head. "Sir, I coordinate with the Sheriff and Detective Mumber all the time. We're all supposed to be partners—"

"Ms. Stanton, you aren't workin' with all the facts. What I'm askin' is in the best interest of the town."

She paused, contemplating her response. She was wading into dangerous waters. As a prosecutor, court rules dictated that she share with opposing counsel. She had extended that habit to law enforcement. It was not in her nature to obscure.

"If you reveal more, it would be easier to align with your current strategy... sir."

"That's enough," Raith said, groaning theatrically. "Trust me and do what I say. If you play your cards right, you never know what doors might open for you in this town." His eyes narrowed. "Or, which ones close. Now, are you onboard, or did I make a mistake in appointin' you to run this operation?"

The yellow tape flapped in the wind, a sharp sound in her ears. A stark reminder of what was in the dewy grass. This was neither the time nor the place to continue fighting. She wouldn't win, anyway. Not this argument, not on the side of the road, and Gamble's corpse fifty yards away.

She raised her chin. "Yes."

"Yes, I made a mistake?"

"No, sir. You did *not* make a mistake. Yes, sir, I get it. We'll coordinate with you first."

"Are you kidding me?" John blurted out. "Annaleigh, what are you doing?"

She held up her hand to him, stopping him. Raith shot a glare at him before reconnecting with Annaleigh's stare. Her lips were the only part of her face that moved.

"All we want is to find the son-of-a-bitch who did this and make him pay. Whatever that takes."

"Good. Get to it."

Back at the Dart and alone, she slumped and leaned against the hood. "I can't believe Gamble's really gone."

John slid next to her and reclined. "I'm sorry about him. You knew him longer than I did. I'm not sure what I can say."

A cool breeze grazed her face, bringing a respite of freshness. Her neck ached from holding steady, her eyes burned as she tilted back, Gamble's absence a weight she couldn't shake. Reading the situation, he said nothing, savoring the fresh air. After a time, she broke the moment.

"I wanted to do this job at some point, but I never imagined it would be like this." She flattened her hand and spied her fingers. "God, they're shaking a little bit. That's new. I'm glad you're here, John. You don't know how much. Listen, back there, I didn't mean to talk down about you about not taking the bar exam yet. I hope you understood what I meant."

"Yeah, I get it. Just facts. Were you serious when you agreed to keep the Sheriff out of the loop? I know I haven't had the best experience with him so far, but locking out law enforcement from what we find?"

"Don't worry," she said. "I just wanted the conversation to end. I have no intention of running a private investigation. You and I are going to be quite busy reviewing every case Gamble worked. As long as it takes. His killer could be someone who still holds a grudge."

John sighed. "Listen, I think I need to tell you something."

"What's that? You're too good for case review?"

"No, that's not it," he said. "I didn't have an opportunity to tell Gamble, so I might as well tell you now. I'm not staying in Coldwater."

Her stomach tightened, a sensation she ignored. It was like she was standing in front of Gamble's body again. "You're leaving? Already? You just got here."

"Not right away. In six months. End of the year."

She clicked her tongue. "John Chance, too good to work in his hometown?"

He shrugged. "Last summer, I interned at the state courthouse in Jefferson City. I helped the guy who is now the County Prosecutor in St. Louis. A long-time attorney on his staff is retiring. He said the opening is mine."

"Oh." She hid her emotion from him, keeping her face stoic. "Well, I guess we'll have to solve this case before you leave. Give you something to add to your CV." She stood and straightened her jacket. "We'll mourn when this is over. Let's get to work."

* * *

JOHN SCRUBBED a grease-smeared plate as warm water splashed his wrists. The casserole's lingering scent mixed with dish soap. Bits of overcooked noodles flopped around as he cleaned, triggering visions of charred skin. He blinked hard to reset his mind.

His mom's shadow darted into his narrowed vision as she dried a glass, causing squeaks against the towel.

"She didn't want me to see it, Mom, but Annaleigh was crushed that I'm going to leave."

Bonnie squinted, shaking her head. "You dropped that news on her right after you both saw a dead body, God rest his soul. Bad timing, son. You'll learn. On the brighter side, she got promoted today, I hear."

John shut off the faucet, water still dripping from his fingers. "Yeah, Raith didn't care about what had just happened. Shoved her up the ladder anyway. She'll do great, but... wait, how'd you know about that?"

"I have my sources, dear." She smirked, stacking the glass with a soft clink.

He snorted, tossing the towel. It hit the counter, limp and heavy. His stomach lurched. The towel's curled landing position caused a flash memory of Gamble's arm lying on the ground, apart from his body. For once, he was thankful for the fuzzy edges of his vision that obscured half of it.

"Your sources? The ones that seem to know all about me?"

"What on earth are you talking about?"

"Mom, everywhere I go, there's at least one person who already knows my name, my whole life story, it seems. Happened on my first day with Parnell, then with Genie, and at the store the other day? The cashier offered me a butterscotch candy. Not from the shelf, Mom. From her pocket."

"Oh, she remembered. I told her those were your favorites." She smiled, and her fingers pinched his sleeve. Her vanilla lotion cut through the kitchen's savory haze. "I may have bragged about you to some friends. Can't a mother be excited that her son is back home?"

He sighed. "Of course, she can. But, maybe not so much, okay? We've talked about this."

"No, you talked, I listened. In fact, I still don't know why you want to move all the way up there. What does St. Louis have that Coldwater doesn't?"

"You're joking, right? About half a million people and a million other things. And, better, probably no burnt corpses at work."

"John Deacon Chance. Bite your tongue. You know what I mean."

John scratched his brow, then pointed towards his mother. "That's it. You just said it. That's why."

She threw her hands up. "Now you've lost me."

"My middle name, Mom."

Bonnie flinched and turned away.

"Deacon," he said, voice low. "You said it was *his* name."

A faint creak echoed from the front porch, but he dismissed it.

Old house, old noises.

She crossed her arms. "Oh, not this again. You're making too much of it."

"Am I? I'm apparently named after a man I've never met."

"If I've told you once, I've told you three dozen times—"

"I know, I know," he said, raising his hands defensively. "You only knew him for a short time. After you got pregnant with me, you both agreed to live separate lives. Yes, you've said all this. But, one time, just once... do you remember this? I asked about him. Normally, you'd say you didn't know where he was. But, that time..."

Bonnie's shoulders dropped, nodding to herself and muttering, "I said that he probably lived somewhere up in St. Louis."

"Yeah, St. Louis. That's why going there is more than the job. If I'm up there, I can look for him. I might still see him. Before this shadow crap covers everything," he said, circling his eyes with his fingers.

"John, about that—"

"I need to find him, Mom. Ask why he ditched us."

Silence fell over the room. Bonnie looked at her son with watery eyes.

"It's complicated. Please, don't hold it against him. Me. Only me, okay? It was the best choice, believe me. But, it was my choice."

He exhaled deeply and embraced her. "You stuck around, and he didn't. I'll blame who I want." He stepped back and leaned over. "Look, I appreciate you bragging about me. I know you mean well. True, it's harder to make my own first impression, but whatever. I'll figure that out. I also wanted to thank you for putting in a good word for me with Gamble. When I found out the St. Louis position wouldn't be ready after graduation—"

"John..."

"I was worried I wouldn't have a job at all—"

"John!"

A look of confusion washed over his face. "What?"

"I never talked to Doyal Gamble about you."

"You didn't?"

"No, it wasn't me."

"Then, how did I..."

"Annaleigh. She was the one who vouched for you."

"Her? We didn't meet until my first day. I didn't know she existed."

Bonnie's lips curled at the edges as she dipped her chin. "She knew you."

The floor groaned again, a jagged edge to it, cutting through the kitchen's fading hum. He managed a deep sigh.

"What did you do, Mom? Is Annaleigh one of your sources?"

"Of course she is, silly. I helped her find a house when she moved here. We talk a lot."

"And, I'm just now finding this out?" He buried his face in his palms. "I feel like the last guy to know everything."

"It's alright. I trust her. You should, too." She leaned in and pointed at him. "And, don't play dumb. Shadows or not, your eyes light up when I say her name."

His cheeks burned. "She's my boss now, that's all." He saw the glimpse of the expression on his mother's face and knew he was caught. He rolled his eyes. "And, my face doesn't light up."

Bonnie took in a deep, slow breath. "Well, son, since we're sharing. It's not only that she and I talk. It's about *where* we talk." John's eyebrows perked up. "She was curious about how you were doing in law school, so the last time she was over, I—"

"She's been to the house?"

"Yes, a few times. Okay, more than that, to be truthful. She's a lawyer. You were studying to be one. You have a lot in common. I thought you two might, you know, be friends, or something."

"I'm twenty-four years old, and my mom is finding me friends?"

"Who knows, maybe more than a friend?"

28

"Mom, I'm not staying. I'm here for a little while, then I'm gone. I won't have time for... whatever it is you're trying to start."

He leaned his head back and closed his eyes. After a moment of reflection, the corner of his lips rose.

"She really was curious about me?"

Bonnie gave him a knowing hug, then retreated upstairs. He drifted into the living room, head buzzing. Too many things were brewing at once. Gamble's tragedy, Annaleigh's multiple visits, and a nudge from his mother towards a new romance. He had intended to put his head down and wait it out, then vanish from Coldwater, only to return after finding his dad.

Easy peasy. Right? It's like a semester at school—

A sharp creak out on the porch split the thought. His neck snapped toward the sound, pulse kicking hard. He lunged to the front window, fingers fumbling the blinds apart.

The night pressed in, thick and black, swallowing the edges of his vision. Crickets screeched, a wall of noise drowning his shallow breaths. Something scraped—wood or metal, he couldn't place its origin. A shadow, tall and broad, sliced past the glass.

He stumbled back, heart slamming against his ribs, hands slick with new sweat. The air went still. A low, deliberate tap on the porch steps.

Not the wind. Not random.

John bolted to the door, threw the lock, and eased it open. He stepped onto the porch, tuning his ear to the night.

Nothing but his own ragged gasps.

He edged back to the threshold, squinting into the void. A faint rustle retreated—soft, steady, then gone.

Someone had been there.

Watching.

Waiting.

5

ALIBIS AND UNHELPFUL ANSWERS

The two-block walk north from the courthouse dulled the hum of passing cars and morning shoppers as the bustle of Coldwater's town square faded behind them. John's shoes scuffed the cracked sidewalk as the county jail's two-story bulk rose above them on the right, its shadow cool against his neck. Annaleigh kept pace beside him, her short heels clipping in the quiet.

At least this trap situated its key buildings within walking distance.

The sun broke past the jail's edge, a blade of light slicing through his narrowed vision. Twenty-four hours ago, that same glare clawed through dense leaves, spotlighting Gamble's still husk. A faceless mess, with one blackened stump, coating the air thick with burnt meat and ash. He blinked hard, but the edges stayed fuzzy, his limited peripheral view locking the memory, central and tight.

"Still with me?" Annaleigh's soft voice cut through, her eyes forward.

"Yeah," he rasped, forcing his gaze ahead. "I keep picturing him."

Her fingers brushed his sleeve. It was fleeting, but accidental. Her arms returned to her sides.

"We're still standing, and we'll fight for him," she said, almost to herself.

His throat tightened, not just from the memory of Gamble but also from the thought of her lounging around on his couch.

The Sheriff's Office squatted across the lot, Parnell's silhouette a distant smudge in the doorway, hands, yet again, on his hips. His default position, it seemed.

John wasn't sure which challenge was worse—identifying a faceless corpse or enduring an interrogation from a sheriff he didn't trust to do the right thing?

Parnell ushered them inside. The inner security door snarled with a low buzz that rattled John's teeth. They entered into a space not unlike their bullpen at the courthouse. A wide space unfolded, jammed with desks and filing cabinets. Multiple oscillating fans circulated stale coffee and ink from a wheezing dot matrix printer through the humid air.

Around the room, two deputies hunched over desks, rustling papers like dry leaves. The hiss of murmurs filled his ears. Parnell's boots thudded somewhere left, a shadow outside his peripheral he couldn't track. A phone shrilled to the right, out of sight.

John tilted his head, straining to catch the sheriff's hushed conversation with a nearby deputy. Too low, clipped, and lost in the drone of the rotating fans. The metal chair bit cold through his slacks as he sat. Detective Hollis Mumber looked up from behind stacks of folders and offered a meek smile.

"No sense in separating you in our interrogation rooms," Parnell said, steeped in drawl as he stood to the rear of the lawyer's chairs. "You'd both request the other to be present to act as your lawyer. So, let's do this out in the open and get it done." He rubbed his hands together. "Hollis, take it away."

Mumber cleared his throat with a swift, hacking cough. "Now, let me see... can you recall what you were up to between, uh... seven and nine o'clock yesterday evening?" he asked, staring at his notepad. He froze, holding a pen, preparing to write. He looked like he had gone catatonic.

John and Annaleigh looked at each other, unsure. She spoke first.

"Sorry, Detective, but which one of us are you talking to?"

Mumber looked up, bothered at the question, and pointed to John.

"You, first."

"I was home with my mother," he said, clipped. "All night."

"Lonely night, eh?" said the detective, scribbling. "And, is there anyone who can confirm your whereabouts during those hours?"

John's eyes widened as he flashed a look of concern to Annaleigh. He received quick confirmation that he wasn't the only one who heard the duplicative question. Parnell sighed, triggering Mumber to correct himself.

"Oh, I mean, anyone *else* that can confirm your whereabouts?"

"No," John said. "As I said, it was the two of us."

He lifted his pen and eyed the sheriff, eyebrows raised.

"Can confirm, Hollis," Parnell said. "Bonnie's backed it up."

John spun around, centering the sheriff in his view.

"Why waste time asking us if you know what we're going to say?"

One corner of Parnell's mouth curled.

"You know the game, Counselor. Never ask a question you don't already know the answer to. Just checking all the stories stay consistent. Hollis, please continue."

John reset himself, trying his best to hide his discontentment. He crossed his arms and folded one leg over the other, slumping deep into the cheap chair.

"Now you, Ms. Stanton... same inquiry."

"I was at the courthouse, upstairs, in my office. After spending the bulk of my time getting John settled in last week, I needed to catch up on some work. I parked in the lot a bit before four, grabbed some dinner at the Wobbly Barrel across the street. Ate at my desk, then left after nine."

It was clear that she was trying to prevent the back-and-forth John had experienced. After hearing her answer, Mumber stopped writing and looked up at her with a vacant expression.

"You were working on a Sunday night?"

"Yes, Detective. It's not uncommon for prosecutors to have to put in extra time. I'm sure you do the same when the occasion requires it."

Mumber bobbed his head. John marveled at how Annaleigh could change her tone and set others at ease. The old, frumpy detective was the current member of her one-person jury, and once again, she controlled the courtroom.

"So, you were alone... the whole time?" he prodded. "Did you make any calls? Or, take any actions, uh, that would help prove you were... where you say you were?"

"Detective, I know these are standard questions. I'm also fairly certain that, as fellow civil servants, we're not suspects. As such, proving our whereabouts shouldn't be the highest priority. But, in the spirit of cooperation, no, I didn't make any calls."

"Again, many apologies. I am simply following our procedures. So, you were alone?"

"No, she wasn't," came a voice from across the room. "I was with her."

From behind the group, Deputy Cason Foley's chair scraped as he stood, like nails down a chalkboard. His inflated confidence cut through the room's awkward haze.

John spun around, swallowing hard. He may have casually dismissed the possibility of anything extracurricular with Annaleigh due to his short stint in town, but that didn't mean he wanted to see some other guy's tongue down her throat, either.

He judged the deputy harshly. Foley's biceps strained his shirt. His chest puffed. Chin held high. Young, cocky.

No way. Not her type. Not a chance.

John sat up straight in his chair. He glanced at her, looking for a reaction to Foley's risqué comment. Her expression gave nothing away.

Say he's lying. Tell them you two weren't together.

Still facing Mumber, she replied with a calm, even voice. "Cason, you occupied the same space as me for a short time. You were not *with* me."

I knew it. And, using his first name to knock him down a peg. Brilliant. Wait, sometimes she calls me John, too...

A crease of disapproval formed between Parnell's eyes.

"Foley, what's this about now? Why is it that I am only now hearing about this?"

"Apologies, Sheriff. Saw her lights on," the young, fit deputy said, shrugging. "Thought I'd check, for safety."

Annaleigh spun, her voice ice. "Check? You barged in, scared me half to death, had the nerve to ask me out—third time I've said no, by the way—and slunk off without a word. Top-notch work, deputy."

"Is this true?" barked Parnell.

"Yes, sir. I left there about 7:25. She was alone." Foley buried his chin into his chest as he sat, randomly moving papers on his desk.

Parnell's focus remained fixed on Foley as Mumber reassumed control of the interrogation

"So... no one else can verify you were there until, uh, nine, was it?"

"No," she said. "For what it's worth, I did look out the window around eight o'clock and noticed the deputy's car still parked in the fire lane outside. I checked again at eight thirty. He was finally gone. Guess he was waiting for me to walk out, *for safety.*"

The sheriff cleared his throat to regain Foley's attention. His raised eyebrows demanded a response.

"Yes, sir, I stayed there for a little while longer. Keeping watch over the square, sir."

Annaleigh's lip curled, a rare crack in her calm.

"Your job doesn't include stalking me after dark, Cason."

John's fists clenched at his sides. She'd faced that corpse with

34

him, steady as stone, and this punk thought he could rattle her? Thought he could woo her? Not if John could help it. He'd break the deputy's jaw first, badge be damned.

Parnell sighed, focused on his deputy with a laser-like stare. "We'll discuss this later, young man." His drawl reduced to monotone. "Ms. Stanton, I'd like to take this opportunity to ask if you feel threatened, and if you'd like to lodge a formal complaint."

Annaleigh grinned, her eyes sparkling. "No, thanks, Sheriff, I think I've got this one handled pretty well."

He tipped his hat. "Hollis, I think she's good."

"Yes... um, I think these two are in the clear."

John's temperature spiked. "That's great, it seems like this has been time well spent. Since we're both innocent, can we talk about something relevant, like, say, the investigation? Any leads you can share with us?"

Mumber looked at John and squinted. "Of course."

He waded through the sheets of paper, mumbling. John, focused on Mumber's digging, didn't hear the sheriff's movement. As Parnell swooped around from behind the chairs to stand at the side of Mumber's desk, he entered John's vision, making him flinch. John sniffed and cleared his throat, trying to cover it up. Parnell lifted his hands.

"No, I think that's enough for now. This is an active investigation and we'll be sure to turn over our findings... once there's a need for prosecution."

Annaleigh's brow furled, sensing something was off. John sensed it, too.

"No," John pressed. "I think we deserve to know. For example, you're asking about our alibis for Sunday night. If he died the night before, why did no one tell us until Monday morning? Are you saying no one found him until then?"

Parnell's trimmed mustache twitched. Silence draped over the bullpen. Heads spun, sending slow glances of fault at an older man sitting at a corner desk.

A wheeze rasped from the corner as old Amos Hinkle, Coldwater deputy since the commercial availability of color televisions, sat slumped. His white hair glowed under the fluorescents. The thin-framed glasses perched on the end of his nose threatened to leap off his face. His eyelids were shut, no doubt taking in a morning nap.

He'd probably doze through gunshots.

John and Annaleigh made repeated eye contact with Parnell and Mumber, waiting for a response. She sensed the discomfort in the room and accepted that no good answer would be forthcoming. She changed the subject. Annaleigh rose, chair sliding back.

"Fine. Any other cases I should know about, Detective?"

Her tone was steel, eyes locked on Parnell, even though she referenced Mumber.

She knows who's really in charge.

Mumber glanced up at Parnell, then returned his focus to her. "Nothing now, ma'am. Not that you'd prosecute anyway," he muttered, papers rustling.

She eyed Parnell. "We live in upgraded times, Sheriff. There's a new prosecutor in town—let's work on rebuilding this bridge." She nodded to John. "Let's go."

From the corner, a Hinkle cough, weak and useless. An old man who'd missed a murder till dawn. Foley reached for the phone and started dialing—distracted, overbearing. Dangerous, maybe. Parnell squinted as his boots shifted, a wall sliding into place.

John rose, squinting back, pulse ticking up.

What a crew.

They stepped into the sunlight, determined to understand the situation. Doyal Gamble's murder wasn't an accident. It was a warning.

Parnell's infuriating games, Mumber's needless jab, Foley's misguided interest, and a body left overnight to rot.

He just needed to last six months, then bolt to St. Louis.

No more mangled bodies, no more crazy drama.

He'd claw himself out of this town before it swallowed him.

Until then, Gamble's past wasn't the only thing they'd have to worry about.

6

ASHES IN THE FILES

The offices above the courtroom hummed with overhead fluorescents with a combination of the stale tang of dust and Genie's perfume clinging to the air. Twenty-four hours since Parnell's squint confirmed their worst fears—trust outside the courthouse walls would be hard to find.

John Chance slumped into his bullpen chair and rubbed his eyes. After arriving at their upstairs office and making their customary shared walk into the building, Annaleigh had stormed into her office. He sat at his desk, pondering his next move. Should he go in and check on her? Ask her for work? He had nothing to do and hated to be bored.

Although how could he be bored when Genie was humming church hymns and deep into a self-care session with the scent of bright blue nail polish wafting around.

From his desk, he couldn't quite see inside Annaleigh's office, but he heard a vast array of noises escaping the cracked doorway—slamming drawers, the screech of file cabinet slides, the ruffling of papers. He imagined her space looking like a crisp fall day with paper, instead of leaves, fluttering through the air and randomly scattered across the ground. His lips parted when she walked out holding a stack of arranged folders, corners perfectly aligned, and dropped them in front of him.

"If it was revenge that killed Gamble, we'll find who did it in here."

He cracked his knuckles.

Time to dig.

In short order, John's desk had become organized chaos. He sifted through the documents—petty theft reports, DUIs, a bar fight from 1991–and placed them into one of three piles: yes, no, and maybe. So far, every case ended up cluttering the "no" pile.

He became familiar with Coldwater's underbelly, but not its killers.

Annaleigh joined him in the bullpen at the desk right next to his. In an almost matching rhythmic cadence, she flipped through manila folders of misdemeanors and plea deals. Her fingers smudged ink as she hunted for fire, for violence, for anything that matched how Gamble died.

He tossed a file aside. Another entrant onto the "no" stack.

Harmless and irrelevant, like most everything in these cases.

Hours ticked by. He reviewed perpetrators and cross-referenced witnesses. Names smeared into haze near the edges. Shadows crept in where his sight frayed. Folders, desks, even Annaleigh—lost beyond the center as he dialed in his focus.

Sweat beaded his neck, the chair's leather sticking to his shirt. Genie coughed across the bullpen, causing him to flinch, half-expecting Parnell's boots behind him.

Come on, focus.

He pinched his brow, willing the fuzz to clear. He was desperate to find a clue. He rubbed his eyes, blinking, squinting.

Gamble deserved justice, and he wasn't going to let his eyes fail, even if they were somewhat broken.

Another case reviewed.

Another dead end.

Eyes still on the papers in front of him, he reached to grab from the top of the next stack. Unaware, as was Annaleigh. Their hands overlapped, his on the outside. He pulled away as his eyes met hers, lingering long enough for John's insides to burn. Her cheeks rose, matching the smile on her lips. Yet, there was no matching emotion in her eyes.

He released her hand and gestured, offering her the next set. She buried her head back into the paperwork.

Following her lead, he opened his next file.

June, from a few years ago. Vandalism, with a twist. It wasn't the type of infraction that he was supposed to worry about. There was no relation to his murder, but Gamble's actions caught his eye.

The case dealt with a nineteen-year-old caught drunkenly throwing things at passing cars. A couple of misdemeanors, usually. Events unfolded in an unlucky fashion for the teen, which added layers of problems for him. A driver, whose windshield was shattered by a chunk of concrete, lost control and crashed into the local Civil War history museum. The damage was both extensive and structural. Gamble recommended two years in jail, well above the standard sentence of thirty days of community service. The advice John received from his boss last week sank in.

"Never miss a chance to burn them with the max sentence," Gamble had advised. "Charge high. You keep the community safe and teach the offenders a lesson at the same time. They can't be repeaters if they're behind bars."

John had nodded then, impressed. In retrospect, the prosecutor's guidance felt off. He was the one who burned, perhaps by someone he overcharged and put away.

Did his strategy backfire?

John shook it off. He flipped until something stopped him cold: Arson, 1988.

The file was heavy, its edges barely starting to yellow. His pulse kicked up as he skimmed through the brittle pages. This case was five years old, but alive with heat.

Clayden Kendrick, the accused, had been arrested for torching a farm outside town. A custom accelerant was involved, although the exact chemical was never identified. First, the barn went up. Then, a separate blaze was started in a steel outbuilding, melting it and its contents into twisted slag and warped claws of jagged metal.

"Unusual fire damage," the report read. "Not standard. Strange burn patterns."

Gamble's face suffered from unusual fire damage and strange burn patterns, too.

John's thumb brushed the mugshot, grainy under his skin. Kendrick's gray eyes glared back, unblinking, a match strike waiting. Mid 30s. Eyes flat. Jaw clenched like he'd chew through any bars that attempted to cage him.

He locked eyes with the picture, unable to look away. The photo's edges blurred, but that stare cut through. Evil, trapped in a frame.

"Found something," he said, snapping her out of a deep focus. "Clayden Kendrick, arson, five years ago. It's him, I can feel it."

"That was before my time. Let me see." She sped-read through the file. "I trust your judgment, but, honestly, there's not a lot in here. Let's check the trial docs and see if they have more details."

They moved their operation into her office, and she began typing on the keyboard.

"Look at this transcript," she said, pointing at the green text splashed across the screen. "Gamble pushed for ten years, the maximum sentence, though it was Kendrick's first offense. After the guilty verdict, the guy snapped. 'One day you'll burn for this!' Word for word."

John's skin prickled. "Oh my god. The bastard finally got his revenge?"

"I mean, it's possible." She flipped to the evaluations, her voice tightening. "Psych called him precise, obsessive. Indicated he was fixated and prone to grudges."

"He swore he was framed. Psychos always do. Guess he faked

good behavior and got out early. He did it. He killed Gamble. Had to have."

Annaleigh's eyes met his, sharp as glass. "If he's out, possibly. Let's check his status."

She entered a few more keystrokes and then traced her finger across the screen. "Kendrick, Clayden T., sentenced 1988, ten years, no indication of any parole hearings. Currently incarcerated at the Missouri State Penitentiary. He's still in. Five years down, five to go."

His chest sank. "He's locked up. Unbelievable." He squinted to read the rest. "No visitors, no mail, no calls."

Annaleigh slouched back into her chair. "He fit the mold perfectly. Just the kind of suspect we were looking for."

"No way he killed Gamble from his cell." He slammed the file folder shut, the thud echoing in the small room.

She rubbed her temples, exhaling hard. "We must be missing something. It's possible he could have directed it from inside. Someone he knew, someone he paid. Or..." She frowned and drummed her fingers behind her ear, as if hesitant to say the words. "If you're in law enforcement, you may not be listed as a visitor."

John recalled their questioning at the Sheriff's Office. Deputies at their desks, heads down, but he still caught their frequent gazes. Maybe Parnell's crew knew more. Too many eyes at that station were too quiet yesterday. A deputy had lingered by Mumber's desk, badge glinting, watching them leave.

Had that guy smirked? Or was it just a crooked smile?

If Kendrick didn't light the match, someone else sure did.

"There did seem to be something off back there. Parnell acted smug, more than usual. Ever since my first day, he's been hiding something. This reeks of him."

"Possible, but unlikely he's part of this," Annaleigh said. "Certainly seems like he's holding something back. Don't quite know what that is yet."

They drifted back out to the bullpens. She grabbed a folder, then sighed. "Look at this. Misdemeanors, noise complaints, vandals. Drunks and shoplifters. Of everything we've seen, Kendrick's the best match we have, but he's still locked up."

He leaned back, chair groaning. "I hate dead ends. Unless he's a puppet master from an eight-by-eight box."

She snorted, but it was cheerless. She started packing the files, each slap of paper a punctuation mark to their shared frustration. John joined her, their fingers brushing again as they worked. It was quick and accidental, but enough to spark a heat in his arm.

Desks now cleared, she returned to her office. He wandered near the corner conference room, then out the balcony door. He leaned over the edge, inhaling country air, smelling a quaint mixture of hay, exhaust, and a faint whiff of cider from the town square.

They'd come so close, only to stall.

The courthouse sat in the town's heart, with cars and pedestrians circling its stone structure like blood. An oddity in the pattern of the bustle caught his eye. A man stood still across the street on the opposite sidewalk, broad shoulders accentuated by crossed, muscled arms. He squinted up.

Was he staring up here?

The hair on the back of John's neck raised when he realized the man's identity. He'd met him only once, but that bulk stuck in his mind like a burr. Raith's hulking friend and bodyguard, Kenneth Roy Atlee.

A breeze licked his face, a siren wailed in the distance. He tracked it to the south, the midday sun glinting off the deputy's back window. As it turned onto a side street, the shrill was swallowed by old pines and brick buildings.

He snapped back to the sidewalk. It was empty.

Coldwater's underbelly, indeed.

Kendrick may have been in prison, but that story didn't feel written.

Not by a long shot.

The dark of Coldwater was threatening to come out and play.

7

TOWN HALL TANGLE

"Prosecutor's Office in St. Louis called today, John," Bonnie shouted from the kitchen.

He hustled through the living room and found her reading at the table. "I wasn't expecting to hear from them until later in the year. What did they say? Do they have an opening?"

"Slow down, son. It's not quite what you think. Although, so you know, I did give them your work number so they can call you next time."

He rubbed his forehead with a fist. "Seriously, Mom? I didn't want them to realize I was working in the middle of nowhere. They'd laugh at me."

"No, they won't." She shut her book and placated him with a smile. "They'll be impressed that you managed to land something so quickly after they pulled the rug out from under you."

"Doubt it."

"Would you rather not have a job at all? Perhaps you'd like to be pouring drinks down at the Barrel? You could be serving wobbly customers right now behind the bar."

"Okay, okay. I get your point." He sat down across from her. "So... what did they say?"

She took a long, slow drink from her teacup, drawing out the moment.

"They do have an opening available for you, if you want it."

John clenched a fist and bounced it on his lips.

"Did they say anything about Gamble? Is that why they're offering it now?"

"No, they didn't mention him. But, I doubt the timing is coincidental."

"I guess it's like a transfer, right? Annaleigh would understand if I took it."

"Don't you want to know what the position is before you start packing your bags?"

"I know what it is. They told me about it months ago."

"You sure?"

"Okay, fine, quit the secret squirrel stuff and tell me. What's the job?" He half-smiled and braced for the answer. She looked at him flatly.

"It's an unpaid internship."

The smile drained from his face.

"And, it's only for the summer. It ends in August."

His head dropped. He sighed and stood up.

"Not ideal. I can solve this." He paced, loafers scuffing the linoleum, his shadow sliding across the table's worn grain.

"Foot in the door," he muttered, voice rough. "Big cases, big names." He spun to face her. "Let's say I take it. It might not be what I want long-term, but I can contribute, I can start networking with important people, and I'll still be practicing law."

"Sweetheart, you're already practicing here. You're neck deep in something meaningful now, aren't you? St. Louis is a mirage. You still need the other guy to retire, don't you?"

He hated how right she was. One week as a lawyer, he was a key player in a murder investigation. With any luck, by the time it goes to trial, he will have passed the bar and could help in the

45

courtroom, too. Who knows, perhaps he'd second chair his first case, maybe get a conviction.

He wouldn't get the same opportunity as an intern.

That's not even counting the fundraiser he attended last week with Gamble. He'd met some of Coldwater's most influential members, even talked with some of its odd members, too. They had welcomed him as an equal, engaging in respectful conversation. Well, mostly respectful.

Would he have gotten that same invite if his responsibilities centered around changing the coffee pot? He didn't even drink the stuff. His shoulders dropped.

"Dad's somewhere up there. Harder to find him if I'm stuck here."

Bonnie's gaze lowered, and she began fumbling with her hands. "You've got a lot here, too, you know," she said softly. "I'm not sure what you're looking for is really in St. Louis."

He moved to the chair next to her, wrapping his arm around her.

"Mom, I love you. I always have. That will never change. But I want to talk to him, you know? Find out what he's like. Is he kind? A good man?"

"What you want and what you need are different, son. Sometimes, what you need isn't that far away. Just my opinion, but I think Annaleigh would rather have you by her side than some strange lawyer to fill your spot. Staying here, for now, won't close any doors up there. You know that." She took a deep breath. "But, leaving... that one would shut."

"You sound like Raith. That's just what he said to Annaleigh."

"Ooh, I hope not. But, you know what I mean."

He knew. To find his dad, he'd have to leave Annaleigh—and the possibility of a relationship with her. Two potential futures for him, colliding against each other.

His mother stood and clapped her hands together.

"Enough talk. Time to get ready, or we'll be late."

* * *

SIGNS HAD BEEN up all day. Phone trees were activated. Word of mouth in the corner stores, salons, and bars took care of the rest. The message was short, but clear.

"Emergency Town Hall at the Community Center, 7 pm Sharp".

John escorted his mother into the gymnasium, arm in arm. She separated and joined some friends in the third row, while he noticed Annaleigh leaning up against the side wall near the stage.

"So," he said, as he slid next to her. "Are you part of this gig?"

"Unfortunately, yeah. I think. I don't know. Whatever way Raith decides to do it, I hope it's quick and painless." The two remained silent for a moment, soaking in her description.

Quick and painless. Was it that way for Gamble?

As with most things related to the county government, the Community Center was located not far from the town square. It rested a few blocks east, one block past City Hall and across the street from one of Coldwater's many century-old stone churches. Its external architecture reminded him of a quaint house of Southern worship. Its insides told a different story, usually bustling with various activities.

Tonight, an eerie silence enveloped the hall, interrupted only by the soft footsteps of attendees and the occasional nervous cough, much different than its typical Bingo gatherings. Metal chairs scraped as townsfolk sat, while a low hum of whispers rose high into the hall's vaulted ceiling. Old cigarette smoke and perfume weaved through the crowd.

Bonnie motioned John to come over, "I saved you a seat", she mouthed, pointing. He tilted his head towards Annaleigh. She swiveled back to face the stage, his hint received.

"The guy who killed Gamble... he's here, I know it," he whispered to Annaleigh.

"I certainly hope not, but keep a lookout, just in case."

Little did she know, he had been doing that the moment he

leaned against the wall next to her. He'd already identified some patterns.

The older generation camped out in the front rows, the same couples and widows here for weekly game nights. A few sat grumpy, arms folded. Perhaps they preferred that their regularly scheduled entertainment had remained intact.

Leather jackets and trucker hats filled the back, while middle-aged and young families littered the center, eager to return home to relieve their teenage babysitters.

On the far wall, Parnell posted up with his deputies. All but one stood with their hands on their belts, looking menacing and serious. One assumed a more relaxed posture, and John recognized him as the deputy who appeared at Detective Mumber's desk after their interrogation. He hadn't caught his name, though. His pose was a stark contrast to the others—inviting, not brooding.

Late arrivals chose spots against the walls instead of squeezing past the earlies and into open seats in the middle. John side-stepped to make room, moving closer to Annaleigh. Their shoulders touched. He felt a slight pressure from her as she leaned into him and pushed his lips between his teeth to hide a growing smile.

Mayor Cameron Raith appeared at the podium, illuminated by a single spotlight mounted on the balcony. He adjusted the microphone, and a deep clicking sound reverberated through the hall as the stand's neck bent.

"My friends," he began, heavy on his trademark drawl, "I'm here tonight to share some truths with you. I don't plan on mincin' words."

He lifted the mic from its holder and stepped to the side, casually leaning against it with his elbow and crossing his ankles. "There's been some rumors. I'm here to say that Doyal Gamble's murder is real. He's gone, folks."

A chorus of shocked whispers and gasps rippled through the assembly, punctuated by the occasional 'ooh' and 'aah' that echoed from shadowy corners of the hall. The crowd quickly quieted, their collective breaths held in anticipation of what horrible news he might reveal next.

He gestured to the wall on his right. "Rest assured, the Sheriff's on it. He and his team will find whoever is responsible in short order."

More random murmurs.

By the look on his face, he's doing a great job of hiding his disdain for the Sheriff.

"Once caught, to ensure this perpetrator is prosecuted to the fullest extent of the law, I have appointed Ms. Annaleigh Stanton to fill the role of Prosecutor, on an interim basis."

He motioned for her to join him on the stage, not stopping until she relented. She trudged up the side stairs and embarrassingly raised a humble arm. "I won't ask her to speak tonight, though I'm sure she had a brilliant speech planned," he chided. "She'll need to conserve her energy as she works tirelessly to bring those responsible for this heinous crime to justice!"

His vocal crescendo sparked a spontaneous spurt of applause. Raith waited for the pockets of clapping to dwindle, thanked everyone for attending, asked for safety, and then dismissed them.

John and Annaleigh remained leaning against the side wall, observing the departing crowd. A few older women from the front rows approached her to offer congratulations and best wishes on finding the culprit.

"I still can't believe this has happened. Been living here for sixty-plus years. Seen a lot, but never something like this. You get 'em, dear," one said, shaking Annaleigh's hand with both of hers. While Annaleigh finessed the well-wishers with her southern charm and pageant smile, John continued to scan the room.

If the guy's here and wanted to send another message, now would be a good time to strike. All this commotion, bad for us, good for him.

This type of chaotic activity was precisely the situation he hated to be in.

With his limited peripheral vision, he had developed a habit of darting his eyes back and forth, and occasionally twisting his head, to keep tabs on his surroundings. In open areas, he preferred to have his back up against a wall, removing one vector from his surveillance. After a few meticulous pranks in college, it was a lesson he'd learned the hard way. Thankfully, Annaleigh picked the exact spot he would have without realizing it.

He panned his head, left to right, like a metronome, moving to a specified rhythm to surveil his entire surroundings. A stir in his gut told him that the murderer was here, watching this spectacle.

Observing the macabre result of his handiwork and plotting his next move, no doubt.

During his sweeps, he kept tabs on his mother, still nestled within a circle of her friends in the third row, gabbing. As law enforcement was on the opposite side of the room, most of the town would be blocking their response should something happen on this side.

The exit doors were handling a surge. It would be possible for the attacker to strike, slip into the crowd, and be out of the building before the Sheriff and his men would even know what happened.

Got to stay vigilant.

As he panned back to his left, something caught his eye. A man walked towards them down the side aisle, against the flow of the meandering people.

There's no exit this way. Where's this guy going?

The man weaved between other members of his community, never seeming to lose track of his intended target—them. His full beard, mangy hair, and tattered jean jacket radiated anger. The man's pace quickened as he swerved between others.

John angled himself, adjusting to get a clearer view. He recognized the familiar features from a recently viewed mugshot.

Clayden Kendrick was no longer behind bars.

"Hey! That's far enough!" John's voice boomed, stopping all nearby chatter.

Kendrick stormed on, finger stabbing at Annaleigh. "I'm glad that cocksucker's dead. You should be next, bitch! All of you!"

John braced, shielding her as Kendrick lunged. He shoved the stranger hard, then gripped Kendrick's shoulder and spun him round. Gray eyes stretched wide, shocked at such a proactive move.

A dull thud echoed as Kendrick's skull hit the wall, his body sagging. John pinned him with a forearm, grinding into his back. The man's neck kinked into an acute angle.

"Admit it, you son of a bitch. Admit what you did to Gamble!"

"I ain't telling you anything... go fuck yourself."

"C'mon, hotshot like you, couldn't wait to break out and get your revenge?"

Kendrick tried pushing off the wall, but John's leverage was stronger.

"Bite me, asshole. I know my rights," he mumbled, face smashing into the painted concrete block.

"Yeah, you've got the right to go back to jail for the rest of your life," John threatened. "We know what you did."

"Wait, wait," he said, smirking over his shoulder. "You think *I* killed him?"

John pulled and spun him around, slamming Kendrick's back into the wall and throwing an elbow into his throat.

"You already admitted it, stupid. Did prison melt your brain that much?"

"I didn't admit to anything, shithead. I said she *should* be next. You need to listen better, dumbass."

"Calling me names won't win you any points, man. You thought Gamble overcharged you? Wait until you see the sentence I hand down."

"Bullshit, you fucking lawyers framed me once," Kendrick said, clawing at John's elbow for air. "Just like you crooked little shits to try it again. Won't work a second time."

"You're the only crook here, Clayden. Hope you liked your

cell. You deserve something worse for killing Gamble. The needle, maybe."

"Jesus, man, I'm telling you, I didn't fucking kill him. I... just wish I did. For what he did to me! But... look, I just got out today, I swear." Kendrick's eyes flicked behind John. He smiled. "Go ahead, ask this pig."

A hand gripped John's shoulder, a slow drawl cutting through the tension. "I think he's had quite enough."

John's head turned, and the kind eyes of the relaxed deputy looked deep into his own. Between the touch and the deputy's inflection, his anger lessened, then subsided. He shoved one final time and stepped back. Kendrick slumped, catching his breath.

"He threatened her," John said, snarling at Kendrick. "What happened to Gamble won't happen to her."

The deputy nodded. "I understand your concern, young man. But, he's telling the truth. Paroled this morning, the warden gave our office a heads-up. Minus all the colorful words, he's right."

Annaleigh, her voice ice, waved a finger close to Kendrick's gasping face. "That may be, but Mr. Kendrick should tread carefully. His threats might be enough to put him back in prison, where he serves out the remainder of his sentence."

Kendrick mustered a weak nod and slinked away. Other deputies arrived and ushered the onlookers towards the exit.

"All right, folks, show's over," Deputy Foley announced, leading the group away, smiling at Annaleigh while he spoke. "Let's start making our way out. This way, everyone, this way."

The relaxed lawman with the kind eyes tipped his cap. "Deputy D. Clyde Brothers, at your service. But only my momma, God rest her soul, called me all that—minus the deputy, of course. John, please call me Clyde."

John shook Clyde's hand, dazed. "You know me?"

Clyde chuckled. "Everybody knows Coldwater's most famous boomerang."

"That's the second time I've heard that term. Not sure if I like it."

"It don't mean nothing bad. It's a compliment, you know? Means you started here, left for a while, then wound up coming back. Around here, we always like to see our own come back home."

"Compliment? Coming back here sounds more like a punishment," John mumbled.

"Thanks, Clyde," Annaleigh interrupted, before John could continue. "We appreciate the de-escalation."

A crooked smile, one final hat tip, and the deputy was gone, guiding the last few stragglers out the door.

John and Annaleigh were left alone in the silent hall, surrounded by a sea of metal chairs in disarray. She put her hand on his shoulder, her touch reassuring and intimate.

"Sometimes, the threat of going back to prison is stronger than physical violence." She exhaled slowly, breathing out through her nose. "Someday, you need to tell me where that rage came from, okay?"

She leaned in and pressed her lips against his cheek, planting a slow and tender kiss. The kind that implied much more than a thank you.

"I do appreciate you sticking up for me," she whispered into his ear.

His heart raced as adrenaline flooded his system, even more than during his scuffle with Kendrick. The hair on his arms raised from the warmth of her breath. She eased away, her skin grazing his.

John stood, locked in the moment. He memorized the feeling of her lips against his cheek, the delicate sound of her whisper, the smell of her lingering perfume.

No unpaid internship could pull him now.

8

DUELING OBSERVATIONS

Annaleigh's car sat parked in the courthouse lot when John rolled in at his usual time, 8:15. He crossed the asphalt, tossing glances back, gut twisting. She hadn't broken their routine before. Their morning walk was his one constant in Coldwater.

Did she regret that kiss last night? Maybe he'd come on too strong?

He scanned the street, then flicked his eyes up to her office window. No sign of her. As if catching a glimpse of her would soften the betrayal of the one thing they shared.

His vision, focused upwards, meant the street and sidewalk retreated into shadow, and he relied on memory of the number of steps to the curb.

It was a decision he'd come to regret.

He slammed into the bumper of a black sedan, echoing across the square with a dull thud. Pain shot through his shin. He dropped to one knee, cheeks burning, praying no one saw. He cursed under his breath, hating his neglect to pay better attention.

A grizzled voice, smooth as Southern whiskey, cut through the throbs.

"Need the siren to wake you up, Counselor, or perhaps a

good kick in the ass?" Sheriff Parnell leaned out the driver's window, smirking.

John rubbed his leg. "I was distracted. Didn't see you."

The door opened, and Parnell stepped out, his large forehead glowing in the morning sun. He walked around to the passenger side of the cruiser, motioning.

"Hop in, son. I think it's time you and I had a chat. Man to man."

John hesitated, eyes darting, calculating a solution. This was not a trip he was comfortable taking.

"Great idea, Sheriff. Let's head upstairs. We can use the conference room for as long as you'd like."

"Get in the car, John."

Parnell peered at him with a steely gaze. His tone left no room for argument. The mutual distrust permeated the air, pressing against them like a tangible force. He drew a slow, deep breath, looking up to the second-floor windows, hoping Annaleigh would see him. If she were to intervene, it'd be two on one. She didn't appear. He relented.

"Fine," he reasoned, his voice tight with unease. "I'm not sure what we have to talk about, Sheriff. You know everything we do, maybe more."

He climbed in, eyes locked on Parnell as the door slammed shut with a bang.

"Maybe, indeed," Parnell said through the open window as he slinked in front of the hood, his eyes never leaving John's. He re-entered, reaching back and grasping the top of the door frame, his fingers curling around the metal with practiced ease. In one fluid motion, he pulled the door closed. The thud echoed with a sense of finality.

As the sheriff settled into the driver's seat, the car shrank around him. This was his real office, not that stuffy station with its vintage furniture and the stench of dereliction. No, this was the place where he felt most at home. He and the cruiser were finely attuned to each other. Without speaking, his presence oozed intensity. His stare remained fixed on John, causing him to shift, uncomfortable with the silence.

"What's this cloak and dagger all about, Sheriff?"

Parnell answered by twisting the key, then revving the engine. After gearing into drive and a slow, deliberate lap around the courthouse, he turned right and headed south, away from the square. The sedan hummed out of downtown Coldwater, where asphalt gave way to cracked state concrete, and eventually to gravel that crunched like bones under the tires.

John's eyes darted between Parnell's steady grip on the wheel and the world sliding past the window. Storefronts faded, replaced first by houses, then sagging barns with roofs caved in like punctured lungs. The morning sun bled through skeletal oaks, casting jagged shadows across the road. Every turn, a step deeper into a trap.

Parnell said nothing, his silence heavier than the engine's growl. His fingers tapped the helm in a rhythm John couldn't decode.

Was it impatience? An earworm? A signal?

John swallowed with a dry throat as he memorized the route, just in case. Left at the rusted grain silo, right after the creek choked with cattails, straight onto a dirt rut flanked by pines so dense they blocked the light. He'd grown up in this town, but didn't know the entire layout by heart, especially on the outskirts. These were unfamiliar roads, and street signs were either rare or unreadable. Landscape markers would have to do.

A pang of dread built in his gut. If Parnell planned to ditch him out here, no one would find his body. Not for weeks. Maybe never.

A weathered "No Trespassing" sign flickered past, half-buried in kudzu, its letters peeling like old skin. John's mind raced through possibilities. Good intentions or not, he'd assaulted a local thug in plain view, and Parnell didn't strike him as the forgiving type. Seemed like for Parnell, revenge is a dish best served soon.

The Sheriff's badge glinted in the dim cab, a cold reminder of small-town justice. Out here, in the backwoods of Coldwater, Missouri, that star meant whatever Parnell wanted it to mean.

The way narrowed and roadside branches scraped against the sedan's sides, like fingernails on glass. A deer carcass loomed ahead, rotting in the ditch, its ribcage picked clean by something unseen.

Flashes of Gamble's body whipped through his head. He shifted, covertly testing the door handle. Locked. Parnell's lips twitched.

"Eyes front, Counselor," he drawled, voice low and thick. "Wouldn't want you to miss the scenery."

The trees lining the way closed in, the air growing damp and sour. John struggled to regulate his silent breaths against his pounding heart. He was a dead man riding shotgun, and the Sheriff was the judge, jury, and maybe the executioner.

"It's come to my attention," Parnell spoke, breaking the silence, "that a certain prosecutor in this town might think himself above the law. I'm curious to hear your thoughts on that."

John crafted a careful response, unsure of Parnell's true motive. "Self-defense is still legal in this state, no?"

Parnell nodded. "Self-defense, Counselor? That's what you're going with?"

"Sheriff, if I hadn't protected Annaleigh, there's no telling what Kendrick might have done."

"Is that so?"

"Yes, 100%. You and your deputies were on the other side of the room. How do you even know what happened?"

"Young man, I have this thing called an investigative division, whose entire purpose in life is to go around, ask questions, and find out."

"Is it really a division if you only have one detective?"

Parnell chuckled deep in his throat. He pursed his lips and nodded, hiding a smile. The vehicle hummed along as he navigated the way with ease. After a few turns, he responded with an even tone.

"Son, I've got more eyes in this town than you've got fancy words. Why *else* would I call it an Investigative Division?"

"Sheer bravado, maybe? Who knows. Of all the skills it takes to be a lawyer, Sheriff, the one I do best is research. The second best? Observation. I've seen your three deputies. Foley, Hinkle, and Brothers. And, of course, your one and only detective, Mumber. You had five vehicles at Gamble's crime scene. Three marked, two unmarked. Those same five cars were in your lot at the time of our interrogation and again, outside the Community Center." John stared ahead, holding in a grin. "I've done my homework. Maybe those aren't the fancy words you were looking for, but we've both got eyes in this town."

Had he been forced to testify under oath, he would have described the Sheriff's mouth as slightly agape. To John's dismay, this wasn't a courtroom, and with his forward focus, Parnell sat in the shadows of his periphery. Regardless, his research hadn't failed him. He knew he had to play it smart and wait for the right time to drop the information he'd coaxed from his mother.

This unusual, perhaps illegal, predicament provided the perfect opportunity to flip the script and gain the upper hand. Pride swelling, John continued, unabated.

"If you don't mind some unsolicited advice, there are a couple of red flags you might want to keep an eye on. Foley's a stalker waiting to snap. Hinkle probably shouldn't hold a gun, much less be allowed to shoot one. Mumber? He seems checked out, maybe nearing retirement. From what I've seen, might want to start a search for a new detective."

Outside the car windows, the world streaked by in a blur of color and motion. Parnell kept a steady pace behind the wheel. He continued driving, unwavering. He offered no resistance to John's detailed analysis and smears against his department. With each sentence, the young lawyer's nervousness vanished, and his confidence grew.

"We're in your black sedan, and Mumber has one like it, except it's a hideous shade of brown. Like I said, you've got a total of five official vehicles, not including the station wagon in your lot, parked in the closest spot most days. I assume that belongs to your clerk." John's tone deepened, hoping to wrestle away the silent control Parnell exhibited.

"That's how I know you have one detective. I notice things. When I notice good things... it gives me hope that maybe the world isn't as dark as it seems. When I see bad things, I use the full force of the law to remedy the situation, applying the appropriate level of justice. Fairly, evenly, and when needed? Harshly. So, tell me, Sheriff Parnell, what should I notice right now?"

His confidence had never been so high. It was as if he were at trial, delivering a closing argument that would result in a guilty verdict from the jury in mere minutes. There was no stopping him now.

Parnell's eyes never left the road. They had driven for about ten minutes, southward out of town, using a series of turns to wind their way into the backwoods. John memorized the entire route and still had no clue where he was. Uncharted Coldwater, at least to him.

Parnell inched down a narrow lane, edged on each side by tall pines of various widths. He brought the cruiser to a stop next to a large dirt bluff on the right. A small clearing opened up on the left, but otherwise this area was remote, surrounded by a mature forest. He flicked the engine off and adjusted his oval-rimmed glasses.

"Not bad, but I notice things, too. Here's what I see, Counselor."

He held up one finger, allowing it to hover. "You didn't account for Gary. He's the fella who mops the floors at night. Doesn't drive to work. He walks, so no car in the lot. Great guy, too, except for when he has to clean up after we have a drunk in the cage. It's the only time Gary cusses."

He raised a second finger. "Sheriffs can do homework, too. I know you've been a lawyer for about one week. And, you're not even a real one, not until you pass the bar exam scheduled in July. So, let's simmer down the talk on the whole *harsh* justice routine. You ain't delivered justice for anyone yet, 'cept maybe a few fake victims in your mock trial classes back in law school."

He exited the vehicle with the same level of confidence he had entered. The slam of the door echoed between the trees.

Inside the cruiser, John's adrenaline evaporated. Reality hit. The upper hand he believed he'd gained was a mirage. He was isolated, alone in the woods, with a man who seemed unflappable.

"Care to step to the back?" Parnell said, talking through the open driver's window.

John rubbed his lips, hiding a silent groan, and pulled himself out of the vehicle. He plodded the length of the cruiser and met Parnell at the trunk. Parnell raised the lid and reached in.

"Your little stunt last night caused quite a ruckus for me this morning. Mr. Kendrick showed up, bright and early, to give me multiple pieces of his mind. You sure ticked him off pretty good, son." Parnell pulled out a long black case. "He wanted you strung up by your toes for the assault you put on him. I told him I'd handle it... my way." With his other hand, he extracted a much smaller container and let both hang by his side. "Shut that for me, will you?"

John's eyes darted, trying to make sense of the situation. He reached up, through furrowed eyebrows and squinted eyes, and closed the trunk. Parnell gingerly set the cases down.

"So you know, Counselor, I imparted to our recent parolee that it was his own fault and sent him on his way. Though, to my detriment, I still had to listen to him rant for thirty minutes, him being a member of the community and all. Reputable or not."

He unzipped one case and snapped the latch on the other. Then, using both hands, he lifted the tops of both and flipped them back.

John's eyes widened as he gazed upon their contents—a pump-action shotgun and a semi-automatic handgun.

Parnell rested his thumbs inside his belt—his default stance—and stared. He raised a single eyebrow and sized up the young man standing in front of him.

Time slowed. The sensation of everything blurred together as John drank in the scene. His eyes raced, scanning between Parnell and the weapons on the trunk. He studied the Sheriff's positioning, his reach suspiciously close to his holstered pistol.

What the hell is going on? Is this a set-up? One wrong move and I'll be Coldwater's next mystery.

Parnell nodded towards the firearms.

"Pick a weapon, and let's see what kind of man you are."

9

TARGET TRUST

"What kind of game are you playing, Sheriff?"

John, adamant in his tone, took a step backwards from Parnell, gravel crunching under his loafers. Hands still at his side, he took no action to reach for either weapon.

"And, move your hand away from your holster, if you don't mind."

Parnell sported a quizzical look, but said nothing.

John's eyes narrowed further. "This has gone on far enough, Sheriff," he said, laced with annoyance. "I'm not interested in your games, or dueling, or whatever else you think this is. And, I certainly don't appreciate being brought out here in the middle of nowhere. You're flirting with an unlawful detention here." His hands clenched at his sides, frustration radiating from every tense muscle. "If you have something to say to me, come out with it. Otherwise, I think we're done here."

"Dueling? Hoo, boy. I think you've been watching too many Western movies to get that impression. Which, by the way, is a wrong one."

"Wrong?" John pointed at the weapons lying on the trunk lid. "What else should I think?"

Parnell breathed in deeply, lips pressed tight, the faint creak of his leather belt cutting through the hum of distant crickets. His exhale burst out, quick and sharp, carrying a whiff of coffee that hung in the dry air.

"Alright, son, let's cut the bull. I'm trying to figure out where your loyalties lie."

"That's funny, Sheriff. I've had that same question about you ever since I got here."

"About me?" Parnell scoffed. "Don't be ridiculous, Counselor. I'm the Sheriff of this town. The time you spent with Gamble makes me wonder about you."

"Are you serious? I knew the man for one week. One week! And, in fact, he warned me about *you*. Don't forget about your little stunt... you're the one who's abused his power. Remember pulling me over for a little chat on my first day? That stop was without cause, and you know it."

"Now, now... you're blowing that out of proportion. I did that to warn you about Gamble. Turned out I was right."

"What are you talking about? You gave me a cryptic word puzzle about 'knowing who to trust'. The only thing it did was make me not want to trust *you*. The mayor, who's also a little creepy, by the way, said basically the same thing. So, it's not just me. Truthfully, nobody around here is looking clean, except Annaleigh."

"Ah, Ms. Stanton," the Sheriff uttered under his breath. "Coldwater's true north star. She's a good one, so we agree on something."

"Yeah, well, at this point, she doesn't know who to trust, either." He paused, looked down, then met Parnell's eyes. "Except me. She trusts me. What does that tell you?"

Parnell dropped his hands from his hips and relaxed them at his sides. "That maybe I should, too," he said, bobbing his head up and down.

"Great. Now, how about we start over and you tell me what the hell we're doing out here?"

"This is my property. Behind that hill is my personal shooting range. If Ms. Stanton trusts you, that gets us close. But, I don't trust no man 'til I've seen him shoot a weapon." He took a step forward and laid his hand on the trunk, tapping it a few times. "Now, like I said before, choose one and let's go see what we're dealing with."

John lifted the pistol, its grip rough against his palm, the steel chilling his fingers like ice pulled from a stream. Instinct kicked in from childhood lessons with his mother.

Deliberate movements.

Safety on, chamber empty, finger on the guard, magazine... light.

Too light.

He exhaled, tension easing, ejected the mag, and handed it back.

"If we're going to do this, I'm going to need one that has rounds in it."

Parnell smiled.

"Impressive catch, Counselor. A very promising start."

* * *

PARNELL LED John to a makeshift booth, its wood splintered and grayed by relentless sun. The structure crouched on the bluff's far side, thirty yards from the mound's scarred face. A two-by-four-foot piece of aged plywood hung in front of the mound, sporting the silhouette of a man, spray-painted in black.

A worn path to the target told the tale of hours of practice. The air carried a sharp tang of gunpowder and scorched earth. Parnell's personal shooting range was a battleground waiting to speak.

John set the pistol onto the wooden top of the stall and put on a pair of ear guards, which mussed his hair more than the frequent gusts that snuck through the dense trees.

Parnell, now sporting a ball cap embroidered with the word

NAVY instead of his trademark straight-rimmed cowboy hat, reached into his back pocket, retrieving a full magazine.

"Eleven in there, young man. Make them count."

John swapped the empty magazine in his hand with Parnell's full one in a smooth, deft motion. He aligned it into the well and snapped it in with a quick smack of his palm. He racked the slide back and loaded the first round into the chamber.

Pointing the barrel downrange, he looked back at the Sheriff over his shoulder. "If I hit center mass, you go deeper into the sinister warning from my first day. I want to know more about what you think... thought of Gamble."

Parnell chuckled. "A game to earn my wisdom? Deal. Try not to waste all them bullets before you get your first answer."

John grasped the firearm with steady hands, using a push-pull grip. With a smooth motion, he flipped the safety off with his thumb, readying himself for the shot. The distinct click of the mechanism made his pulse quicken.

A slow squeeze of the trigger kicked the pistol hard in John's palm, sending a jolt that buzzed up his arm. The shot's echo reverberated against the bluff. The plywood swayed on its rusted chains.

Center mass. Dead on.

"Hmm, wasn't expecting that," the Sheriff uttered. "Not bad for a desk jockey."

John shrugged. "Deal's a deal. Let's hear it."

Parnell sighed. "I've long suspected Gamble of either slow-walking prosecutions or dismissing them outright."

"I guess that explains Mumber's wisecrack to Annaleigh at your station, you know, about not following through. Prosecutorial discretion gave him a lot of latitude on which cases to take or drop, in case you didn't know."

"Oh, I'm familiar, but it started happening more and more over the last few years. When he first got here, nothing slipped by him. He was a hard ass, came down pretty strict on about anyone. Kendrick's a good example of that. But..."

"But, what?"

Parnell crossed his arms and nodded at the plywood. "Two more, center mass. Gotta keep earning it."

John returned his focus downrange and steadied the weapon. Two more shots shattered the quiet of the backwoods.

When the target slowed down from swinging, Parnell confirmed two additional holes in the center, separated by six inches. He reverted to habits as if instructing recruits.

"The force of impact swings it backwards, so compensate for that on the aim of your second shot."

"Yeah, yeah, Sheriff," John said, waving him off. "Don't change the subject. Keep going."

"Gamble hitched his wagon, so to speak, to some questionable people." He sat down on a stump, staring off into the trees, searching for the words. "He found the company of Cameron and Kenneth."

"Cameron, as in Mayor Cameron Raith? That Cameron?"

"Yes, sir, the same one. Cam and I go way back. Kenneth ran around with us, too. Grew up together. Some years back, though, we had a falling out. Things got... complicated." He pointed at the target again. "Head."

Another shot whizzed through the air.

"Damn son, you got quite the aim. I'm surprised. You were a little jumpy at the station, so I figured you for a pansy in a suit. No offense."

"I wasn't being jumpy."

"Really? You about launched out of your chair. Tried to cover it up by clearing your throat, but I clocked it."

John took a deep breath, the scent of sagebrush bitter in his nose. A twig snapped somewhere in the brush, sharp enough to make him flinch. He hated talking about his condition.

"I don't see very well on the sides, that's all. Makes it difficult to see sometimes."

"You're telling me, with that shot, you got some kind of vision problem. A disability?"

"No!" John barked, then composed himself. "A few unfortunate surgeries caused some blind spots, that's all. I'm not disabled."

"Well," Parnell said, peering in, "your eyes look fine to me, son."

"My central sight is fine. That's all that matters. When I focus on something, nothing can distract me. No matter what it is."

Parnell raised his hands, realizing he'd hit a nerve.

"My fault, then. Message received. The man can see just fine."

"Don't tangent. Tell me why Gamble talking with the mayor was a bad thing."

"You first. Try something different. Turn away, left side, then rotate back and fire. One to center mass, one to the head. Now, fast!"

John pivoted at the hips and swung back, squeezing the trigger as soon as the plywood blur came into view.

Hesitation. Blinking. Refocusing.

He fired off a second round.

The first shot had grazed the edge of the board, splintering the layered wood. The second pierced the target's painted shoulder.

"Interesting." Parnell scratched at his chin.

John sighed.

"No worries, Counselor. At least you still hit it... somewhere."

"I earned my answer, then. Out with it."

"Your tone aside, I'll keep up my end. There was an incident with Cameron's wife, Evelyn. One day, she up and disappeared. Abandoned him, her boy, the house, this town... everything. Didn't tell a soul and vanished into the Coldwater breeze. As Sheriff, I wanted to know where she went and why she left, so I started digging around. He disagreed with my approach."

"Disagreed?"

"To me, leaving without a peep is... suspicious. The first suspect in a case like that is always the husband. I pressed in. He pushed back."

"Makes him look guilty, doesn't it?"

Parnell yanked the bill of his cap, fingers scraping sweat-slicked hair, at least what little remained, as he grimaced. Behind him, the mound loomed, its pockmarked face catching shadows that twisted like unanswered questions.

"Now you see my predicament. He was adamant she left on her own. Others weren't so sure. Didn't have no proof, though. When Kenneth vouched for Cameron's side of the story, that sealed the investigation's fate."

"How so? He doesn't run you."

"A mayor—especially a small town one—can make life pretty difficult if they really want to. Soon after my investigation started, there were 'complications' with the budget. *My* budget. Would've cost a lot of jobs... and the safety of this town. So, I backed off. What do you know? City Hall suddenly found the money."

"Bullshit corruption," John muttered. "That crap wouldn't fly up in St. Louis."

"What's that?"

John shook his head, waving. Parnell rubbed his mustache, straightening out the edges.

"To me, Evie's case will always be open until I find her, dead or alive. Cameron knows that, and holds it against me. He and Kenneth are on one side of this. I'm on the other." Parnell stood up and shuffled the dirt with his shoes. "Two more, center mass."

Crack! Crack! The Sheriff waited for the target to stop swinging, then looked at John, confused.

"You missed."

"Check again. I got bored. I put both into the other shoulder instead. Gave it a matching pair." John paused to watch Parnell squint, then nod in acknowledgment. "So, who do you think did it? Who killed Gamble?"

"Counselor, if I knew that, they'd already be rotting in jail. Now, mag dump the last four. Then, you can ask the one question you've been dying to ask."

"Just one problem, Sheriff. Only *three* shots left." He smiled, proud he hadn't fallen for the trap. "You knew that, though."

"That I did, son. That I did."

Three more rounds exploded from the barrel. Each shot thudded into the target, splintering plywood under the center mass hits. It swung wildly, chains screeching like a trapped animal, as the echoes faded into the hills, swallowed by an unsettling hush.

John lowered the pistol, pulse racing. The pistol's slide snapped back with a sharp, metallic clack. The magazine was spent. He set the gun and the ear guards down onto the wooden counter, then faced Parnell.

"What could have done... that... to him? It's almost indescribable."

"That, son, is the mystery that Coldwater may never solve. In all my years, it's the most unique—and gruesome—way to die that I've encountered in all my years on the force. It's perplexed me ever since I saw what had happened." Parnell picked up the handgun and verified the chamber was empty. "Coroner thinks the arm went first, ante-mortem. Critical, but not what killed him. The injuries to his face and head did. Still no idea how. Could be a blowtorch, arc welder, hell, maybe a plasma cutter. Gotta be a kind of heavy-duty equipment to generate that level of directed heat. We've checked and cleared anybody who owns anything like that in the entire county."

"So, no weapon, no leads." John looked downward, pursing his lips. "Not your fault, I get it. Between you and me, I still can't get the image out of my head at night."

Parnell extended his hand to John, genuine warmth radiating from his outstretched palm.

"Truce?"

John clasped it, gripping tight.

"No." He leaned in. "Trust."

Parnell's grin widened, then froze as the cruiser's cackling radio echoed from behind the mound.

"Sheriff? Sheriff, come in."

With a single finger, he left John at the booth and hustled

back to respond. A roaring whistle, paired with frantic waving, drew John's attention.

"We need to go," the sheriff yelled.

John raced towards him, shouting. "Why? What happened?"

"Someone has been reported missing. The courthouse is on lockdown."

His eyes bulged as his stomach flipped. "Oh my God, who did they take? It wasn't Annaleigh, was it? Who's missing?"

"*You* are."

10

SOMEONE DIDN'T R.S.V.P

I t didn't take Sheriff Parnell long to untangle the chaos.
Annaleigh had arrived early, and Genie was right on time.
In the gap, no one had seen John slide into Parnell's cruiser and
drive off. Bad timing had fueled the entirety of the morning's
panic.

After being tardy for the first time, Annaleigh spotted John's
empty car in the lot across the square. A quick call to Bonnie
confirmed he'd left home on time, and everyone braced for the
worst.

"One big misunderstanding," Parnell insisted. His twang cut
through the courthouse clamor—radios crackling, deputy boots
scuffing the floorboards, and the faint whiff of leather shine
mingling with the stale air.

As law enforcement dispersed, Genie's hug enveloped John in
a warm, perfume-soaked crush. Sharp diamond sequins pricked
his arms, her bangles clinking with the squeeze.

"Sugar, we were fixing to call out the bloodhounds!"

Across the office, Annaleigh appeared in her doorway, looking
stressed. He grinned, trying to politely wriggle free from Genie's
embrace.

"Parnell's lousy at making reservations. At the time, it didn't feel like much of a choice."

"There's always a choice," Annaleigh scolded from across the room. "Next time, do better and skip the joyride."

Her tone was harsher than he'd expected. She sank into a nearby desk chair and spun to face the other way. Genie clapped her hands and shuffled towards the stairs.

"I, for one, am glad everyone's safe and sound. I'm gonna take an early lunch. Two birds, one me. I can surprise the Mister and give you time to mend some fences."

A hush covered the room. John wasn't sure how long to let it linger. He dropped into his chair, rolled closer, and lowered his voice.

"Didn't mean to make you pace a hole in the floor, Annaleigh. I'm sorry."

"I know," she murmured, still turned away. Her chair creaked as she stood, the air around her filling with a faint scent of lavender. "I'm not mad at you. But, I'm billing Parnell for my morning cardio." A shaky inhale. "I thought we'd lost you."

She sank back down, aimlessly shuffling papers and blank legal pads. Her hair grazed her shoulders, catching his eye despite the tension. Her eyes were glassy, holding back tears. She pulled a few strands and covered her face, hiding from his prying eyes.

It wasn't the first time he'd stolen glances at her, but he was doing it again, at the most inappropriate time. He looked away, only to be struck by the unmistakable sensation that he, too, was being watched in return. He cursed his lack of peripheral vision to confirm.

Heavy footsteps thudded up the creaking staircase, a cold draft slithering through the office. Both heads snapped toward the sound.

"Genie?" Annaleigh asked into the void. "Forget something?"

A deep, gravelly voice echoed from around the corner, shudder-inducing.

"Nope, but you can rub my lamp, little missy."

That voice. John knew it, though, until now, he'd only heard it speak a single word.

Kenneth Roy Atlee hit the top step, turned into the court-house office, and John's gut wrenched. Within no time, his second encounter had already become as awkward as the first.

Last week, John's first day lunch with his new boss, Gamble, at a local Italian joint had soured fast. As they settled in at their candlelit table, surrounded by clinking glasses and the rich tang of garlic and marinara, a deep, country voice disrupted the moment.

"Didn't expect to see you here, Doyal."

Mayor Cameron Raith, with a wide-brimmed hat tipped low, led a trio towards them. His brooding son, Wesley, followed right off the mayor's hip, staring at the ground. The last time John saw him, Wesley wasn't even a teenager. After the years John was gone, that young kid looked old enough to buy beer.

Kenneth, a brute, lurked, observing. The mayor was stocky—the kind from sitting behind a desk, not riding a tractor. Kenneth, however, stood a full head taller than the mayor and sporting shoulders wider than John thought possible. His menacing scowl, complete with a sociopathic stare, bored into John's forehead as he shifted his position to the other side of Raith, closer to the table. He exuded the notion that he wrestled bulls as a hobby. And won.

"Cameron," Gamble said, gesturing wide. "I was treating the young man to a work lunch—"

Raith cleared his throat, causing Gamble to restart his intro-duction.

"Mr. Mayor, pardon me. Sir, this is my new attorney, John Chance."

John scooted to the edge of his chair, attempting to rise and shake the mayor's hand. Anything other than that felt improper, per Bonnie's instruction. Making a good first impression could make his life easier, no matter how long he intended to stay in this town.

Kenneth's burly hand interrupted his rise and slammed him back down with unimaginable strength.

"Sit."

A short, searing pain radiated through John's shoulder. Raith raised his hand, gesturing.

"Stand down, Kenneth. The boy is on our side, after all."

Kenneth removed his large, warm hand and retreated a step backward, but not before drilling John with another stare that promised trouble. John slumped back, eyebrows lowered, and rubbed his shoulder. The pressure was gone, but the ache remained. Raith tipped the brim of his cap.

"Apologies for that, young man. My friend Kenneth gets jumpy around strangers. He means well, though. Don't you, Kenneth? Anyway, Cameron Raith, at your service. Please, call me *Mayor.*" Raith's tone flipped from jovial to commanding in an instant.

John absorbed the moment, locking eyes with the mayor. He'd met the man years before, as a child, but no need to bring that up now and invite further conversation.

"Nice to meet you," he lied. A quick nod towards Kenneth. "Maybe your buddy isn't Coldwater's best spokesperson, though."

Raith chuckled. "That's sound advice, son. Sound advice, indeed," he said, his voice flipping back to conversational once again. He rubbed his hands together. "Doyal has told me all about you. For what it's worth, I didn't think we had the work to sustain another lawyer. But, Doyal insisted. It's his budget to waste, I reckon."

Raith motioned to his left. "This is my son, Wesley. He's pleased to meet you."

Wesley briefly raised his chin and then lowered it, saying nothing and directing his eyes back to the floor. As he dipped his head, candlelight reflected over the side of his face like waves on a lake, illuminating wrinkled and leathery skin. Keloid scars, John knew them well. The scar tissue in his own eyes was the result of numerous surgeries. Wesley's, though, looked different. Organically shaped, stretching from his eye to his sideburn.

Those look like burn scars.

John nodded at Wesley, his eyes darting away from the young man's disfigurement.

"Welcome back to Coldwater, son," the mayor said, emotionless. "And, thank you for your service to the town."

Raith maneuvered between the tables with familiar movements towards the front entrance, snapping at Wesley to follow. Kenneth eased close to their table, knocking twice, then dragging himself away. Once at the door, he took one last, determined stare back before disappearing outside and onto the sidewalk. John raised his eyebrows in confusion.

"What the hell did I do to that guy?"

"No, no," Gamble said, half-smiling. "That's just how Kenneth is. It's not often that you see one without also seeing the other skulking in some nearby corner. Sorry about that. I was hoping not to expose you to, well, him, on your first day."

"Part of me wants to charge him with assault." He adjusted his shoulders, trying to stretch the soreness away.

"I get it, he and Cameron are both pretty intense, but I wouldn't worry about them. The best thing for you to do is put your head down and do the work. As long as I'm around, I'll be your shield. Annaleigh's, too." He drew a slow, deep breath. "No need for either of you to get involved with... any of that."

John peered at the shades covering the front windows of the restaurant. The mayor's enforcer was still out there. Lurking.

Kenneth Roy Atlee's boots stomped closer inside the courthouse office, nearing Genie's desk.

"What the hell did you say to her? You apologize. Now!"

Annaleigh launched out of her chair, arriving at John's side, hands on his shoulder. "It's fine. I'll handle this." She turned her attention back to Kenneth. "What is it that you need today, Mr. Atlee?"

"Updates. Mayor's investigation. Now."

John scoffed, "You're not part of this. The exit's behind you."

"The man sent me here himself," Kenneth growled. "Tell me what you've found."

Annaleigh stepped in front of John. "Mr. Atlee, with all due respect. You don't work for the mayor. Or the town. We'll deliver updates to the mayor personally."

Kenneth inched closer. "I don't think you heard correctly. Spill it. Now."

John stepped forward and covered Annaleigh. "I'm not sure *you* did. Have a nice day," he said, waving Kenneth off.

A fire grew inside the brute. His face reddened, his fingers began needling in his palms, fists inflating and deflating and matching each huff from his mouth.

"Could've been easy, Chance. You picked hard."

"Is that a threat?" John strode again, coming within arm's reach of the mayor's bodyguard.

"If you don't know what one is, you'll find out soon enough."

Kenneth flashed a smirk, turned, and headed back down the stairs. Annaleigh leaned against a desk, shaking her head and letting out a long breath. John remained alert, eyeing the stairwell, in case the footsteps returned.

"Jesus, every time that guy shows up, it's a new shade of creepy."

"Agreed. Your mom told me about him. Said to cross the street if you see him coming."

His eyes narrowed as a bright light washed over the stairwell, spilling into the office and momentarily blinding him. It vanished as quickly as it had appeared. He rubbed his eyes as a whiff of charred wood hit his nose.

"You smell that?" he asked, following it to the stairs.

He waved Annaleigh over. Together, they peered around the corner and found the stairs empty.

"Smells like a campfire, doesn't it?" she asked.

"Yeah, but no smoke."

They descended, one step at a time, and froze at the bottom. She gasped.

A handprint with five blackened, spread fingers was burned into the wood paneling, still warm to the touch. A faint orange flicker lingered around the scorch mark.

"What the hell is that?" he whispered, pulse racing.

11

DRAWER OF SECRETS

"Farmers around here use all kinds of custom brands," said Deputy D. Clyde Brothers after examining the burn on the woodwork at the foot of the stairs. He was first on the scene to investigate the allegations, and upon his arrival, he seemed perplexed about its origin, eventually settling on the only logical explanation.

"You don't think this is a warning? A threat?" John snapped, disagreeing with the reasoning. "This courthouse isn't a cow, deputy."

"We've seen this kind of vandalism before, in different shapes," Clyde explained. "I can't imagine the mayor's guy doing this, though."

"You didn't hear what he said. The words he used."

"I understand, Mr. Chance. I'll find out from Hollis, I mean, Detective Mumber, to see if we have records who might be using this one. We'll get to the bottom of this, don't you worry."

"Thanks, Deputy," Annaleigh interjected, shaking his hand. "We appreciate you coming back so quickly."

Clyde reflected a warm smile. "Anything for you, Ms. Stanton. I'm just glad Mr. Chance didn't go missing again." He ignored the roll of John's eyes, smiled with his own, and left.

"We need a steel door up here, like Parnell has. Put it right there at the top of the stairs," John joked after he and Annaleigh returned upstairs.

"Great," she scoffed. "Swap sneaky intruders for a heart attack when they start pounding."

"Fair point. I'd rather not die of fright before we solve this." He crashed into his chair, causing it to roll backwards. By the time he stopped it, he was clear of his desk and facing Gamble's door. The door had yet to be opened since his murder.

It might stay sealed until I leave for St. Louis, who knows?

Maybe, eventually, Annaleigh would move in. It was bigger. Nicer.

Her office only had room for a single bookshelf, in addition to her small desk. And, if she were sitting at it, the door couldn't swing all the way open. On her shelf, books were crammed in unusually, with unmarked folders teetering on each shelf's edge. It's the way she preferred—her system. Every time he saw it, it made John wince. Her chaos was oddly endearing.

Gamble's office was almost twice as wide, ample room for two bookshelves *and* a full-length table. Everything was always straight. Too straight, perhaps.

Nah. Things can't ever be too straight. Ninety-degree angles. Everything in its place.

Tucked into the corner of the bullpen, it was a shrine to order. Legal volumes aligned with military precision, pens parallel, nameplate squared to the desk's edge. The kind of structure John loved, a commonality he and his boss shared. He noticed it during their initial meeting on John's first day. While sitting down in that ugly chair with the paisley upholstery, he accidentally kicked the back of Gamble's desk, and a single pen rolled out of formation. Gamble quickly reached out and set it back into place. Then, his long, thin fingers touched every other pen and notepad on the surface, confirming their position. The attention to detail did not go unseen.

Behind that closed door, all those details sat, perfectly

preserved. It was almost odd that no one had been in there since his death. Or, at least since they'd heard about the murder.

No, he remembered, since they were *told* about the murder.

"Instead of pounding on the door," he said, pointing towards the office, "what if someone crashes through like Raith did?"

Her confusion shifted to realization. "You mean the day Gamble died?"

"Yeah, we interrupted whatever he was doing in there. He exploded out," John said, picturing the mayor's flushed face, his tie askew, hiding guilt behind authority. The door had slammed so hard the framed county map rattled on the wall. "You jumped a mile. I remember it clear as day."

"Are you kidding? *You* jumped," she shot back, arms crossed. "Scratch that. You probably didn't even see him. You only jumped in reaction to my jump—" She caught herself, then pointed at him. "That smirk? Erase that. Now."

He grinned. "Yes, ma'am. Whatever you say, ma'am."

They stood outside Gamble's office door, waiting and wondering who would make the first move and touch the handle. John spoke first.

"Parnell said Gamble was burying cases. Maybe Raith knew too, and was looking for answers?"

"There's really no reason for us to make prosecutions disappear. The real question is, *who* was he dropping them for? Who else would benefit from it?"

"I guess secretly searching a dead guy's office is one way to find out. Does the mayor strike you as someone who would act out of sheer curiosity?"

She hesitated. "Not at all. It must go deeper, then. Perhaps, whatever's in there might burn him, then. Or us." She raised her knuckles, then dropped her fist to her side. "Muscle memory wants me to knock first. Wait for him to tell me to come in."

"Don't," he said, hand on the handle. "He won't answer." He exchanged another glance with her, eyebrows vaulted. "I could twist this knob, and we can see for ourselves. Or, we could go ask Raith what he was doing in here. Your choice."

"I don't know about you, but I'm not overly eager to have another conversation with that man yet. Or, anyone else close to him, for that matter." She nodded, convincing herself it was the right play. "Let's see what Gamble left behind."

John rotated the handle, the faint click of the latch echoing in the silence. As he inched the door open, the hinges groaned a low, mournful creak that seemed to protest the intrusion. He peeked in, half-expecting the man to still be sitting in that ornate high-back chair, flashing an annoyed look for entering without permission.

Instead, greeting him on the edge of the desk, Gamble's nameplate. "Doyal Gamble", it read, etched in bold letters, hovering over the italicized text, "Prosecutor, Coldwater County". With him gone, it served no purpose other than to act as a grave marker. A chill ran down his spine.

He stepped inward to make room for Annaleigh, though she did not follow. The air carried a faint whiff of polished wood and old leather, laced with the stale tang of a room sealed too long. John scanned the office for signs of disturbance, his eyes again latching onto the nameplate glinting on the desk.

It was askew.

In fact, everything seemed a little bit off its expected layout.

John's fingers brushed the mahogany desktop surface, its grain marred by a subtle stickiness. Smudged fingerprints, perhaps. The pens, the antique banker's lamp, the phone, the legal pads—all shifted away from their usual precision. One pad lay face down, its corner curled. Even the lamp, its default location aligned with the desk's edge, sat crooked, shining half its light onto the floor.

He fought the sudden urge to start tidying.

The phenomenon affected the entire office. The volumes on the bookshelves, once expertly arranged, were uneven. Some books were pushed all the way back, while others leaned against their neighbors for support. Oddly, the folders on the full-length table remained, all in their perfect, original placement. White corners of pages stuck out from their confines, hinting their innards had been rifled through. He looked back and waved her in.

"Come in and see this."

She took a single step into the room and sighed. Dust motes danced in a slant of gray light spilling through the blinds, casting faint stripes across the empty high-back. Her head turned, as if looking around, but her eyes stayed fixed.

"Tell me what you see, John. I can't stop staring at that chair."

"Well, Gamble kept everything pristine. Every object, arranged and in its place," he explained. "I'm a bit like that, too." He shrugged, his gaze dipping low.

"Don't worry," she said softly. "I noticed that about you. It's cute."

John walked around the other side of the desk and surveyed the disarray.

"There's no doubt someone's been snooping in here, moving things."

"For what reason, though? That's the question."

"Let's find out." He pulled out Gamble's chair and gestured to it. "This is yours now, Acting Prosecutor Stanton. *You* should be the one to search it."

Taking a deep breath, she gripped the arms and sat down. "This feels wrong."

John, hesitant at first to touch anything to preserve the scene, switched to hands-on when the shadows ringing his vision played tricks on him, showing him clues that didn't exist. He yanked books from the shelves, checking behind them, finding only spare pens and a pair of forgotten reading glasses. He flipped through each legal volume, hoping the name of Gamble's killer would be written somewhere inside.

No such luck.

As he searched, the sharp screech of wooden drawers pierced the room's silence as Annaleigh tugged their handles.

He continued to eye the rest of the office, contemplating the next location in a mental search grid. He paced around to the front of the desk and leaned against the door frame, stealing a glance at her. In this morbid moment, though they were rummaging through a dead man's things, she still had an aura about her.

Her perfect, scrunched nose almost made him forget why they were in there. Perched on the edge of Gamble's chair, her focus trained on the contents of one of his drawers as she inclined forward to get a better look. In a fluid motion, she gracefully swept her hair behind her ear with her right hand, the gesture momentarily revealing a strained expression.

"Find something?" he asked.

"Nothing relevant," Annaleigh said, lifting a mostly empty bottle of peppermint schnapps from the drawer. The sharp, medicinal sting of peppermint floated up, biting her nostrils.

"No glass. I guess he drank straight from the bottle." She frowned. "I thought he just liked breath mints."

A faint thump echoed from out in the bullpen. They froze, eyes darting to the door.

"Tell me that was the wind. This place creaks like a normal, old building, right?" he whispered.

Annaleigh's hand hovered over the desk phone, ready to call for help.

Silence.

Held breaths.

He tiptoed over and eased the door shut, just in case.

Slow, determined exhales.

More silence.

She softly tapped the desk. "Back to it. One more to go. If anything is hiding, it's doing it well. Come out, come out, little clues." She tugged at the drawer, but it stuck. Locked. "Of course," she muttered, scanning for a key.

"Problem?" John asked, pausing mid-step.

"Gamble's not making this easy. Bright side, though, this lock might have stopped Raith from getting in." She fished a paperclip from the pencil drawer, bending it with deft fingers. "Learned this at my sorority. Don't ask."

He raised an eyebrow. "You're full of surprises."

"Keep searching, neat freak."

"Hell no, I'm watching this."

The paperclip scraped inside the lock, a faint click signaling success. She smirked, but her triumph faded as she peeked inside.

He stepped closer, causing a floorboard to creak. The unexpected noise made them both jump and look toward the door. Realizing, they exchanged relieved glances and turned back to the drawer. She inched it out.

"Oh my God. Look at this."

She pushed back with her feet, rolling the chair backward, letting him peer over her to take a look.

The drawer's treasure was a pile of manila folders, bundled together with a thin rubber band. She lifted it out and set it onto the desk, hands visibly shaking. Her breath caught as she spied a sticky note, in Gamble's scrawl, staring back.

"Annaleigh. The truth."

12

THE LAST SCRAWL

Doyal Gamble switched off the fluorescent bulbs and tugged the bronzed pull chain of his antique banker's lamp. The soft glow of the sixty-watt bulb cast gentle shadows across his office in Coldwater's courthouse. It was well past midnight on Saturday night. He wanted ambiance, not a spotlight.

Not that he had much to concern himself with at this hour.

The downtown district, with the courthouse as its focal point, has long since gone quiet. Shops and restaurants shuttered after the dinner rush, leaving only the Wobbly Barrel as a landing spot for the slow-sipping retirees nursing quarter-full tumblers of bourbon. If they had glanced up at the courthouse's second-floor windows and seen a light, they'd likely forget by morning.

Nothing to worry about.

The late May air, thick with the sound of cicadas, drifted through the open window. Summer's heat was creeping into the evenings, but Doyal wanted to savor the breeze while it lasted.

He lived a few blocks south of downtown, a privilege that meant his evening walks could easily lead him to the courthouse's quiet steps. Working at odd hours allowed him to focus, with the silence sharpening his thoughts. It also kept prying eyes from seeing the kind of work that twisted his gut with shame.

His hands trembled as he sifted through the manila folders strewn across his desk, their edges frayed from countless reviews. Each was a piece of his penance, or maybe his punishment. A treasure trove of secrets, gathered through back channels and subterfuge, stared back.

Many of those secrets came easily. Prosecutions that flowed through his office as County Prosecutor, only to vanish from the docket and wind up in this stash, for safekeeping. Others, like falsified permits or doctored zoning reports, required charming the County Clerk, a retired widow stuck in her sixties and clinging to purpose. Doyal, no socialite, had even joined the fire chief for weekly breakfasts at the station, securing access to arson investigations that never saw daylight.

This multi-pronged effort built a dossier on the man whose family had a grip on Coldwater's soul—the town's mayor, Cameron Raith.

Tonight, guilt pressed heavier than ever.

Doyal leaned back in his creaking chair, the leather cracked like his conscience. He reeked with remorse, hiding in an out-of-touch office, a stubborn relic of a town where fax machines were novel and personal computers a fad, destined to fade like Betamax tapes. Even its rotary phones and handwritten ledgers told of a backwards time where political power, not logic and common sense, ruled over all.

He had once loved this place. It had simplicity, both in its buildings and its people. That love had soured into a slow poison, seeping through his veins. His hands were nearly as dirty as Raith's, because Doyal was a witting, though unwilling, participant in every scheme he'd documented in this stack of secrets.

Five years ago, it started with a late-night visit from Mayor Raith. The man's smile was all teeth, his offer cloaked in charm and laced with menace.

"You've got a daughter in college, Doyal," he'd said, leaning across this very desk. "Med school's expensive. Debts pile up. Help me out, and I'll make sure she's taken care of."

Emma, his pride, was a product of a marriage long since broken. He hadn't seen her in two years, kept away by a scornful mother who no longer loved him. Perhaps this opportunity would be the gift that could set things straight, and his daughter might love him again.

Doyal had nodded and accepted the deal, thinking it a one-time infraction. Surely, it would only be a single dismissed charge or a file lost behind a cabinet.

One favor became a dozen, then more, links in a chain forged by blackmail. Raith's whims bent the law, and Doyal, once its guardian, turned into its gravedigger.

Every folder he flipped through was a brick in the wall of his shame, built to protect Emma but now threatening to crush him. His eyes stung, not from dim light but from the weight of his betrayal. He'd perverted justice, silenced witnesses, and buried cases, each a violation of the oath he'd sworn decades ago in this office.

He thought of John Chance, the young lawyer, fresh from law school, eyes on a prize job in the big city, but stuck in Coldwater's gravity. A hometown black hole. John's ambition mirrored Doyal's younger self. He was too smart. And, too bold.

Then, there was Annaleigh Stanton, his assistant prosecutor, with her sharp mind and even sharper principles, untainted by the town's rot. She'd joined last fall, her hunger for justice a faint echo of the man Doyal used to be.

He'd keep them clean of his sins.

This was his cross to bear.

A creak from the stairwell snapped him upright. The courthouse should be empty, the janitor long gone, but the old wooden steps groaned under the weight of an unexpected visitor.

Heart pounding, he shoved the files into the drawer, their edges catching as he forced it shut. Footsteps outside his office echoed, deliberate and heavy. The door stood ajar, the bullpen beyond lit only by the faint red glow of an exit sign. His breath shallowed as a shadow appeared.

"Doyal?" a voice called, young but edged with something sinister. Wesley Raith, the mayor's son, stepped into the light, his thin frame peering into the doorway. His eyes, cold and unreadable, locked onto Doyal's. "My dad sent me. He needs to see you."

Doyal slumped, masking his shaking knees.

"Wesley, it's late, I'm wrapping up and about to go home—"

"No, now. I had to check your place first. Then, I came here. We can't keep him waiting any longer."

Doyal's stomach twisted. Wesley, barely twenty, was his father's errand boy, all loyalty and no spine, his face scarred by a life under Raith's thumb. He'd never set foot in this office before. Tonight's visit carried with it an ominous feel. Doyal forced a nod.

"So be it. One second, though."

He grabbed a sticky note, his usual careful script reduced to a frantic scratch.

Annaleigh. The truth.

No time for more.

If this visit with Raith went south, those files might be his last chance to undo the mayor's empire. He slid the note onto the top folder, locked the drawer without a sound, and moved with calculated calm under Wesley's watchful gaze.

"Alright, Wesley. All done. Let me grab my coat." He reached for his suit jacket, mind racing.

Another meeting with the mayor meant another demand, or worse, he had sniffed out Doyal's plan to flip the script. Those files held proof of corruption that could topple Coldwater's king. If Raith sensed betrayal, this wasn't a courtesy call.

It was a reckoning.

Wesley's sneakers squeaked on the worn floorboards as Doyal followed him into the hall. Doyal glanced back at his office, the drawer's secrets hidden, but vulnerable. He hesitated, fingers brushing the doorknob, itching to lock it.

Wesley's impatient stare stopped him.

With a slow exhale, he pulled the door shut, the click resounding like a gavel.

The courthouse's silence pressed against him, replete with the ghosts of buried cases. If Raith's patience had snapped, Gamble was sure Annaleigh would discover the files, see the note, and unravel the web of lies. She was relentless, sharp enough to expose the truth and free Coldwater.

As long as she doesn't lose faith in me.

Outside, the mayor's Blazer loomed at the curb. Doyal's fear sharpened into certainty. He'd pushed back one too many times, his second chances worn thin.

As Wesley disappeared behind to enter through the driver's side. Doyal silently tossed the drawer key into nearby bushes. If Wesley saw him lock the drawer, he couldn't bring it with him and give the mayor easy access to the evidence. He'd retrieve it later, after he was free from Raith's beckoning.

He climbed in the passenger seat, heart heavy with what he'd done—and what he hadn't—he could only hope that, if needed, Annaleigh would find the courage he'd lost.

13

GRIME AND WINE

Annaleigh's knuckles rapped on John's wooden front door, the sound sharp against the quiet of Coldwater's southern flank. A cool evening breeze brushed her bare legs, carrying the earthy tang of pine from the nearby woods past the edge of the property.

Her pulse ticked up, not from nerves, but from the thrill of what she carried. Hidden from view were two bottles of peach wine behind her back and a mind buzzing with the weight of Gamble's secret files.

She'd changed out of her courthouse armor, opting for jean shorts that hugged her hips and a simple black tee that teased a sliver of her toned midriff. The outfit was a calculated choice. John's reactions were always a treat, and even though a heavy conversation was about to happen, she had to keep dropping hints.

If I don't, he might never figure it out.

The door swung open. John's breath caught, eyes wide, lips parted. She suppressed a smirk, tilting her head to let her hair spill over one shoulder.

There's the look. Gotcha.

"Hope you don't mind me popping by," she said, tucking both bottles behind her back. "Thought we could debrief a little."

John swallowed hard, his fingers fumbling with his shirt collar. "Yeah, uh, not a problem, um, Counselor. I can never get enough of you, er, I mean, you're welcome here anytime."

Haven't seen him tongue-tied before. Adorable.

She quirked a brow, revealing one bottle. "I brought entertainment. Peach wine." She flashed the second with a flourish. "We're unwinding tonight. Coldwater style."

John's shoulders eased, his lips curving into a grin. "Never heard of the stuff, but who could refuse an offer like that?"

"Better not be you," she teased, stepping inside and kicking off her sandals, the worn hardwood floor cool beneath her bare feet. She plopped onto the couch, folding her legs criss-cross and grabbing a thin plaid blanket that had been draped over the back. She patted the space beside her.

"I know I'm in your spot. I'll let you in on a little secret. It's kinda mine, too. Usually, you're not here. Sit where your mom does, okay?"

John settled stiffly next to her, leaving half of a couch cushion of separation. "Hold up, something's off. You're being too nice. You went back to the office after we both left, didn't you?"

Annaleigh's stomach twisted. She'd hoped to ease into this.

"I... may have looked at a few of those files." His expression darkened, and she rushed on. "Fine. I looked through *all* of them. I had to know what Gamble was up to, John. I couldn't wait."

He leaned back and crossed his arms. "I thought we agreed to do that starting tomorrow... together."

She met his gaze, voice soft. "He meant a lot to me. That note was personal. It was haunting me. I needed answers. I hope you're not mad."

He sighed, shaking his head. "It's fine. I understand, I do." He exhaled again, his tone softening. "Was it useful? Does anything in there point to who killed him?"

"It certainly wasn't what I thought it would be."

Annaleigh uncorked the first bottle with a pop, and sugary peach scent swirled into the air. The wine glugged as she poured two glasses. He watched intently, seeing its golden hue catch the light. She handed him one with trembling fingers.

"It's bad," she said. "More awful than I imagined. Dozens of cases. More, maybe, I didn't get through all of them. All kinds, too. Vandalism, conspiracy, embezzlement, you name it. Gamble buried them all."

"Unreal. I didn't realize he had it in him."

She rubbed her temple, frowning. "It gets better. No... worse. Every file had a handwritten timestamp next to a little note. Each one read, 'Per Cameron.'"

John's glass froze halfway to his lips, his knuckles whitening. "Mayor Raith? Seems like about everyone's on a first-name basis with that guy."

"Not me." She sipped her wine, the tart-sweet flavor clashing with the bile rising in her throat. "If these files can be trusted, it looks like Gamble was in Raith's pocket."

"Holy shit, Annaleigh. I knew that son-of-a-bitch was dirty." She flinched. He quickly added, "Raith, I mean."

She returned a soft smile. "What I don't understand is why leave them for me? More importantly, why would he think I'd go snooping in his desk to find them?" Her fingers tightened around the glass. "I respected him, John. Now, I don't know what to think."

"Sounds like he wanted you to finish what he couldn't. The irony is, we wouldn't have found them at all if it weren't for Raith's nosiness."

"Still, those notes aren't enough to convict. Even if I provided the jury with the right context, it's all circumstantial. Any good attorney will argue that those scribbles could mean just about anything. They don't read 'Dropped, per Cameron' or 'Bribe received from our corrupt mayor.' Just 'Per Cameron.' We can assume it meant Raith was calling the shots, but we'd get unbelievably chewed up on cross-examination." Annaleigh set her glass down, making a loud clink in the otherwise quiet room. "We can't walk into court and show the judge scribbles. We need more. Lots more. Raith's too slippery. He's got half the town either charmed or bought."

"So, what's the play, boss?" he asked, swirling his wine.

She matched his grin, the spark of a plan igniting. "First step, observe. We watch him. Quietly, though. Follow his moves, dig into his meetings, his money. If he's dirty, he'll slip."

"Let's not forget his lackey, Kenneth. If one of them is dirty, I guarantee they both are."

"You're not wrong, especially the way he came barging into the office wanting updates. There's no daylight between them."

His eyebrows arched, a glint in his eyes. "There's a chance that what Gamble did with these cases, you know, making them disappear... is what got him killed."

"Just as much chance that it's not," she snapped back, before pausing. "Sorry, even after what we've found, there's still a built-in instinct to defend him."

"No need to apologize. Until we can prove otherwise, he's earned our defense." He raised his glass. "To catching the bastard."

She clinked hers against his.

"To justice. For Gamble."

* * *

JOHN REFILLED their glasses and emptied the first bottle. They decided to move to the backyard patio, which meant passing through the kitchen. Bonnie sat reading at the table, a mug of chamomile tea steaming in front of her. She stood and grabbed Annaleigh's arm, pulling her into a warm embrace.

"Hello, dear. He finally let you come and say hi to me?"

"You know these Coldwater men, Bonnie. They fawn all over me. Couldn't shoo them away if I tried. Forced me to sit on the couch and talk. Yuck."

Bonnie fixed John with a mock glare, his lips twitching.

"Johnny? This true? You put your fawn away this instant and quit bothering this young lady."

His cheeks flushed. "All right, you two. This is weird. Spill it. How in the world did the two of you cross paths?"

The two women looked at each other and giggled. Annaleigh stood at Bonnie's side, arm still wrapped around her shoulders.

"When I came to Coldwater last year, your mom was the real estate agent who helped me find a place. Ran into her at an open house—"

"We hit it off right away," Bonnie interjected.

"—and not only did she get me a great deal, she waived her commission. I couldn't thank her enough—"

"Save your thanks, kiddo."

"—and ever since then, she sort of adopted me."

John's eyes darted between them, settling on his mother. "You didn't mention that you both appear to be one human with two heads."

"I *also* didn't tell you she stayed here until her close date," Bonnie admitted, smiling.

"Stayed?" he asked, eyes bulging. "That's quite a different word from visited, Mom."

Bonnie looked at Annaleigh, then back to John. "And, she slept in your room."

His lips parted in shock. "In... my room?"

The two women shared another laugh. Annaleigh pivoted her attention to John, slinging her arm around his shoulder in an act of reconciliation.

He wriggled away and grabbed a napkin from the table, mashing it into a ball and tossing it at his mother. "I can't believe how much you're enjoying this. I'll be right back. I'm going to go fetch my baseball glove, and the two of you can have a nice catch."

"Oh, dear, that's nonsense. We'd rather look through old photo albums at your naked baby photos. Again."

Amidst hearing a final round of giggles, John waved his mother off and rushed off.

Annaleigh followed him outside, the night air cool against her skin. Stars glittered above, and the distant hum of crickets wove through the rustle of leaves in the breeze. She sank into the wicker chair next to his, its woven strands creaking, her flushed cheeks showing the wine's warmth was spreading through her. After a few silent sips, her soothing voice filled his ear.

"Hey, partner. How ya doing over there?"

"In case you weren't aware, none of this is fair. You apparently know all about me. Everyone in this town apparently does. For God's sake, you've slept in my bed." He gulped down the remaining mouthful from his glass. "I'm pretty much in the dark about you, however."

"Fine, let's even the score. Ask me anything... well, for anything we need a lot more wine. Ask me *something*."

He thought for a moment, then grasped the second bottle she'd brought with her. He uncorked it, unleashing its potent, fruity aroma.

She shot a stern look. "Pace yourself, John Chance."

"Okay, then, here's an easy one. Why didn't you tell me you knew my mom?"

"It was her idea. She wanted you to focus on your job and not be distracted by anything else. We didn't mean to keep secrets from you. I promise. We thought it would help you."

He took a long, slow sip from his glass.

"To be honest, she already let it slip. But I didn't quite know the extent of it. You sleeping here? Now *that* is new information."

"In my defense, it was like a bed-and-breakfast stay, nothing weird. It was only for a few weeks, if that helps with anything. Like, six—"

He gasped, inhaling a bit of the wine.

"Six weeks? Six whole weeks? Please tell me you were *not* going to say sixteen, Annaleigh."

"Look, the whole time, I was worried you'd pop home for a visit, but—"

"I didn't, I know. I hear it from mom all the time." He dipped his head. "I wonder what would have happened if I did."

"Not sure we've had enough wine for that hypothetical." She pursed her lips. "Maybe someday, though."

A late evening breeze blew through, rustling the youthful green leaves on the nearby trees. Their eyes locked for a moment before he turned away. She leaned back and looked up at the stars.

"Just beautiful."

"Gorgeous," he said, eyes on her.

A hint of a smile grew on her face as she stared upwards.

"You're not looking up, John."

He glanced away. "Dammit. I forget other people can see sideways."

"Yeah, your mom and I talked about your surgeries one time. It didn't work out too well, huh?" Through the dim porch light, she stretched over the chair's arm and peered into his eyes, searching for the flaw. "What's it like?"

He sighed, looking around on the ground, trying to conjure the words to explain. His moment at the range with Parnell flashed in his mind. Normally, he hated talking about his condition. It made him feel weak. Less than everyone else. A private anchor around him that no one else even realized was there.

But something felt different with her. Annaleigh made him feel safe. He cupped his hands around his eyes, like binoculars.

"Kinda like this. Center's fine, but nothing but shadows on the outside, where my hands are."

She mimicked his hand placement and moved her head around, taking in the limited view.

"Wow, thrilling. So, I'm teaching you law and have to check both ways for you when we cross the street?" A giggle escaped her. "Seriously, though. There's no way to fix them?"

"It's been tried. Multiple attempts, all failures. Each time made it worse, ironically. You can only cut something so many times before you run out of it." He pointed at his eyes. "These aren't mine. Two corneal transplants."

"Oh my God, John, you have somebody else's eyeballs?"

He let her question dangle in the evening air. Multiple head nods from her silently begged for an answer.

"No," he chuckled. "Not the whole thing. Just the corneas. It's the clear part on the front. Like wrapping a Christmas gift with plastic wrap. Only a thin layer on the front. That's my cornea. Well, not mine, I guess. Though I think I heard somewhere that possession is nine-tenths of the law."

She rolled her eyes, sinking deeper into the chair. "Well, I assume law school. Although, fun fact? It's not an actual legal principle. More of an idiom to help teach—"

"Nah. The playground. Fifth grade. Let's just say I didn't eat lunch that day. Oh, one more thing. This color? These brilliant, speckled greens? All me, baby."

He knew it sounded weird as soon as it came out of his mouth. His neck grew hot, more than the wine's warmth. Interestingly, she didn't react. Instead, she leaned in towards him, narrowing her eyes.

"Good. I kind of like those speckled greens. It wouldn't mean as much if you just plugged somebody else's in."

"Wanna hear an *actual* fun fact?" he grinned, not waiting for her response. "Corneal tissue is only *sometimes* sticky."

She choked on her wine. "What on earth? No, sir. That's not a fun fact at all. What in the hell does that even mean?"

He laughed as she coughed. "The donor tissue is supposed to stick to the eye in about thirty seconds. Mine didn't. Doc set it in place, waited a bit, then told me to blink to test it. I blinked. He leaned over to his nurse and said, 'Suture kit, please.' I asked him why. He said, 'Because your cornea popped out and is on your cheek right now.'"

"Oh my God, John, that's disgusting! A cornea on your cheek? A needle in your eye? Sounds gross. And painful. And you were awake for the surgery? Your mom didn't mention that part."

"Awake and alert for every single second, even the part where he carved a hole into my eye to make room for the transplant. I thought he was going to push my eyeball into my brain for a second there."

"John, I had no idea..."

He couldn't stop himself. He usually masked some of the specifics when talking with his mother. No need for her to worry even more for him than she already did. It was the first time he'd really talked about the truth with anyone, and the details kept spilling out before he could stop them.

"The knots from the stitches rubbed against the back of my eyelid for three days. Probably only slept for an hour that whole weekend. I almost OD'd on painkillers, too. No matter how much I took, it still rubbed every time my eye moved."

"That's horrible! But, I get it. In REM sleep, don't your eyes wiggle back and forth?"

"Exactly. And, because of those stitches, the transplant tissue didn't heal properly. And, they were sewn along the edge of the round donor tissue, which led to the—"

"Shadowy rings! Oh, I get it now. Still gross, by the way," she said, sipping wine with another shudder. "Subject change. I want to get serious for a second. After what happened to Gamble, I wouldn't blame you if you want to call it quits."

The turn of the conversation surprised him. He sat up. "Quits?"

"Yeah, you've been a trooper through all of this. I can call the Wayne County Prosecutor and ask to borrow one of his staff attorneys, at least until I can hire someone new. You knew the man for a week, John. Anybody else would've run away after going to the crime scene. I'll understand if this doesn't feel like the right place for you anymore."

His expressionless face crunched inward. She could see the wheels turning inside him.

"Don't answer now," she continued. "I want you to know you

wouldn't be leaving me alone." She took a long sip, letting her offer sink in. "I'm giving you an out."

He nodded, lips tight. "What are you talking about? Of course, you wouldn't be alone. Deputy Foley will be there to keep watch over you, right? Outside the courtroom. Outside your house. The guy could be out there in the trees as we speak." He chuckled, motioning to the woods. She scanned the tree line.

"Um, that's a negative from me. Too creepy. When I found out that he hangs out in his car, waiting for me? I mean, who does that?"

John's eyes widened, realizing she wasn't talking about Foley anymore. No more white lies. Bring out the peach wine, and all pretenses drop away.

"First," he explained, "sometimes waiting around to escort a woman inside the courthouse is chivalrous, not creepy. Second, there's no way I'm leaving you to solve this on your own. And, third—"

"How many of these do you have?"

"Third," he said with reinforced enunciation, "how about I sleep on the couch tonight? Two bottles of wine, peach or otherwise, means you shouldn't be driving. You can have the 'Chance Suite', like old times."

"Don't be silly. I'll take the couch. We've already got it all worked out. Your mom's setting a pillow and blanket out for me."

He threw up his arms in disbelief. "Is there anything you two don't plan without me?"

She laughed hard enough that she almost spilled what was left in her glass.

"So, about tomorrow..."

"What's tomorrow?" His words were starting to slur.

"Very funny. We start small," she said, tucking her legs under her. "Raith's got a fundraiser at the Armory. Perfect place to eavesdrop."

"You want us to crash a fancy party? I'm not exactly black-tie material."

"Please." Annaleigh rolled her eyes. "You'll clean up fine. Besides, I'm the Acting Prosecutor for the County of Coldwater. I can get us in. Plus, I'll do all the talking. You just show up looking pretty and keep those fake eyes peeled."

"Come on, now. Between the two of us, there's no way I'm the eye candy." He grinned, but his gaze sharpened. "Seriously, though, if Kenneth is there, or if Raith figures out what we're doing, that's a lot of extra variables to account for, Annaleigh."

"Don't worry, we'll be careful." Her voice hardened. "We blend in, get what we need, and get out. Easy peasy."

He nodded, but his jaw tightened. "And, if we happen to find something big?"

"We build the case and put him away," she said, leaning forward. "Witnesses, documents, recordings, whatever it takes. Raith thinks he's untouchable. We prove he's not."

14

COVERT INFERIORITY

John doubted Annaleigh's ability to talk their way into the fundraiser. He shouldn't have. Not because she wouldn't be able to do it. Subterfuge simply wasn't required.

The National Guard Armory buzzed with small-town elite, parading around in tweed suits and teased hair. A crackling PA system played southern gospel from a corner speaker, while folding tables sagged under potluck cheese plates and punch bowls. A truly Coldwater-esque scene.

John and Annaleigh walked in, unnoticed amid the gossip and clinking glasses.

His pulse quickened at the sea of familiar faces as he scanned the Armory's open hall. Town council members, farmers, the diner's chain-smoking cook—all dressed and ready to rub elbows with their favorite hometown politician. A backwater masquerade where everyone played a part.

If only they knew the whole story.

He tugged at his ill-fitting tie and nudged her toward a corner table piled with campaign flyers.

"We've got to blend in," he murmured, grabbing a stale iced oatmeal cookie from a tray. "In addition to Kenneth, we've gotta believe Raith's got eyes everywhere."

She nodded, her gaze darting to Mayor Cameron Raith, who stood near a faded American flag, shaking hands with a practiced smile. John's gut hardened at the sight of the man. He knew now, for sure, that Raith's charm was a veneer, polished over years of secrets.

Secrets he and Annaleigh were determined to crack.

He caught a glimpse of Kenneth lurking close to the rear exit, blocking the door like a sentinel. The man's stare swept the room, and John turned away, pretending to study a flyer touting the mayor's new "Farm to Table" initiative.

"For the Farmers", my ass. I'll bet this is somehow lining his pockets.

He leaned closer to Annaleigh, speaking softly over the hum of gossip.

"Okay, we're here. What now?"

"We listen," she said with a spark of defiance glinting in her eyes. "There's no way he can remember all his lies. He'll slip up and say something he's not supposed to."

"Sounds easy enough, I guess. Let's get closer."

They hovered near Raith, out of eyeshot, ears straining for any damning word. Raith's voice, smooth as polished oak, droned about budget cuts and other inane topics. With Kenneth's looming shadow keeping them at bay, shrinking the distance any further risked exposure, so they had to be content hearing fragmented conversations.

Forty-five minutes slipped by. They'd gleaned nothing. John leaned against a corner table.

"He's better at lying than I thought... we're getting nowhere. This is such a waste of time," he muttered.

"Well, did you think he was going to come out and admit everything?"

"Not everything. Part of me thought we'd hear *something* useful."

"This isn't some assignment in law school where things fall into place, John. This is the real world, and sometimes, most times, we don't get the answer we want. It doesn't mean we just quit."

He sighed, raising his brows. "I know it's not law school, Annaleigh. I thought that someone with Raith's ego would love to brag. It would have been subtle, but it would at least still be, you know, a way to show what kind of power he's got. The kind where nobody realizes its true size. We didn't hear anything like that."

Annaleigh's eyes narrowed, her fingers drumming the table's edge. "Oh, sorry, I thought you were just... never mind. Didn't mean to snap at you. I think we're both frustrated."

"I also don't know how much longer we can avoid his psychopathic bodyguard, either. I'm pretty sure he's already seen us a couple of times."

"Raith's got to be playing us, right?" she asked. "Acting the saint, on his best behavior in front of his donors?"

"Maybe." He bit into another iced oatmeal cookie. "I hate to admit it, but other than these awful cookies, I think we're leaving empty-handed tonight." He stuffed the other two cookies he was holding into his suit jacket's side pocket. "We won't learn anything new. We can't even get close enough to hear all the good stuff, anyway. Let's call it and regroup in the morning."

She nodded in agreement, slapping the table with solemn finality, then led the way towards the exit. As they wove through the Armory's crowd, John felt Kenneth's gaze like a weight on his back, the man's scowl a silent warning. With a hand on the small of her back, he quickly ushered her outside, out of view, and to a safe distance.

Neither talked on the short drive across town back to the courthouse parking lot. Dashed hopes and feelings of failure were indeed a strong silencer. John parked his Dart next to her vehicle, and Annaleigh hopped out.

"I see that look in your eye, John. No lone wolf," she said, turning back and leaning on the passenger window.

"You mean, like you did by looking at those files without me?"

"I already apologized for that, and you know it. If they catch on to us, we lose the upper hand. Right now, Raith has no idea what we know. We need to keep it that way."

He gave a mock salute, his smirk holding tight. "Got it. No Evel Knievel stuff. Office, tomorrow. New plan."

As he watched her drive away, he had no intention of going home. He didn't intend on playing the hero or performing any death-defying stunts, either.

What's the harm in a bit more reconnaissance?

He tucked his Dart into a shadowed side street, the Armory's lot glowing under a single flickering streetlamp and its entrance in clear view. In this town, where every face was familiar, the pale green car of one of the county's prosecutors might as well have been a neon sign. He sank low, eyes locked on the building, praying no neighbor drove by.

If Raith recognized it, he was sunk.

If Annaleigh figured out where he was, he might be in even more trouble.

He killed the Dart's engine, the silence of the side street pressing against him like a held breath. He cranked the windows down, letting in the cool breeze and cricket chirps. As he slouched in the driver's seat, the cracked vinyl creaked at the shift.

The weight of his lie to Annaleigh sat heavy in his chest, a stone he couldn't dislodge. She'd trusted him to stick to the plan. Nothing reckless. Yet, here he was, playing lone wolf, exactly what she asked him not to do, chasing a low percentage hunch that Raith might publicly do something incriminating.

A single firefly's light shone in the back of the parking lot.

No, not a firefly. Someone smoking.

John half-smiled, thankful he'd never started the habit. A glowing cigarette, in this situation, would be a beacon in the dark, and he couldn't afford to be seen by Raith, by Kenneth, by some nosy local itching to gossip. He watched the man take a few more drags, then climb into a two-seater and drive away.

A dog barked in the distance, sharp and insistent, pulling his focus back to the bigger picture. He squinted, tracking the slow exodus of cars, each one a reminder that Raith could slip away any moment. He gripped the wheel, resolve hardening. He'd wait. Whatever it took.

She went through the files without me. Is this really any worse?

A guilty head shake and a sigh. Maybe. Maybe not.

He could've driven off, and no one would have ever known he was there. The guilt would have evaporated into the late spring Coldwater air.

What if he uncovered something helpful? Something tactical they could use at trial? The mere possibility was too good to pass up.

The Armory's entrance swung open. John squinted through the fading light, hoping for Raith, but a middle-aged couple emerged, arm in arm, their laughter carrying across the lot and into the Dart. Thirty minutes passed, and each time the doors parted, John tensed, only to be disappointed.

He could count the number of cars that remained in the lot with one hand. Another set of donors left the building, making their way to a paneled hippie van. He wanted to keep his eyes focused on the opening, waiting for Raith, but the ridiculous rainbow swirls and swooshes on the side of the van drew his focus. He watched as it eased backwards out of the spot and drove away. He clocked no less than twelve bumper stickers, plastered on at random angles.

Then, his eyes widened as he looked back at the van's empty spot. Previously hidden, parked in the next slot was something John had been hoping to see.

The mayor's jet black Chevy Blazer.

He's still here. Need to wait him out.

A sudden realization sank in. What was he expecting? A whispered confession? A shady deal in plain sight? What was he actually going to do when Raith exited the building?

He wasn't close enough to hear any conversations, so it's not like he could document anything. No pen or paper. No camera, either. So, John would be unable to capture photos of any hypothetical shady deals the mayor might conduct. He realized he hadn't thought any of this through very well.

Plus, on the infinitesimal chance something did happen, how would he contact Annaleigh? Or the sheriff? Out here, with no phone booth to call for help, he was on his own, eyes on the door, heart in his throat.

What is the point here, other than lying to her?

He knew he should drive home. But the thought of Raith slipping through their fingers gnawed at him and kept him watching. He needed the man to make just one wrong move, and John could witness it. That's all he needed to crack the mayor's facade.

The Armory doors burst outwards once more. Mayor Cameron Raith stepped out, surveying the scene as if he were looking for the red carpet to walk on. A hulking man lingered behind. Kenneth Roy Atlee.

It was the moment John had been waiting for. He stared intently at the two men, letting the rest of the world disappear into the shadows. His target was in his sights, and he wasn't going to take his eyes off it. Nothing beyond the edges existed. It was just him and the mayor, locked into a one-way staring contest.

Out of view, the passenger door of the Dart flew open, and a tall, thin figure dove into the seat.

"Caught you red-handed," Annaleigh said, her voice low.

"Jesus!" John jolted, his heart slamming in his ribs and his feet into the floorboards, accidentally stepping onto the round, silver push button in the far left corner. The sudden click of the relay caused John's eyes to widen as the Dart's high beams glared to life.

They pinned Raith and Kenneth in a harsh glare, their figures stark against the Armory's brick wall. The light carved every detail into sharp relief. It highlighted Raith's tailored suit and Kenneth's clenched fists. Even the faint scratches on the mayor's Chevy Blazer parked nearby shone like accusations.

The high beams weren't only a huge mistake. They were a flare, broadcasting his presence to the one man he needed to outsmart. Across the lot, Kenneth's head snapped towards them, his eyes narrowing like a predator's. John's stomach lurched. If Kenneth crossed the street, if he got close enough to see them, what would they do then?

"Turn them off!" Annaleigh barked.

His fingers slipped on the wheel, slick with sweat. He fumbled with the button, stomping wildly, the beams flickering as he fought to kill them. Every moment lasted a lifetime. The illumination was a noose tightening around their plan. Raith raised a hand, shielding his eyes and signaling toward Kenneth.

"Shit!" John hissed, his foot pounding, over and over. Unintentional presses first killed the brights, then flashed them back on. "Damn it!" A final, deliberate press plunged the lot back into dusk's haze. The entrance was a soft glow of streetlights once again, but the damage was done. He grabbed Annaleigh's arm.

"Get down!"

They slumped below the dashboard, hearts thudding. John's mind raced. Had Raith seen them? Had he recognized the Dart?

"Oh, this is all my fault. I'm so, so sorry," Annaleigh whispered. "I had this feeling that you were planning something. Figured this might be your way of evening the score for me going through Gamble's files without you."

"Where the hell did you even come from?"

"I'm parked a few cars back. You didn't see me come up the sidewalk?"

"Of course I didn't," he said, breath ragged, circling his eyes with a finger. "Never mind that. Do you think he noticed us?"

"You lit him up like a fireworks show, John, so he saw something, but maybe he didn't realize who it was. What kind of jalopy has a foot pedal for brights?"

"Hey, my Dart is cool," he shot back, shaking his head.

Her eyes glinted, probing. "What was your plan, anyway? Catch Raith confessing to the moon?"

"I had to try again to find something, anything," he snapped, words clipped. "It was eating me up that we know he's dirty and can't prove it."

She squeezed his arm. "I had a hunch you'd pull something. But, I forgot how much you hate surprises."

"You didn't see him standing right there at the entrance? Horrible timing, truly awful... no offense."

John swallowed and raised his head to peek over the dashboard. The mayor's vehicle was nowhere to be seen, its parking spot empty.

"Damn," he said, sitting up. "He's gone."

Annaleigh exhaled, face scrunched. "I spooked you and ruined your stakeout. On the bright side, it's possible he thought it was some random car. Hard to be sure. It was a good idea, though."

He craned his neck towards her. "Wait, you're not mad? That I'm here? That I lied?"

Annaleigh's smile thinned. "Because I expected it, doesn't mean I like it." She paused, eyes on the darkened lot. "Just don't make it a habit."

Her words pounded inside him. It hurt more to hear she knew he would do this.

Is that what she thinks of me?

"There still might be time to tail him."

"We have no idea where he went," she said. "Even if we were to drive out near his place, the entrance road at his property winds through the trees. You can't see the house just driving by, so we'd never know if he was there." Seeing John's creased forehead, she quickly added, "I had to drop off some papers there one time."

John exhaled, shaking his head. "If he did realize it was us, that we're following him—"

The weight of their exposure sank in. If Raith suspected them, their shadow investigation was as good as dead, along with any chance of exposing his secrets. He glanced at Annaleigh, her face half-lit by the streetlamp's flicker, and saw the same grim resolve mirrored back.

"We need a new angle," he said, voice low. "Something Raith can't hide behind his smile."

Annaleigh's eyes narrowed, a plan forming. "The Armory's back office. One of Gamble's files referenced the Guard's commander. If Raith's been cozy with him, and if there's paper-work—permits, deals, anything—it might be in there."

"Break in? Are you serious? We're not criminals."

"It's not as bad as you make it sound."

"I'm not sure, Annaleigh. This is quite the heel turn for you, isn't it?"

"Come on, most of the crowd's gone. Whoever's left is drunk on punch and promises. We slip in the side door, poke around. Ten minutes, tops."

"Didn't figure you for a rule breaker."

"Look, if I had a badge, nobody would bat an eye. Raith himself asked us to play detective, so, in a way, we've already got probable cause. Right?"

His pulse quickened, the thrill of action overriding his doubts. Courage building, he locked eyes with her, reluctantly nodded, then reached for the door handle. Before he could open it, a thud rocked the Dart's rear. The car dipped under an unseen weight.

Startled, they spun to the back window, but were blinded by a searing white flash. Bright as lightning, a low hum buzzed as it pulsated. Sizzles and crackles cut through the night, sharp and bitter. They shielded their eyes, unsure of the cause.

Had another vehicle collided with them? Was Parnell back there, playing a joke? Was he lighting them up with his cruiser's spotlight?

As quickly as it had begun, the light vanished, leaving them with sunspots in their eyes. John scrambled out, Annaleigh behind him, both rubbing their eyes. They locked onto the trunk, freezing.

Two handprints, mirroring each other and seared into the paint, glowed under the streetlamp's flicker. The Dart's green paint curled up around the outline as red-hot chips scattered into embers. The acrid tang of scorched metal stung their noses as eerie shadows danced across the mark.

"What the hell happened to my car?"

Annaleigh's voice trembled. "It's like... the brand on the courthouse wall."

"Why would somebody do that to my Dart? It's just an innocent bystander. Come on, man..."

John stepped back, the night's chill seeping through him, and scanned the empty lot. The Armory's lights had dimmed, the last stragglers gone, leaving only the hum of a distant generator.

Though they had no direct proof, they were sure it was Kenneth who left the mark at the courthouse. He had exited the Armory along with Raith, but as they were ducking out of view, there was no way to know if he drove away with the mayor.

Whoever had left these marks had vanished, but the message was clear.

They should watch their backs.

He leaned against the trunk, his fingers hovering over the seared metal, as if touching it might unravel its secrets. His mind churned. The courthouse brand had been a public act, a defiance splashed across the town's heart.

But this? This was intimate, carved into his car, his sanctuary. Now it was marked, tainted by the same force that had gotten Gamble killed.

"You think Raith planned this?" Annaleigh asked. "Planned on us watching him?"

John shook his head, exhaling slowly.

"The better question is... who was watching *us*?"

15

LAST CALL FOR LIES

Hank's Three Pump, Coldwater's grimiest dive, lingered on the town's edge like a derelict shrine. Its Budweiser neon panel flickered, casting jagged light over a gravel lot strewn with cigarette butts and shattered bottles.

The converted '60s gas station poured whiskey instead of fuel, and for budget reasons, kept its faded "Hank's Three Pump" sign, though the name "Hank's" had long since been scratched off. Two rusted pumps stood like gravestones. The third lay toppled, mangled by a drunken hit-and-run no one ever claimed.

Annaleigh, sparked by the burned handprints on John's Dart, decided to follow up on a lead of her own. A single brand at the courthouse was a one-off instance. A second brand was a pattern. After John had left the scene and headed home, she made her move.

She recalled a few obscure details from their review of Gamble's old prosecutions. In one case, she remembered Eddie Tate, a short-haul trucker who lived out his nights at this backwater hole. She arrived at Three Pump, armed with a rumor, courtesy of courthouse gossip Genie Glitter, that pegged Eddie as the hit-and-run driver.

"Hope it's something you can use to make him sing," Genie

had said. "Maybe it's time that man paid for something more than drinks."

More crucially, the vandalism case buried in Gamble's records mentioned Eddie witnessing "glowing hands." Coupled with the desecration of the Dart's trunk, she had to learn more.

And, she had to do it alone.

Not as payback for John's stakeout. If she showed up solo and anything went wrong, trouble would only have her name written on it. Annaleigh would keep John and Bonnie safe by putting the crosshairs of this dive on her. Even though it was the opposite of what she told him to do.

This is for his—and Bonnie's—own good.

She pushed through the heavy door into a haze of stale beer, cigarette ash, and sweat. Merle Haggard's twang wailed from the juke-box, half-drowned by clattering mugs and coarse laughter. In a nice blouse and jeans, she stood out among the flannel and grease. Her flats crunched peanut shells on the sticky floor as she scanned the scene.

A dozen grizzled patrons in trucker caps eyed her like a fox in a henhouse. A drunk at the counter, face pockmarked and ruddy, leered with yellowed teeth. He sported an aging suit, complete with an inner vest that was buttoned using the wrong holes.

"Well, damn, darlin', ain't you a sight. Get lost on your way to a fancy bar?"

Annaleigh's smile, sharp as a razor and honed from court-room battles, held steady.

"Save the sweet talk for your whiskey, pal," she said, voice cool, but edged. "I'm not here for you."

The drunk slid closer, undeterred. "You sure? We'd look good together, tho' a pretty thing like you don't belong here. How 'bout a drink, on me?"

She leaned in, enough to make him think he had a shot, then locked eyes.

"How about you keep your thoughts—and hands—to your-self, or else *your* drink will be on you."

He waved his hands, slurring, "These things? Hey... look, I got six fingers!" He squinted, tapping them one by one. "Wait... where'd my finger go?"

"You counted your thumb twice, genius," she said dryly.

The bartender, wiry with a long, graying beard, wiped the counter with a rag filthier than the floor. "Not that I mind the business, but what's a lady like you doing here?" he asked, voice low, eyes darting nervously. "You might fit in better down at the Barrel."

"Yeah, what's a barrel doing in a lady like you?" the drunk repeated.

Annaleigh ignored him, eyeing the bartender. "I'm looking for someone—"

"I'll be your someone..." muttered the drunk.

"Heard he's a regular—"

"I come here all the time—*hiccup*..."

"He's got something I need—"

"I need you to show me what's under that blouse..."

She spun and slammed her hand onto the bar, rattling the glasses.

"That's enough, buddy. Shut your beer hole or I'll have the sheriff haul you in for harassment before you finish that glass."

Her tone was honey over steel, and the drunk blinked, backing off with a mumbling curse.

"It's a whiskey hole, not a beer hole, just so you know..." He stumbled off the stool and tottered over the jukebox, leaning on it for support as he drew on the glass with a finger.

Fellow patrons at the bar snickered, and she felt a prickle on her neck, like eyes boring into her from the shadows. She shook it off.

The bartender smirked. "Was wondering how long you were gonna let that go on."

"Eddie Tate. Know him?"

The bartender's eyes flicked to a shadowed corner booth over her right shoulder, so quick she almost missed it, then back to his rag, wiping faster.

"What if I said he's the dumbass you just shut down?"

"I'd say you're full of it. Truckers don't wear out-of-date, wrinkled three-piece suits."

The bartender clenched his jaw and tongued his gums.

"Eddie's over there," he muttered, nodding toward a lone figure hunched at a table over her left shoulder, nursing a beer.

"Tell you what, I'll have what Eddie's drinking." She pointed at the drunk, now kissing the jukebox's lid. "On him."

"Don't expect much," he replied, tipping a glass under the tap and yanking the handle. "He ain't talked straight since whatever it was he saw." He slid the mug across the bar. "Most nights, he mutters to himself until he passes out. Best of luck."

He turned, grabbing the lime-green rotary phone from the counter. His fingers jabbed the dial with a nervous twitch, spinning it rapidly.

Annaleigh's gaze settled on Eddie, then flicked to the opposite corner booth—the one the bartender seemed to fear. A broad-shouldered silhouette sat half-hidden in gloom, light shying away. Couldn't make out anything else, though. Her gut twinged, but she dismissed it as nerves.

Eyes on the prize. Get what you need from Eddie and get out.

She grabbed the beer and headed for Eddie's table, dodging a pool cue swung by a burly man arguing over a missed shot.

"Watch it, sweetheart," he growled, breath sour with bourbon.

"With that aim, you might want to sit down next time you take a leak," she tossed back. His buddies laughed as the man scowled.

She approached the table and laid eyes on Eddie Tate, forty years old and well-weathered. His darting, red-shot eyes stared downwards into the abyss of his empty mug.

"Eddie?" she asked, sliding into the chair across from him. She set the fresh beer down in front of him. "Brought you something. I'm Annaleigh Stanton, Acting Prosecutor. Maybe you remember me from the town hall a few nights ago?" He grunted without looking up. "I guess not. Well, I was hoping to talk to you about a case from a few years ago. About witnessing some vandalism?"

Eddie's eyes widened, and he buried his head into his shoulder.

"So you do remember it," she said, pushing the new drink closer to him.

His hands trembled around his old mug, eyes dropping.

"Got nothing to tell."

She leaned in, voice softer. "I've got it on pretty good authority you almost turned this place into Two Pump, Eddie," she said, testing the waters.

He chuckled, hops on his breath. "They still pour me my drinks, don't they? Idiots." His eyes shot up to hers. "Wait, who told you? Damn that Genie..."

"Tell me about what you saw, and I won't tell the owner what I know."

He scoffed. "I don't know what you want from me, lady. Told the sheriff it was dark, didn't see much. That's all I know."

"Bull," Annaleigh said, her voice a quiet blade. "You said 'glowing hands'. I see it's got you scared. My boss buried that case. I want to know why."

A faint sulfur whiff cut through the bar's stench, acrid and fleeting. She glanced at the booth again. That same dark shape sat, unmoving, menacing.

Focus.

"You don't get it, lady. It didn't make sense then, doesn't now."

"That's fine, Eddie. Some things don't make sense, but they're still worth hearing. What you have to say is worth hearing to me."

"I... don't know how to describe it..."

"Try your best. I'm here. Nothing's going to get you."

His eyes bulged. "I was in my truck cab, sleeping off a little too much one night. There... was a bright light. It woke me up... I peeked out the window. What I saw... it was..."

"Yes...?"

"They were glowing like coals, hot enough to melt a tire rim. And... that rumble!" Eddie swallowed hard. "He saw me, I froze... he yelled at me to keep quiet... or I'd burn. So, that's what I'm gonna do. I've got nothing else to say to you." His knuckles whitened on the glass mug. "Maybe your boss got the same talk. Maybe that's what killed him."

Her pulse quickened, but her face stayed calm, empathetic. "I believe you, Eddie. I've seen some strange things, too. I'm trying to find him, to put him away. What did he look like? Or, his name? Come on. Give me something. Anything."

Eddie's eyes flicked to the bar and the man behind it, who had been wiping the same spot since Annaleigh sat down. The bartender glanced at the corner.

"Big guy, mean," Eddie mumbled. "Didn't see his face. Don't know who he is."

Most of the bar fit that description. She pressed further, but he clammed up. After a glance at the bartender, she noticed his gaze snapped again to the corner booth. A glass clinked there, sharp in the din.

Something made her look there again. It was empty. No more silhouette, only a vacant table and a half-drunk glass. Her heart thudded.

Alright, time to go.

"Eddie, if you remember anything, come find me at the courthouse." She slid a business card across the table, avoiding spilled beer. "You're not alone."

The sulfur smell hit again, sharper. The air became heavier, warmer. She wove through the crowd, ignoring a slurred catcall from the jukebox corner, and burst into the crisp night. The breeze had died, and the acrid tang carried outside with her. She hunched as she steadied her breathing.

"Counselor?"

Detective Hollis Mumber's voice rasped from the shadows, startling her. Annaleigh spun, flats crunching gravel, and spotted his portly frame shuffling toward her. His hat was tilted at an odd angle, like he'd slapped it on in a hurry.

"Detective? What are you doing here?"

Mumber offered a lopsided, closed-mouth smile. "Sheriff Parnell asked me to keep an eye on you. Got a call from that barkeep in there, fretting about a young lady showing up where she might not be wanted. I figured it was you, Miss Stanton." He fumbled with a toothpick between his teeth, nearly dropping it, then caught it with a clumsy swipe. She crossed her arms, jaw tight.

"I'm flattered, Detective, but I can handle myself. Been in worse places than Hank's Three Pump."

"No doubt, no doubt," he said, raising his hands like a man surrendering to a scolding. "Hank's been dead a few years now, but I'm sure hearing his name carried on would've made him smile. You see... Parnell's got this crazy notion you're diving headfirst into some sticky situations. And me, well..." He chuckled, a dry, wheezing sound, and patted his badge, pinned crookedly to his suit jacket. "I'm still on the payroll, so I reckon I'd do something useful before Sheriff shoves me out to pasture."

Annaleigh's eyes narrowed.

"No offense, but useful would've been showing up before I had to dodge drunks and play nice with a scared-witless trucker. That is, if I needed you. Which I didn't."

Mumber winced, scratching the back of his neck.

"I lost track of you after the fundraiser... figured you'd called it a night. Then, the call came through on the radio." He tapped the bulky police box clipped to his belt, its antenna bent like it'd seen better days. "Took me a minute to get here. These old bones don't move like they used to, y'know."

She sighed, softening despite her annoyance. Mumber's eyes, rheumy but earnest, caught the flickering neon, and for a fleeting moment, she saw the cop he'd been before time had dulled his edge.

"Look, Detective, I appreciate the effort, but I'm not some damsel needing a babysitter. I got what I came for. Sort of."

He nodded, slow and thoughtful, toothpick rolling to the other side of his mouth. "Heard you're chasing ghosts in there. Eddie Tate, right? Fella's been spooked about something for a while now. Searches for answers at the bottom of a mug, these days. You get anything outta him?"

Annaleigh hesitated, the memory of Eddie's trembling whisper flashing through her mind. She wasn't quite ready to spill that to Mumber. Sheriff Parnell, sure. Not this detective, even if he did show up here to check on her. She'd rather limit the size of their trust circle.

"Enough to keep me up tonight," she said, voice clipped.

Mumber's smile faded, and he looked down, scuffing his shoe in the gravel. "I got no nose for trouble anymore, but, believe me, that bar's crawling with it. Other places, too. You watch yourself, hear? We don't have many friends in there, and..." He glanced at the shadowed lot, his hand resting on his holster like a reflex from younger days. "Something's different about Coldwater."

Her gut twinged, the same prickle she'd felt inside the bar. "Preaching to the choir, Detective. I'll be on my way." She spun to leave.

"Hey, Miss Stanton?" Mumber called, his voice softer, almost sheepish.

She paused, half-turning. He rubbed his jaw, looking like a man who'd forgotten his lines.

"Back when I was your age, I thought I could handle anything. Nearly got myself killed chasing a hunch back then. Lost a partner, too. Don't be me. Don't let this town chew you up, alright?"

Annaleigh's annoyance flickered, replaced by a pang of something she didn't want to name. "Thanks, Detective," she said, quieter now. "Get some rest. You look like you need it more than me."

He chuckled, tipping his hat properly this time. "Reckon I do."

Annaleigh watched the detective's taillights fade into the night, his cruiser's rumble swallowed by the silence of the empty lot. She angled for her car, the sulfur tang from the bar still sharp in her throat.

The Cavalier's red roof, right above her driver's side door, glowed with a handprint. Its edges were seared like a blowtorch's kiss, causing the air around it to shimmer, leaking radiant heat.

Her breath exited her in a jagged gasp. Her sedan begrudgingly sported the same mark as John's Dart.

The bar's neon flickered behind her, its buzz drowned by the blood pounding in her ears. The lot's shadows crept in, alive with threat, curling around her.

Was he still here, watching her?

She glanced at its grimy windows—dim, smudged, and holding in the country twang and drunken voices. If she screamed, would anyone inside hear? Would they care enough to stumble out into the dark?

Fear clawed at her chest. She was exposed, a lone figure in this godforsaken corner of Coldwater, where the town's edge bled into nowhere. Her eyes locked on the handprint, its unnatural glow burning into her mind, narrowing her world to that single, searing mark.

Leave. Now.

She fumbled for her keys, hands trembling, and slid into the driver's seat, the vinyl cold against her clammy palms. The engine roared to life, and she peeled out, gravel spitting under her tires as she fled the lot's suffocating shadows.

Her pulse raced, but she gripped the wheel, forcing herself to focus on the road ahead.

What have I done?

16

PAYBACK'S PROMISE

John and Annaleigh sank into their desk chairs in the upstairs courthouse office, the tension easing from the night before. Old wood creaked beneath them as they waited for Parnell's arrival.

John exhaled, glancing out the window. No flashing lights speeding by, just the quiet hum of a new day. No sirens had wailed at dawn, no frantic calls demanded they identify bodies. Perhaps the day would pass without anything unusual happening.

Sunlight spilled across the courthouse's second-floor balcony as Genie bustled in with a Tupperware full of warm cinnamon rolls.

"No need to thank me, sugar—I know you two were out late." She set the container down, her grin teasing.

Last night, after John's failed stakeout, they had used the Armory's phone to call Sheriff Parnell and report the incident. His arrival came with a flushed face and tight jaw. He was irked that the two lawyers had staged multiple stakeouts, both inside and outside the fundraiser, without his advice or consent.

"Only the first one was planned. Opportunity knocked after that."

John's comment drew a sharp glance from the sheriff, his

scowl deepening. It also elicited an odd reaction from Annaleigh, as she looked away and covered her face with her hair.

"It's pure dumb luck you two are okay," Parnell had snapped, his voice caught between ally and exasperated parent.

John figured he was as furious as they were, maybe more. They'd seen yet another incident occur with these unusual burns, and no one had uncovered the brand's origins. After reviewing the scene with Clyde, Parnell leaned close to Clyde and whispered something. Clyde hurried off, and the sheriff then promised he'd have answers first thing in the morning.

John glanced at his scratched Timex and nodded.

"Nine o'clock. Sheriff said he'd be here by now."

He tapped his pen on his desk in a gentle rhythm, each tap sharpening the unease gnawing at him. Parnell's delay wasn't usual. As Sheriffs go, he was a punctual one.

"I gotta say, vandalism on my trunk aside, for a few moments, being a spy boosted my adrenaline more than researching case law in old books."

"What, trading law books for a C.I.A. badge already?" Annaleigh leaned back, smirking, and pointed at the shelves. "Those dusty volumes over there? I don't care what you say, that's the real thrill. Nailing a verdict for your side with one perfect precedent. It's where our actual fight is."

"Says the girl who wanted to break into the Armory last night?" She blushed. "I'm just saying, being out there felt different."

"I'm sure Parnell will love to share his opinion on your new favorite hobby. No doubt we'll get another lecture when he gets here."

"Ten after nine," he said, checking his watch. "Genie, how often is the Sheriff late to something?"

"Not since the courthouse got its first typewriter, sugar," Genie said with a sly grin. "I'll call over there and find out."

Eavesdropping on Genie's one-sided conversation, John watched her face drain of color. Her knuckles whitened as she squeezed her hand into a fist. The muffled voice of the Sheriff's clerk filled the courthouse's stillness, too soft for him to make out.

She hung up, exhaling shakily. "Honey, I'm sorry, but there's been trouble again. Y'all need to get to the hospital. Everyone's waiting for ya in the ER."

"Oh my God," Annaleigh gasped. "What's happened now? Is it the Sheriff? Is that why he isn't here?"

"I don't know, darlin'. That was his clerk, and she didn't say more. But, you two gotta get there." She rose and gathered her purse. "There's nothing I can do from here, so my new job is to go home and start cooking. I know from experience that hanging around hospitals makes people hungry. I'll come by later, bring some food, and check on everyone."

John hung his head, Gamble's crime scene flashing back, with images of blood pooling on the Coldwater dirt and a severed arm lying nearby.

Had it happened again?

* * *

JOHN SLAMMED the Dart into park and leapt out. His eyes locked on Coldwater Memorial Hospital's glass doors as he rushed toward them.

"John, wait!" shouted Annaleigh, trailing behind him.

He didn't stop. He couldn't.

Parnell had trusted him, stood by him, even with his missteps. Now, his reckless stakeout might have cost the Sheriff his life. He had to know.

"John!"

Ignoring her pleas, his hand reached for the door pull when Annaleigh grabbed at his arm.

"John, stop."

He jerked his arm free. "No! I need to know what happened to him!"

"Stop, you dummy!"

Her crass shout froze him. Eyes wide, he looked back at her like a scolded child.

She pointed to a familiar black police cruiser, emblazoned with the words "Sheriff" on the door, parked crooked, next to the sidewalk. The driver's side front tire sat awkwardly on the curb, and a faint trail of smeared rubber was etched on the pavement behind the rear tires.

"Look, that's his car," she said. "He looks like he was in a hurry, but if he drove it here, then—"

"He's still alive," he admitted, inhaling and trying to compose himself. "Or, at least, he was when he got here." He pursed his lips and opened the door. "Time to find out."

They hustled through the glass doors. John scanned the bustling emergency room for any sign of the Sheriff or his deputies. The hospital's fluorescent lights buzzed overhead, casting stark shadows on the linoleum. Each beep of a distant, muffled monitor cut through his thoughts.

Parnell was here, hurt, because of him.

On the far side of the lobby, he spotted two uniformed men, staring down the hallway, facing away from him. He recognized Amos Hinkle, Parnell's eldest deputy, and Cason Foley, his youngest. John also could tell it was Foley because he was the shortest deputy, too.

Those two were blocking a third uniformed individual, a man he assumed would be Deputy D. Clyde Brothers. A warmth rippled across his shoulders, as it did when he first met Clyde and welcomed his steady gaze. John trusted him to tell him the truth, so he headed for him.

Bracing, he strode forward, loafers squeaking as he neared the deputies, their heads bowed in hushed conversation. Each step felt heavier, the whispers amplifying his racing pulse. His rapid pace approaching the group from behind caught the attention of Deputy Foley. In one swift motion, Foley spun, arm outstretched, and blocked John's shoulder, stopping him cold.

"Hey now, slow it down," Foley commanded, before dropping his arm. "Oh, it's you."

The others realized it at the same time, and Deputy Hinkle pivoted, allowing John to catch sight of the unknown deputy. Although it wasn't a deputy at all.

It was Sheriff Dane Parnell.

John silently gasped. Parnell stood tall, unharmed, hands on his hips, his familiar presence cutting through the hospital's buzz. Relief flooded him, then he froze, realizing if Parnell was fine, that meant someone else was the victim.

"Sheriff?" he said, voice tight. He glanced at Annaleigh. "I thought when you didn't show at the courthouse... I assumed... you were..."

The older man's face was stony, his gaze heavy in a way that chilled John.

"John," said Parnell, his twang thick with emotion, "it's not me."

The words hung as their meaning seeped into John's consciousness. His relief evaporated, replaced by a growing sense of dread. Parnell placed a hand on his shoulder, his grip firm but gentle.

"It's Bonnie... It's your mother, John. She's been in an accident."

The world tilted.

Parnell's words struck like a blade to his chest. His mom—whose laugh filled their kitchen, her infectious smile filtering through every room with love—was here somewhere, hurt. He clutched the air, as if he could hold her strength, but the ground seemed to crumble beneath him. Parnell pointed to a hallway around the corner.

"Clyde is standing guard outside her room now. And, she'll have protection the whole time, until she goes home with you. Even then, we'll keep a close watch."

Time slowed as John parsed the Sheriff's wording.

She needs protection? From an accident?

His legs moved on autopilot. With each step, he dragged himself down the corridor. He plodded around the corner and saw Clyde. His familiar eyes were red-rimmed and glistening. He stood underneath the placard for Room 7, where a paper with a single handwritten name caused lumps in John's throat— "Chance."

"I'll give you a moment," he said, stepping away. "Don't worry, I won't go far."

John stepped into the room, frozen solid at the sight of his mother. She lay unmoving, pale, fragile, and broken, her arms and face swathed in white bandages. Tears stung his eyes as he approached her to brush a strand of hair from her forehead.

He sat by her bedside, eyes watering. He grasped her hand. It felt frail and lifeless, like the brittle pages of her old recipe book.

Regret gnawed at him. He knew he'd spent too much time at law school and too little with her. He could have visited home more often, like she'd urged. His hatred of the road, of driving at night, of driving, period, had clouded his judgment. He'd let his vision issues not just ruin his life, but rule it.

"Mom, I should've come sooner," he whispered over the hum of the hospital's ancient equipment. Her fingers twitched in his grip, a flicker of the strength he remembered. He leaned closer, searching her face beneath the bandages for a sign she heard him, but her eyes stayed closed, locked in a place he couldn't reach.

He rested his head on her hand, the coolness of her skin a stark contrast to the warmth of his tears. They slid down his cheeks, pooling where his face met her fingers, a quiet confession of all he hadn't said.

The world blurred, and for a moment, it was just the two of them, tethered by love and regret.

* * *

ANNALEIGH LINGERED in the hospital lobby, dodging glances from Deputy Foley and pacing a worn-down line across the floor.

John's mother lay injured because of her, because she'd rolled the dice once too many times last night. She hadn't yet shared her late-night dalliance with John, convincing herself that she hadn't found the right time. Part of her wanted never to find it.

She was certain her actions had tipped the scales, and someone had chosen to hurt Bonnie to send a message. She was sure that whatever she'd done had tipped the scales, and someone went after Bonnie to hurt John, but also herself, too. Once a stranger, this woman had grown into Annaleigh's best friend in Coldwater. Maybe closer than that.

Sheriff Parnell stood by the lobby's coffee machine, his shoulders slumped, hat in hand. His eyes were teary, mirroring her own. He was her ally, and she needed him now.

"Sheriff," she said, voice low, crossing to him. "Can I buy you a cup?"

Parnell nodded, his twang soft but heavy. "No thanks, Ms. Stanton. Already hit my quota for the day. How you holding up?"

She leaned against the wall, the cold plaster grounding her. "I did something stupid. Bonnie's in there because of me."

"Now, little lady, I doubt that."

"I went to Three Pump last night—"

"Yeah, I know. Hollis filled me in. Didn't believe it at first, but you got a stubborn streak in you, don't ya?"

"I thought by going alone, I could shield everyone from any blowback, but..." Her voice cracked, and she swallowed hard. "I think I stirred something up... and it hit Bonnie."

Parnell's hand rested on her shoulder, firm but kind.

"Don't go blaming yourself. You didn't set the fire. Whoever barred that shed door is at fault here."

"I led them to her!" she snapped, then lowered her volume as a nurse glanced over. "I pushed too hard, Dane. Eddie knows a powerful secret, and I asked too many questions. Someone was watching me, and now Bonnie's hurt. It's easy math."

His eyes narrowed, but his tone remained steady.

"You're doing your job, Annaleigh, same as all of us. Digging for the truth. We'll get who done this, but you gotta keep your head clear. John's gonna need you, not some guilt-ridden shadow of yourself."

She rubbed her face. "If John finds out I might've caused this..." Her chest ached, picturing his anger, those clenched fists. "No, I need to tell him."

"I agree, but tell him when he's ready, and make sure you are, too," Parnell said. "Don't carry it alone. And, please realize what you're carrying isn't as heavy as you think."

Annaleigh nodded, shoving the guilt deep.

"I hope he doesn't hate me after this."

"IT'S NOT AS bad as it looks," Annaleigh said from the doorway of Bonnie's room, her voice catching. "Doctors say minor burns on her arms, some on her face. She got out fast, thank God." She crossed the room, placing a hand on John's shoulder, caressing it. "She's tougher than both of us, John. She'll pull through."

John couldn't tell if her words were meant to reassure him or steady her own nerves. His heart ached with a mixture of anger, sorrow, and relief. Anger at whoever had caused this harm, sorrow for the pain his mother must be enduring, and relief that, despite her injuries, she would make a full recovery. A recovery. With permanent scars.

"They're keeping her overnight, then she can come home. That's good news. Hang on to that."

He stood, turned on his heels, but was held back by a frail grip. His mother had reached out to grab his hand.

"It's going to be okay, Mom," he said. "We'll get through this."

Her mouth moved, but no words escaped. John leaned in.

"Don't try to speak, save your strength."

"Your father..." she rasped, gripping his shoulder to pull him closer. "Get your father. He can protect us." Her voice weakened. "Annaleigh needs you, too. Lean on her."

Bonnie's eyes closed, and she drifted off to sleep.

John's jaw clenched, and his hands shook. He hated seeing his mother in this drug-induced state. Injured, scarred, and apparently delirious, too. His father? Get him? He had no idea who the man was. And why did she think he could protect them?

Without a word and his eyes locked onto his mother, John surged to his feet, his mother's frail grip burning in his palm. A line had been crossed, and he knew who would be made to answer for it.

It was time for a talk with the mayor. But, this time, on his terms. He stormed out, vision blurred with tears and fury, blinking them away. Annaleigh hustled after him, her steps quick, voice urgent.

"John, wait!" she called, grabbing his arm just outside the door, out of Bonnie's earshot. Her eyes were wide, glistening, her face ashen. "I need to tell you something. I hurt your mom."

John froze. "You did what?"

"I mean, I'm the reason she's here."

"What are you talking about?"

Annaleigh's breath hitched, her hands twisting together like she was wringing out her guilt.

"Last night, after the stakeout, after what happened to your Dart, I remembered something unusual I'd seen in Gamble's files." She squinted, as if bracing for his reaction. "So, I went to Three Pump to chase down a witness. To get some info."

John's anger flared. "You went where?" he snapped, stepping closer, his shadow looming over her. "To that hole? Alone?"

"That's where the witness was. I thought he could give me a name." Her voice cracked, tears spilling. "I think someone was watching me, and when I went to leave... there was a handprint on my car, like yours. I think I caused Raith to hurt Bonnie. To hurt the both of us."

"Both of us? She's *my* mom, not yours!"

"Come on, John, you know what she means to me, too."

"Let me get this straight. After crashing my stakeout and ruining everything, then telling me not to go solo, you went off on your own and poked some kind of maniac. Now my mom's burned up. What the hell were you thinking?"

Her face crumpled, but she held his gaze, voice shaking. "I was trying to protect you, John! Her, too! I thought I could get answers. I didn't think..." She raised her hands, then let them fall. "I'm so sorry."

John's chest heaved, his rage shifting. He pictured her, out there alone, chasing a killer. The thought of her in that bar, out there with the crazies that go to that place, and to wind up with a handprint on her car, too? She could have been in a bed next to his mom, all wrapped up and burnt, too. It twisted him.

"You could've been hurt, Annaleigh! Or... it could have been so much worse. You go off playing hero, and for what? Where did it get us?"

"I didn't mean to," she whispered, tears streaking her face. "I thought I was doing something to save us, John. The guy didn't even give me anything we could use... I was wrong to go out alone. Maybe we both were."

Her vulnerability hit him like a cold wind, dousing his anger. She'd been reckless, sure, but so had he, tailing Raith without a plan. Bonnie's words, "lean on her", echoed in him. Then, he saw Annaleigh's fear. He reached out, his hand brushing her arm, voice softening.

"I'm sorry. We're in this together, okay? From here on out, we're a team."

She nodded, wiping her eyes, a shaky breath escaping. "Yeah."

The fire in John's chest reignited. It wasn't directed at Annaleigh, but at the one who'd done this.

That person needed to pay.

He turned, storming down the hallway, fists clenched so tight his nails drew blood.

"I know who's to blame. And I'm going to end this," he

growled, his voice echoing as he headed for the lobby. He ignored the concerned looks and murmurs of the deputies as he forced himself into the group's middle, facing Parnell.

"Tell me what happened to her. Now." John's raised tone caused multiple heads around the room to turn towards him. Parnell steered John to a quiet corner, sighing.

"She was in the shed when it caught fire."

"The shed caught fire? By itself? Bullshit. What really happened?"

"The door was barred from the outside. It was arson, son."

"She was locked in there... to burn to death?" John's hand smacked the wall as he stepped back.

"Keep it down," Parnell said, guiding him closer. "Very few people know these details. I haven't even told all my deputies the full story."

John squinted his eyes, staring into Parnell's. He was done mincing words.

"Who the hell did this to my mom?"

"Shh." The sheriff gestured again for him to lower his volume. "We don't know the exact cause yet, only that it wasn't natural. We think it started by the door, then spread. It was lucky the fire burnt through one of the walls quickly enough that she was able to bust out before we got it under control."

John dipped his head, imagining the scene. His hands shook as he pictured the action.

"So, whoever did this was just there? This morning?"

"That's our thought, too. We didn't find any timers or anything."

An exhale exited John's throat, sounding more like a growl. "I was just there. It means they waited until I left. They chose hurting her... on purpose."

"John, let's keep our cool—"

"It was Raith," John said, voice low and certain. "Last night, we followed him. He spotted my car. Now she's in that room. Two and two is four, Sheriff."

"Son, let's not jump to conclusions. Let us do our job, and we'll find who did this. When your momma comes home tomorrow, I'll have Clyde sit outside the house, just in case. I trust him with my life, and he'll protect your family."

John's shoulders tensed as he took in a long, deep breath. He exhaled in a flurry.

"Gotta go, Sheriff. Need to take care of something."

"John, don't do this."

John stopped, turning his head and talking over his shoulder.

"He's gone too far. Now, it's my turn."

17

WESLEY'S WARNING

"I'm going to fucking kill him!"

John's hands shook as he stormed across the hospital parking lot, the asphalt radiating late morning heat through his soles. He ignored Annaleigh's hurried steps behind him.

"Raith needs to pay. For Mom, for Gamble, for every damn thing he's buried in this town!"

He finally stopped after she gave his arm a forceful tug.

"John, that's not the right way to handle this, and you know it." She stood beside him, her hand hovering near his wrist, her eyes softening for a fleeting moment before she pulled back, voice steady. "You're a good man, and good men don't do that."

He spun, eyes blazing, to face her. "Then... I'll drag him to that shed myself and make him confess what he did to her!"

She paused, crossed her arms, and replied, her tone calm.

"Fine. Go ahead. Realize that any confession you force won't hold up in court, though. He'll walk free. Is that what you want?"

"You think I want him to go free? Are you serious?"

"I understand what's driving this, John. I really do."

"No, you don't! My mom—she's in there, wrapped in bandages, and I can't even see how badly she's hurt!" The image of her frail frame under hospital lights burned through his mind.

He'd been gone too long, chasing law school dreams while she faced this town alone. "I want revenge!"

Annaleigh stared at him with raised eyebrows.

"I understand more than you know, John. I want payback, too. But we need to do this the right way. That's what Bonnie would want."

He exhaled, irked by her patience.

"How the hell would you know?"

She stepped back, arms crossed, then jabbed a finger at John.

"Yes, I would know, you idiot." Her gaze locked on his with a raw intensity, tightening his chest. "Since I moved to Coldwater, I've spent nearly every day with her. When you were off at law school, never coming home, I was here. With her. You weren't. Don't try and pull rank on me." John's eyes widened as her words poured out. "When she says she had *company* over, that was me. When she told you she went out to eat *with friends*, that was me."

"You've spent almost every day—"

"No," she said, pointing again, "it's time for you to listen. She was alone. You were away and never came to visit. So, she turned to me. I was what she needed, though I could never measure up to the great John Deacon Chance. At least, in her eyes. And, honestly, she gave me what I was missing, too. We bonded in the absence of you."

Each of her words struck like blows, unearthing the years he'd abandoned his mother, chasing a degree while Annaleigh became her confidante. Had he so utterly failed his mother by staying away? Guilt twisted in him, sharp and cold.

We bonded in the absence of you.

A wild thought erupted in his mind.

Wait, did I hear that right?

"What are you saying, Annaleigh? Are you in love with... my mom?"

In that moment, she did something he had yet to witness in his short time in Coldwater.

She lost her temper.

Her arms flailed, her nostrils flared, and she shouted—loud enough to rattle parked cars—"NOT WITH *HER*, YOU MORON!"

The parking lot fell silent. John was unable to do anything but blink as he tried to process the meaning of her words. They stared at each other, the humid air thick between them.

Her cheeks flushed red, her eyes fierce, contrasting with her trembling arms. He read anger in her clenched jaw, but maybe something softer in her gaze, though he couldn't be sure. His heart lurched, balancing shock and a feeling he couldn't quite pin down.

His finger inched toward his chest, asking a silent question.

She gave a small, quivering nod.

He opened his mouth, words faltering, when a rustle in the shadows jerked his head around.

From between two cars, a young man with leathery skin on one side of his face stepped out.

"Did you just say you were going to kill my dad?"

* * *

JOHN TENSED, palms slick with sweat. He spun and spotted Wesley Raith.

"Wesley, what on earth are you doing here?" Annaleigh demanded, her voice firm.

Wesley's gaze flicked to a vintage, yellow pickup parked nearby as he stuffed his hands into his jeans pockets.

"None of your business, lady, but somebody needs to start explaining why this guy is threatening my dad. You know, the mayor of this whole place?"

Startled and a little embarrassed, John quickly backtracked.

"No, no, no," he stammered. "You misheard. It was a figure of speech, that's all."

"Yeah, right. I heard it just fine. Where exactly did you say you were going to drag him to, huh?"

Annaleigh stepped in between, raising one hand to Wesley and patting John's chest with the other.

"Listen, Wesley, he's a little upset. No, no, don't look at him, look at me." She pointed at herself, redirecting his gaze. "He's going through a rough time. His mother was injured in an accident this morning."

"And, you think my dad did it? You can't be serious."

"We don't know who did it," she said, still using one hand to push back on John, preventing him from joining the conversation. "It only happened a little bit ago. The investigation is underway."

Wesley tilted his head. "When?"

"When, what?"

"When did this accident happen?"

Annaleigh dropped her hand from John and faced Wesley.

"Around eight-thirty. Why?"

"Oh, it wasn't him, then."

John stepped out from behind her. "Forgive us if we don't trust you—"

"What he means," she interrupted, "is we need to know how you're so sure?"

Wesley scoffed. "Aside from him being the mayor?"

Her eyes narrowed, her voice cutting through the morning air.

"Yes, aside from that. No one's above the law, Wesley. Your dad's got loyal dogs, I mean, folks who'd do anything for him, maybe even burn a shed to send a message." She leaned closer. "You know who runs in his pack, don't you?"

Wesley's grin faltered, a nervous laugh escaping him.

"Sure, he's got friends. Who doesn't? So what?" He kicked a pebble, avoiding their stares. "Doesn't mean they torched anything." He shot a look at the pickup again, voice tightening. "You're fishing, lady."

She pressed, sensing blood.

"Loyal friends, like Kenneth? Or someone else who's been cleaning up other... messes?"

"I'm surprised you don't already know. He had a morning meeting today with some hotshot attorney. He's looking to replace you." He looked right at her and smiled. "Check with his secretary if you want, but he got up super early and he's been there since like seven or something."

John shook his head. "That doesn't mean he didn't set it up beforehand. Or coordinated the whole thing from City Hall." Raith's shadow loomed in his mind. Whether he was playing mayor or puppet master, he always seemed one step ahead.

Slippery like a greased pig.

"Whatever, dude. Do you even hear yourself? You're just, like, thinking with your trauma brain. I'm telling you, he didn't do it."

"Doesn't matter," John said, teeth gritting. "This will just be one more charge to ensure he only sees sunlight through prison bars for the rest of his life. We know what's been going on around here. He's up to his neck in all of it."

This piqued Wesley's curiosity, his brows rising slightly.

"All of what?"

"All the crimes he's been covering up," John said.

"Like what?" The young man shuffled his feet and bit at his lower lip.

Annaleigh stepped forward. "Wesley, do you know something about it?"

"The only thing I know is you're about to be out of a job, lady."

"Come on, Wesley. Enough of the bravado," she said. "You know what kind of man he is. This is all getting out of hand."

"Look, we just got here, me and Kenneth," Wesley said, pointing to the yellow pickup. As he gestured, his sleeve rode up and John glimpsed a faint burn mark on the cuff, like a cigarette had grazed it. He yanked the fabric down, covering it. "We wanted to see how his mom's doing. We heard there was some kind of accident."

John made a lunge towards Wesley, breath heavy. "Heard how? Was Kenneth there? Did he do this?"

"I don't know what you're talking about. You really need to calm down, man."

Annaleigh flashed her eyes at John with an expression he interpreted as "slow down and breathe".

"Wesley," she said, "answer the question. Where was Kenneth earlier this morning? In fact, where were you, too?"

Wesley's eyes flicked to the pickup. "We were at home making waffles when we heard the shed went up in flames. Town gossip spreads faster than lawyers think."

John's instincts flared as Wesley's flippant tone didn't match the nervous twitch in his neck. That cuff burn nagged at him. Had Wesley caused it while smoking? Probably not. He didn't smell of nicotine. But sporting scorch marks was no coincidence. Not when this mark looked new while his facial scars looked old.

And not when every wrong thing in this town somehow revolved around fire.

Annaleigh's brow arched. "Home? Anyone else—besides you two—that can verify that?"

"I dunno, the griddle still might be hot. Wanna go touch it?"

John grabbed Wesley by his shirt and pulled him in close.

"God dammit, tell us what you know and lose the attitude."

A door slam echoed across the parking lot, jerking his attention. He turned to see Kenneth step from the truck. His hulking frame towered beside the hood and shimmering heat drifted upwards from it.

"Lay off the kid," he snarled from afar, voice like gravel. "Or else."

Wesley's smirk widened. "Sorry, bud. My uncle Kenneth don't take kindly to your type."

Fear prickled John's spine. Kenneth's bulk and Raith's reach could crush him, but he wouldn't back down. Not with his mother in that hospital, not with Gamble's killer still free. John leaned in, whispering so only the two of them could hear.

"He's not your uncle. And, if he weren't here, you'd be on your ass right now." He shoved Wesley lightly as he released him.

The young man regained his footing, smiled, then nodded at Kenneth, who returned inside the truck.

"Whatever. This has been real fun, but I've got business inside." He took a step towards the entrance. John surged, planting himself in the way.

"You're not setting foot near my mom, you smug little bastard."

Wesley halted, eyes gleaming with defiance. "Move, dude, or you'll wish you had."

Annaleigh grabbed John's shoulder, her voice urgent.

"John, don't."

The hospital doors swung open, and Deputy D. Clyde Brothers stepped out, blocking the entrance.

"Wesley, this ain't the place for you, son. You best be off now." His tone was calm but unyielding.

Clyde to the rescue, again.

Faced with a deputy, Wesley's tone unexpectedly flipped. "I, uh, was just going to, uh, my dad wanted to know..."

"Back to the truck, young man." Clyde blocked the doorway and waved for him to leave. "Don't you worry, we will brief the mayor on Ms. Chance's condition. Get up and go now, ya hear?"

Wesley drew a deep breath. A snarl spread across his lips.

"Fine. Hospitals are lame, anyway. Bunch of sick and, hopefully, *dying* people."

John's blood boiled as Wesley retreated. The overemphasis on the word 'dying' flipped his stomach.

My mom's going to be fine, you jackass. If you were dying in front of me, though, I'd sit and watch it with a bowl of buttered popcorn.

Kenneth started the engine as Wesley hopped in, and they edged out of the parking spot, throwing glares and scowls. A short yelp of screeching tires accentuated their exit from the lot. Clyde walked up to John and placed a hand on his shoulder.

"You flew out of here looking pretty angry, John. Everything okay?"

John's racing heart slowed as he peered into Brother's understanding eyes, still tinged with redness.

"Yes, sir," he replied, head drooping. "Better now. Just lost my head there for a minute."

"Bonnie and I go way back, so I know how you're feeling." He squeezed, and John's eyes flicked to him, surprised at the previously unknown relationship. "Ms. Stanton is correct. You gotta do this the right way."

"You were listening?" Annaleigh asked.

"To every word," Clyde said. "From now on, whenever the two of you aren't safely in the courthouse, I'll be keeping an eye on you, just so ya know."

After a long inhale, the rush of anger inside John fully subsided as he expelled the Coldwater air.

"Thanks for stopping me," he said to Annaleigh. "What do we do now?"

Clyde cleared his throat. "I ain't no hotshot lawyer like you two," he said, "but I figure the boy showing up here might tip you off."

"Tip us off?" John asked, head tilted.

"Everything means *something*, don't it? Old lesson I learned from Detective Mumber."

Annaleigh snapped her fingers. "That's it! Why would Raith send his son down here? That's not his style. It only draws attention. If the mayor had shown up himself, fine, that's an official act. He's visiting one of his constituents. But, to have Wesley and Kenneth—"

"Maybe those assholes feel guilty about something," John interjected.

"Cussing don't make you cool," Clyde said, shooting him a stern look.

"Even if that description is dead-on accurate? Fine, whatever.

Maybe those two unlikeable and evil-at-heart individuals are checking on their handiwork. Is that better?"

A thin smile grew across Clyde's stubbled face.

"Yes, your theory is possible. And, your mother would be proud of your improved vocabulary."

Annaleigh waved to gain their attention.

"Eyes on the ball, folks. Kenneth wouldn't light a match without Raith's say-so, right? Maybe they went rogue." She glanced at John, her eyes softening. "And, like John said, they're checking if their little mission succeeded." She winced, catching her words too late. "Sorry, that came out wrong."

The image of his mother's bandaged form flashed in his mind. The shed fire wasn't a random attack. It was personal, a shank stuck, then twisted, in his gut. He forced a smirk, masking the churn of anger and fear.

"I'm sure he knows you meant nothing by it," Clyde said, nudging John with his shoulder.

Annaleigh grinned. "Yeah, sure he does. I think it's time we take what we know to the judge. He can give us—"

"Hold on, now," Clyde interrupted, stroking his chin, his kind eyes glinting with calculation. "I know Judge Chapel. I see him in the church pew every Sunday. Soulful voice he's got. We talk over coffee afterwards quite a bit. I know for a fact he'll want more than suspicions. Let me take our boomerang back to his place, poke around a little. We'll dig up something solid to bolster your case, Ms. Stanton. Can I borrow him? A few hours, tops. I promise."

His voice carried a steadiness, something John didn't share. Instead, he felt a jolt of dread.

Return to the shed? Right now? Where Mom nearly burned alive?

He nodded, swallowing hard.

Annaleigh's gaze flicked between them, then she snatched the Dart's keys from John's hand with a playful smirk.

"Agreed. I've been itching to take this beast for a spin. See you back at the office, boys!"

As she strode away towards the parked Dart, Clyde clapped a hand on John's back, steering him toward the cruiser.

"Let's go and see how your hero of a mother escaped this fire, shall we?"

18

KINDRED SPARKS

The late morning sun hung high over Coldwater, layering the gravel drive outside John Chance's childhood home into a patchwork of thin, interlocking shadows. A restless breeze stirred the air, carrying the scent of damp earth and rustling the gnarled oaks and pines that lined the property.

John shifted uncomfortably in the passenger seat of Clyde's cruiser. It felt strange to approach his own house this way, like a visitor in his own life. Annaleigh had absconded with his Dart, returning to the courthouse, leaving him with Clyde to examine the place where Bonnie had nearly been burned alive.

He stood in front of the shed, his eyes watering at its weathered planks, now charred into black remnants. The thought of his mother in this death shack haunted him. She had been trapped in there to burn.

He wanted answers. No, he wanted more.

He needed someone's head on a spike.

Clyde shadowed him, scanning the shed with a quiet intensity. His face, soft despite its lines, seemed out of place in this hard-edged town.

"You up for this, young man?" Clyde asked, his voice low and steady, almost encouraging. "I know we're already here and all, but ain't no shame in taking a breather after what happened."

John shook his head, his gaze fixed on the shed's warped door.

"I'm good, Deputy. Need to figure out who did this."

Clyde nodded, stepping toward the small building.

"Alright, then. Let's give it a look-see."

He pushed the tattered door open, the hinges groaning, and a blast of scorched wood hit John's nose. The interior was a mess. Shovels and rakes lay scattered, a metal toolbox tipped over, half-melted, its edges curled like wax. The two men entered, soles crunching on ash-dusted dirt.

"Looks like our initial thoughts were a bit wrong," Clyde said, rubbing his forehead. He moved to the back and slipped outside through a gap in the wall. He crouched to spy a blackened patch. "Two points of ignition. Didn't only start at the door. Take a look here," he called, pointing to a handprint blistered into the wood, its edges unnaturally sharp. He stepped back inside, inspecting the mark from within. "Burned clean through. Looks the same as that courthouse brand. But I can't see no cattle iron doing this."

John silently agreed. The handprint matched the one he and Annaleigh had seen, both at the courthouse and etched onto their vehicles. His gaze swept the rest of the shed, but instead of finding clues, his mind conjured horrors beyond reality.

On the ground, Bonnie lay crumpled, one arm severed, face melted and gone. She also leaned against the bottom shelf of the workbench, lifeless, amidst scattered potting soil, in a state of crispy decay. And, she was splayed in the ash-filled corner, random shards of terracotta forming an outline around her lifeless body. Behind him, at the scorched door, blackened claw marks smudged where she'd fought to escape. The images choked him.

"I can't see anything else but her," he mumbled, eyes glazing over the floor.

Clyde's brow furrowed, his eyes flicking to John. He brushed ash from the bottom of the door, revealing a second handprint, smaller, its fingers slender, burned deeper and blacker than the first.

"Well, I'll be," he muttered. "Two sets. Did you catch this?"

John's face flushed. He didn't, but should have. He had been staring right at it—and past it—at the same time. This time, it wasn't his surgically impaired vision that had betrayed him. It was something more. He didn't want to admit it. Instead, he crouched beside Clyde, studying the prints.

"Yeah," he lied. He leaned in and pivoted between the two marks, comparing them. "This one is smaller. Different sizes might mean two brands? Maybe even two suspects."

Clyde's eyebrow arched, a faint, knowing smile tugging his lips. "Sharp catch, boomerang. See? You're thinking like one of us now."

That nickname—*boomerang*—landed softer this time, warmed by Clyde's tone. Something about the deputy felt like an old friend John couldn't place. Perhaps he'd known Clyde years ago, as a child, but forgot? But, if so, why wouldn't Clyde have said something?

John stood, wiping ash from his hands. "We may not know the source, but these marks link Kenneth to both the courthouse and here. It should be enough to get a warrant for additional questioning. Let's head back and—"

"Hold up," Clyde interrupted. "Let's take a beat out front. Got coffee in a thermos in the car."

"No offense, Deputy, but we don't have time. Plus, coffee's not really my thing."

"Pop, then," Clyde said, grinning. "I'm sure Bonnie's gotta some stashed away somewhere. Grab us a couple. Meet you on the porch, two minutes."

John sighed, realizing resistance was futile. He snagged two Dr. Peppers from the fridge and exited through the front door. He stepped out and saw the deputy on the wooden steps overlooking the gravel drive. He handed one over, and they clinked bottles before popping the caps.

"Sit a spell," Clyde said, patting the step. "You're running hot, John. Give yourself a minute. Let's talk."

John hesitated, then sat, the top step creaking under him.

"Summer's coming fast, John. Coldwater's heating up, you know? I don't know about you, but for me, it seems like it's getting more difficult to keep cool. Maybe it's time to pull out the short sleeves."

"Are we here to talk about fashion, deputy?"

"John, we can talk about anything you want to."

Bonnie's pain, coupled with the unreal images flittering in his mind, lingered.

"I don't really want to talk about anything, honestly. But, yeah, of course I'm running hot. Why wouldn't I be? You've seen what's going on around here. And I'm damn sure I don't know how to slow down," he admitted. "Not with mom in the hospital. Not with that shithead mayor roaming around free—"

After a hearty throat clear from the deputy, John reevaluated his word choices.

"Fine. *Darn* sure. And... *bastard* mayor? No, that might be borderline. Jerk, scum? There may not be a better word for him, truthfully."

Clyde nodded, trying to hide a smirk. He gazed out over the property with a distant stare.

"When stuff happens to family, it's personal. I know there ain't no stopping that fire in your gut. But I'll bet your mama would gladly wear any burn if it meant protecting her son—you. That's a parent's job, you know." He swirled his Dr. Pepper. "Never raised any kids myself. Always wondered what it'd be like to guide a son right. I'm sure my words can't fix everything, but I hope they at least bring some comfort."

He frowned at Clyde's odd phrasing, then moved on.

"Well, you're not too shabby of a guide, Deputy. I appreciate you talking me down at the hospital. I was ready to tear Wesley apart."

"You do have spirit, I'll give you that. Coldwater's got more to

teach you than you think, John. Doesn't need to be a pit stop."
His eyes met John's, kind but piercing, like he saw something
deeper.

John leaned back. The porch step dug into his spine, but he
didn't care.

"Parnell told you, huh?" Clyde nodded, chewing at his lip.
"Look, St. Louis is the plan. Has been my plan for a while now.
Got a job waiting with the prosecutor there and everything." He
hesitated, the words spilling out before he could stop them. "And,
I'm looking for my dad. Never knew him. Mom's never said who
he is, but she dropped some hints that he lives there, and I think
St. Louis is where I'll find answers."

Clyde's hand froze on the bottle, his jaw tightening for a
heartbeat.

"Your dad, huh?" he said, voice steady but softer. "That's
quite a quest. Pretty sure you were born here, weren't you? Are
you sure up there is the place to start?"

John shrugged, staring at the gravel. "Gotta start somewhere.
The longer I wait, I feel like the further away he gets." He glanced
at Clyde, that strange ease settling in. "Might miss this town and
some of the people in it, though. Didn't see that coming when I
got here."

"Honored if you're lumping me into that crowd. But I think
we both know that it's a young woman you're really talking
about." Clyde's smile was small, almost sad. "You're a good kid,
John. We'll get justice for Bonnie. For Gamble, too. Stick with me
and the Sheriff, and we'll see it through, alright? Then, you can
decide what you want to do next."

"Deal."

He clinked his bottle against Clyde's again. The moment felt
right, like a missing puzzle piece slotting into place. They sat in
silence, cicadas humming as the sun climbed higher. John's eyes
drifted around, soaking everything in. Leaving for the city meant
leaving this view. He'd done it once for school. A second time
would be harder.

Climbing the trees that grew along the long drive. Fishing in the pond beyond the ridge. He remembered playing basketball on this gravel, trying to control a dribble that wanted to bounce in every crazy way possible on the bumps and grooves in the pea gravel.

A realization pulled him out of his memories. Something caught his eye, an unusual rut in the driveway. A set of tire tracks, deep and uneven, smashed into the loose stones. He stood, squinting.

"Clyde, you see those tracks?"

"Ain't from your Dart," he said, getting up and kneeling to get a closer look. "Not Bonnie's sedan, either. Or my cruiser. Too deep." His voice hardened. "Someone else was here. Recently."

John's pulse quickened, his mind snapping to Kenneth's battered pickup.

"Bet you those tracks match a certain vintage, yellow truck we saw back at the hospital."

Clyde's chin dipped, hand on his radio. "Could be. A truck, maybe a van. I'll call for the camera kit to match 'em to vehicles owned by Kenneth or Raith." He keyed the mic. "Mumber, come in. I'm at Bonnie Chance's place. Bring the kit, now. We've got something."

John's heart pounded, a grim satisfaction taking root as he strode toward the house, the phone receiver already in his sights to call Annaleigh.

The tire tracks were a solid, real lead. The uneven ruts burned into his mind, his ire pointed straight at the mayor's lapdog, Kenneth Roy Atlee. His hulking frame, cryptic warnings, that courthouse handprint. It all screamed of his guilt.

John's fists clenched. He'd make him pay for Bonnie's pain, for the fire that nearly stole her. He could see it. Kenneth cornered, his smug grin fading as justice landed, with the bang of a gavel and a lengthy prison sentence. A flicker of doubt crept in, like the haze at his vision's edges.

But, what if it wasn't Kenneth?

Mayor Raith's calculating eyes flashed in his mind, his voice dripping with control at the crime scene. Raith had the power and, based on his name showing up in those secret files, he also had the motive to bury Gamble's murder.

Could Raith have set the shed ablaze? Was Wesley lying to cover for his dad?

John shook his head, clearing the fog.

No, it was Kenneth. Had to be.

His mind locked on and shut out the broader picture. He grabbed the receiver, its cold weight steadying him, determined to tell Annaleigh they were closing in.

19

TRESPASS AT MIDNIGHT

Annaleigh Stanton's breath fogged the window pane of City Hall's side door as she crouched with a screwdriver clutched in her trembling hand. The lock, a flimsy relic like everything in Coldwater, yielded with a single twist, the door creaking open like an invitation to ruin.

"Guess I won't be needing this after all," she said, shoving the tool into the back pocket of her jeans. "Scratched up my back door lock, practicing for nothing."

"Practicing? Is it really that different from a desk drawer?"

"Actually, yeah. You should get out more, learn new things, John."

"Well, I learned you've upgraded from paperclips to screwdrivers. Perhaps you'll get more chances inside," he joked. His eyes told a different story, though. He was worried.

An unlocked door in Raith's domain wasn't carelessness. It was confidence, and that chilled her more than the night air. Tonight, they'd look for proof of his corruption, or lose everything trying.

John crouched beside her, his scrunched face weighing the consequences of their decision.

"Come on," he whispered, "is it really breaking in if the door opened like that?"

"Seriously?" she replied, flashing a look of surprise. "Trespassing? Remember that from law school? You know, the place you graduated from, like five minutes ago?"

"You know what I mean." He flushed and turned his head. "This is a bold move. Still not sure it's the right one."

"Think of it this way... Raith's tipped the scales already. All we're doing is trying to balance it out." Her legal savvy justified bending the rules. Sometimes, justice required a heavier hand. "Plus," she argued, "the documents we're looking through are public record. We could wait, walk in tomorrow morning, and get them, if we wanted to—"

"Raith would know what we were up to then."

"Exactly," she whispered, pointing. "So, let's pretend we're picking up an advanced copy. That way it won't feel like theft."

"Trespassing, remember?" A half smile creased his lips.

"More proof he can learn. Come on, let's go find what we've come for."

John nodded, his reluctance clear, but his loyalty to her was stronger. They eased into the building. Once they were both inside, she pulled the door closed.

No turning back now.

The dark corridor became a tunnel, swallowing the dim red glow of the exit sign.

Each step risked an errant squeak, alerting anyone listening to their presence. Who would be at City Hall at midnight when the whole town was asleep? This jaunt would be a simple in and out, with no witnesses.

Exactly the way she'd planned it.

Annaleigh's heart thudded as they inched down the hallway, ending up in front of two opposite-facing doors. The entrance on the left—territory she was desperate to avoid.

She eyed the frosted glass pane housed in the door's upper

half. In arched, golden letters, a name boldly pronounced the office's occupant.

Cameron Raith, Coldwater Mayor.

They were in the belly of the beast now.

Her focus narrowed to the door on the right. The records room—their target. That's where evidence of Raith's poisonous touch on this town would be, she was sure of it. She glanced at John, his eyes darting nervously, his hand grazing hers for reassurance. She'd vowed not to go alone again, but bringing him dragged him further into her fire.

Annaleigh froze. The door stood ajar, a sliver of shadow spilling in.

Why is every door in this place either open or unlocked?

"Trap?" John whispered, his breath warm against her ear.

"Maybe," she murmured, inspecting the gap. The desire to prove Raith's crimes pulled her inside stronger than the feeling to run back to the courthouse and never look back. She crept into the room, peering into the darkness.

"Coast is clear. Come on in."

John followed her in, his footsteps soft but unsteady. The room was a maze of sagging file cabinets and dusty shelves, a rotary phone hanging in one corner, and a few sporadic desks pushed together, providing a make-shift table.

She flicked on her flashlight, casting flitting shadows and illuminating John's face, exposing his blur of worry. Once they were in, she eased the door shut. She winced at its faint groan.

"City Contracts are over there," she whispered. "That's where we start. You take the left drawer. I'll start with the right."

Annaleigh's fingers shook as she flipped through the folders. Her pulse raced. This was so far out of her comfort zone she might as well have been across the Mississippi River, somewhere in Kentucky.

Keep it steady, girl. You've got this. Raith left you no choice.

A folder labeled "Consulting Agreements" caught her eye, remembering a reference from one of the files from Gamble's secret stack. She rifled through its contents, eventually pulling out a page. The document listed payments, the vast majority directed to a single entity.

"Look at this," she whispered, flagging John over. "Tens of thousands of dollars for consulting on projects I've never heard of. A bridge, a park, an extension to City Hall. And, get this... computer upgrades for the courthouse?"

"Pretty sure that last one never happened," John added, stifling a snort. "Our tech is ancient."

"Most were given to one company. KRA Industries." She pointed to a column on the ledger. "Looks like they received about 75% of all city contracts. Seems odd."

He scanned it, his eyes narrowing as he absorbed the page.

"KRA Industries," he repeated. "KRA. As in, Kenneth Roy Atlee? They wouldn't be that stupid, would they?"

She shook her head. "There's no way the mayor would be that brazen about it."

"I don't know. With the size of his ego, it's pretty much on brand. He thinks nobody is as smart as him. That we wouldn't connect the dots."

Her heart leapt. This tied Kenneth's corruption to Raith's schemes, and though the mayor's name was absent, at least it provided the next domino to fall.

She folded and pocketed the page when the presence of additional light caught her peripheral vision. She snapped her head toward the door, looking over her shoulder. A faint white glow from down the hallway pulsed under the frosted glass door, warm and unnatural.

John stiffened. "You see that?" he whispered. "Flashlight's off. Now."

Her breath hitched as slow and heavy footsteps echoed in the hall.

A young voice, sharp with anger, muttered.

"Why doesn't he just get rid of her? It would make things so much easier."

Another voice, colder and deeper, replied.

"She's being watched. Besides, can't do anything so soon. Not after the other one. You know that. *I know you do.*"

The hallway flickered with white light, like flashlights, but the glow beneath the door burned steadily, pulsing like a heartbeat.

"Under the table," Annaleigh hissed, dropping to her knees, scraping the floor. John scrambled beside her, squeezing in close. The air grew heavy. Warm. Thick. She pressed against the table, hiding behind its one full panel side.

John joined her, both their breaths shallow and hitching. The glow brightened, casting shadows through the door's frosted pane.

The footsteps paused outside, the younger voice muttered.

"Next time, it'll look more like an accident."

Her stomach dropped.

Were they talking about Gamble? Or perhaps, Bonnie?

Annaleigh's lungs burned, refusing to breathe. Maybe it was the break-in, maybe it was the voices. Control threatened to leave her.

John's hand found hers, trembling but steady, grounding her. The figures paced beyond the door, inches from their hiding spot.

The older voice hissed.

"Well, what are you waiting for? Get your ass in there and get what we came for. It's supposed to be on the desk."

Annaleigh glared at John with wide eyes. The table they were under would only conceal them in the dark. If those voices came into this room flashing those pulsating lights, they would have no escape.

She stared at the door's handle, squinting, hoping she wouldn't see it turn. A click sounded—the unmistakable sound of a doorknob twist.

Is this really happening? There's nowhere else for us to hide.

A groan bellowed from the hallway. A door had swung open, and the footsteps scurried inside.

My mind must be playing tricks on me.

She narrowed her eyes, straining to bring the records room door into better focus.

It was still shut. The two men had entered the mayor's office across the hall.

"Really?" the younger voice said, full of annoyance. "His stupid hat? That's what he needed us to get?"

"What the boss wants, the boss gets, right?" The older voice, gruff and tired, sounded just as irritated. "Shut the door and let's go."

The door across the hall slammed, echoing throughout the still hallway. Annaleigh was certain she'd stopped trembling, but John's warm grip squeezed her, confirming otherwise.

The footsteps retreated, and the white, pulsating lights faded until she and John were left in darkness once again. She counted her breaths, her pulse a drum in her ears, thankful for silence's return. She nodded to John, and they crawled out, her legs shaky.

She reached a hand into her pocket and confirmed the ledger page was still there.

They slipped back into the corridor, leaving the records room door ajar, as they had found it. After checking that it was clear, they sneaked out the side door and back into free air.

John's eyes met hers. "What now?" he whispered.

"We use this," Annaleigh said, holding up the page.

"How? Can't do a lot with stolen evidence, can we?"

"I've got an idea, but you may not like it."

John's brow furrowed, his focus boring a hole through her. "Try me."

In her head, a plan formed bit by bit. A risky play to expose the truth, but it could also cost them their careers.

"Not here. Let's go." Her voice was steady, but her hands still shook.

She'd bent the rules tonight.

To achieve justice, those rules might need to be shattered completely.

* * *

ANNALEIGH SLID into the driver's seat of her two-door Cavalier. The vinyl from its front seats, cool from the midnight chill, bit through her jeans. John settled across from her, his breath still ragged. The engine sputtered to life, and she pulled onto the empty road, desiring to put as many deserted Coldwater streets between them and City Hall.

The ledger page, folded in her pocket, weighed like lead. It was proof of Kenneth's corruption and provided a thread to Raith's building. The only problem? It didn't connect to Raith directly. Even still, merely possessing this bombshell, given the context of Gamble's secret files, could be a noose around their necks.

Her hands gripped the wheel, trembling, the white glow from the records room seared in her mind. The younger man's words chilled her more than the night air. Make *what* look like an accident? Was it Gamble's murder? Bonnie, frail in the hospital? Or was a new attack brewing?

John broke the silence, voice low, nearly lost in the engine's hum.

"I thought we were done for back there. We were *that* close to getting caught." His fingers fumbled with his seatbelt strap, a nervous tic she'd noticed him do before.

"Well, we weren't," Annaleigh said, sharper than intended. Her eyes flicked to the rearview mirror, half-expecting headlights or that unnatural glow. "We're not out of this yet."

He turned, face pale in the dashboard's dim shine.

"The ledger had KRA Industries all over the place. Even if we prove it's really Kenneth's company, there's still no mention of Raith."

"Yeah, but Kenneth's the muscle, not the brain. Raith may have covered his tracks on this, but this puts us one step ahead."

Her mind raced, piecing together the plan she had hinted at before driving away. Going to the Cedar Creek Times was a long shot. Its editor, Earl Boone, loathed Raith, but his salacious stories about the mayor always seemed to fade, without fanfare or traction. Perhaps this ledger could change that.

But leaking it could end their careers, given the way it was procured. Or worse.

Stolen evidence wasn't a prosecutor's badge of honor.

"Your idea... what is it? You said I wouldn't like it."

She sensed his patience wearing thin. Eyes on the road, she exhaled, trying to control her racing pulse.

"We go public. The Times. Boone hates Raith. We leak the ledger, let the town turn on him."

His brow furrowed. "Leak? To that rag? Annaleigh, that's not us. We're prosecutors, holding stolen evidence—"

"*Public* evidence, remember."

"Doesn't matter. We still took it after hours. Tonight just doesn't seem like you, Annaleigh. We could lose everything. Our jobs, our licenses, our freedom. And, if Raith finds out it was us—"

"He'll already know it was us, John," she snapped. "He gave us that phony investigation as a way to distract us. A way to control us. That's why he didn't want us to go to Parnell. Because what we were doing wasn't real. But, he didn't realize we'd catch on to him." She waved the paper at him. "With this, we've got the upper hand. Those voices—no doubt Wesley and Kenneth—were talking about cleaning up his mess. We're the mess, John. We're the mess they need to clean up."

Her own scars flared in her mind, dredging up feelings of powerlessness. She wouldn't be cornered again.

John's hesitation about her plan wasn't wrong, though. This was a line they couldn't uncross. He rubbed his neck.

"No. This can't be how it ends. Going public is not enough."

"Well, we can't kill him, now can we?" she muttered. She caught a side-eye from him and felt the shadows start to creep in on them both. She shook her head, clearing the darkness. "The

Times hits harder, faster. That kind of pressure could give Parnell leverage."

"*We* can provide that leverage, Annaleigh. Don't let what happened to my mom break you. I'm broken enough for the both of us." His hand trembled as he laid it on her arm, seeking the reassurance he'd given her under the table back at City Hall.

She pulled the car to the roadside, leaving the engine idling. The ledger page crinkled in her pocket as she twisted to face him.

"You're not broken, John," she said, softer, fear surfacing. She placed her hand on top of his, interlocking her fingers with his, staring deep into his eyes. "I know I've been a little reckless, especially since your mom. Look, we've bent the rules pretty far already. If we stop now, Raith wins. Gamble's still dead, your mom's still hurt. There's no telling who might be next. We can't let this keep happening."

"You're right. We need to stop him. Going public isn't a given, though. Boone can twist it. Worse yet, Raith can spin it—"

"Okay, okay, I get it. Too much at stake to hand the reins to someone else," she said, voice steel despite her bouncing hands. Her fingers rapped the wheel, mind racing for options. She dropped her shoulders.

"There... might be another way. I swore to myself I'd never do it. But, I don't see any other way."

"Do what?" John pressed, eyes narrowing. "What's the way?"

"With you there, I'd be able to get away easier..."

"Annaleigh, don't start this cryptic crap again. You're not making any sense. With me, where?"

She slapped her thighs, making her decision.

"We're going to the bank in the morning. For a withdrawal. Sort of."

His face clouded with confusion and dread. "What in the world does that mean?"

She forced a tight smile, the weight of her choice settling in.

"I never wanted to play this card. This time, it might be worth it."

They'd crossed a line tonight, but to burn Raith's empire down, Annaleigh would have to break a vow she swore to keep forever.

20

BANKROLL BLUFF

John walked into the lobby of the First Bank of Coldwater and was blasted with the smell of wax and old money. Its wood-paneled walls and brass fixtures screamed small-town pride, frozen in the '80s like the rest of Coldwater. The bank had just opened, and they were the first entrants.

Annaleigh leaned close, her voice low as they passed desks with placards reading "Financial Representative."

"Reginald's been after me since I moved here," she murmured. "Always asking me out, never taking no. Follow my lead, and whatever I do, don't flinch."

"Don't flinch? Annaleigh, you're not robbing the place, are you?"

Deep down, his resentment lingered. Her solo mission to Hank's Three Pump had landed his mom in the hospital. On the flip side, he blamed himself just as much.

It was his foot that had hit the high beams in the Dart, not hers. That was the first domino to fall.

Still, her raw guilt had softened him. He was eager to move past it if it meant putting Raith behind bars.

To achieve that result, he'd play along. For now.

She dropped her gaze, her flats scuffing the marble floor. "I'm going to bend a few more laws here, John. I'm also going to flirt with that guy over there. Don't judge me."

They reached the back corner, where a desk twice the size of the others squatted under a copper nameplate, reading "Reginald Windermere III, Bank Manager" in an overly bold font.

The man behind it wore a three-piece suit with a haircut so coiffed it looked sculpted. His posture dripped privilege. John's gut soured.

Smarmy. This guy looks like he'd sell you something that he knew didn't work.

"Fancy seeing you, Annaleigh," Reginald said, standing to take her hand. He bent, planting a quick kiss on its back, his lips lingering a beat too long.

She let him.

John's fingers twitched, itching to ball into fists.

Reginald straightened, still well below Annaleigh's chin, and extended a hand upward to John. "Who do we have here?"

John stifled a smirk, leaning down to shake.

"John Chance, Prosecutor. No need to kiss my hand."

"Pleasure," Reginald said, tone clipped, eyes flicking back to Annaleigh. They sat, his chair creaking under his ego.

"John, I'd like you to meet Reginald Windermere. He helped set up my accounts when I moved—"

"The third," Reginald said, nose aimed high.

John's brow furrowed. "Sorry, what's that?"

"Reginald Windermere, the third." He shot her a patronizing glance, head tilted. "When we introduce people, Annaleigh, we should strive for accuracy."

John gripped the chair's arms, resisting the urge to leap across and twist the man's head right off.

After I get out of jail for killing him, I'm going to need a long shower.

"My mistake, Reginald," she said, leaning forward, hands on his desk, voice honeyed. "I hope you'll forgive me."

"Of course, anything for you. I know you mean well," he replied, stars in his eyes. "How can I assist? Are you accessing the prosecutor's business account today?"

A coy smile grew on her lips as she dialed up the courtroom charm. "Why, yes, Reginald. I am. You always know what a lady wants."

I'm going to throw up.

John shifted, biting his lip to stay quiet. He saw through her act, knowing deep down she meant none of it.

To Reginald, though, she was convincing. Very convincing. His eyes gleamed, lapping it up.

"Anything, of course. You've come to the right man."

"As Acting Prosecutor, I'm tying up loose ends after... Prosecutor Gamble's passing," she said, her voice catching enough to sell the grief. "I need account statements for the prosecutor's office, the last two years. I feel like I'm drowning trying to get everything running smoothly. You know, like you have with this bank."

John marveled at her play. She was using Reginald's crush to let him "solve" her problem, though those records weren't their true target. Reginald was a juror being swayed, oblivious to the game. He preened. His fingers raced, pressing a sequence of keys, and the dot-matrix printer screeched to life.

"I'll add you as an authorized user, Annaleigh. Mrs. Johnson's a user on the account, too, just so you know." He flicked an annoyed glance at John. "I assume he's not important enough yet?"

John gritted his teeth, forcing his cheeks high. "Maybe one day I'll be a bank manager—"

Annaleigh's elbow came out of nowhere.

Reginald's smile tightened, indifference flashing on his face. He slid a form across the desk, eyes locking with hers, grinning like he'd won a prize.

"Sign here. If you're elected Prosecutor, we'll make you primary."

Annaleigh scribbled then leaned closer, her voice a velvet whisper.

"One more thing, Reginald, and it's delicate. Just between us." She glanced at John, then back, eyes wide, pleading. "We found an invoice in Gamble's things, but it only has the company name. No address. We're not sure where to remit payment. Can you look and see if they have an account here?"

"Absolutely, most businesses in Coldwater bank here. We are the best, after all. Thanks to me, of course." Reginald sat up straighter in his chair.

"Of course," she placated. "The business we're looking for is called 'KRA Industries.'"

He typed as she spoke it, hitting the Enter key with a flourish.

He really thinks he's winning her over. This is part magic, part torture.

Reginald inspected the screen and nodded to himself.

"Yes, it looks like we do indeed have an account for them. I can provide their company address so you can remit payment—"

"I was *really* hoping to get the owner's name, too."

The bumbling grin on Reginald's face vanished. "Annaleigh, that information is confidential. An address is one thing, but the owner? You know I'm not supposed to give it out. We protect our clients here."

"I know that, Reginald, I do. I also know you call the shots around here. You're the big man, aren't you? You make the rules, you can bend them, just this one time. I'd be... so very grateful..."

Her tone, soft and sultry, made Reginald squirm. He tugged at his white collared button-up, desperate to loosen his necktie.

"I... uh, I'm not sure..."

She leaned further onto his desk, sliding her hand next to his keyboard. Her index finger dragged down the edge of the plastic, slow and deliberate.

Oh. My. God.

"Just one... little... name." She emphasized each word by tapping on his keyboard with a fingernail.

Reginald rubbed his forehead, which had blossomed into beet red. A vein on his left temple bulged, throbbing in pace with his visibly racing heartbeat.

"Okay. I'll do it for you, Annaleigh." He pressed the Enter key one more time and read the contents of the new screen aloud. "Says here, Kenneth Roy Atlee. He's the primary account owner. And, the only authorized user."

"Mr. Atlee?" she exclaimed, feigning surprise. "That is the mother of all coincidences, isn't it?" She slapped John's arm to sell the performance.

"A coincidence? How's that?" Reginald's smile faltered, hand pausing over the keyboard. "Wait a minute. Atlee? Isn't that the mayor's friend? That's sensitive information."

"You're never going to believe this, Reginald. We recently heard an accusation—in a separate case, you see—that Mr. Atlee had run afoul of some financial reporting requirements. We put it on the bottom of the stack, you know, in deference to the mayor. But, since we're here, in light of this newfound evidence you've discovered, you may be in a position to help us clear up his unfortunate situation."

"Newfound evidence? That *I* discovered?" Reginald's eyes darted around, as if he were searching for it.

"Yes, of course," she said, her tone morphing into one she would use in a closing argument in the courtroom. "A warrant would become public, possibly even ruin him. With your assistance, we might be able to scratch his name off quietly and move that accusation from the bottom of the stack... right to the trash can."

"If anyone found out—"

"Everyone knows you value discretion, Reginald. Like you said. *You protect your clients.* Your actions will do that for Mr. Atlee."

Protect him from getting away, that is.

"My actions?"

"Bank statements for the last five years. For KRA Industries... and for Kenneth's—I mean, Mr. Atlee's personal account?"

Reginald, in a daze, looked at her in confusion.

"His personal account, too?"

"I know it's a big ask," she soothed, voice silky. "You'd be doing Raith a favor, too, by ruling his guy out. And, of course, it'd be a favor... for me." She batted her eyes, enough to make John's skin crawl. "Please, Reginald?"

"Why not call Mr. Atlee for permission? If it's to clear his name, I'm sure he'd agree to the release." He reached for the phone, but Annaleigh placed her hand on his.

"Because I just *know* this information will clear him, and I'd rather he not know some idiot witness pointed a finger at him. All I need are the statements. You already saved the day once with our business account. Please, Reginald Windermere... the *third*. Be the hero again."

Reginald licked his lips and disappeared into her eyes.

He was sold.

She settled back into her seat, elbows on the desk, chin resting on her hands. He pressed a few more keys, and the printer whirred once again, spitting out page after page of precious data.

"For you, Annaleigh, I'll keep this quiet. But..." He leaned in, voice oily, sliding the pages across the desk towards her like contraband at a night drop. "Since I'm doing this favor, how about that dinner? You never have quite answered, and I've asked multiple times now."

Calling in the favor already? Don't flinch, remember? She's got this.

Annaleigh's hand found John's under the desk, squeezing tight. She stood, pulling him up, and flashed a grin.

"The only issue is that timing is everything, Reginald. And, my boyfriend here—" She swiftly grabbed John around the neck with both hands and pulled him in.

He could tell it was only supposed to be a peck. She'd started

164

to pull away, but instead, her eyes locked with his, and she pressed her warm, moist lips deeper against his.

Reginald, the bank, Coldwater, and the entire world vanished from John's mind.

He was kissing the most beautiful woman within a hundred miles, maybe even a thousand, without any other care. He wrapped his arm around her waist and forgot about Gamble, his sunken face, missing skin, and severed stump. He reached up with his other, palming the back of her head, and didn't care that the mayor and his vicious bunch of thugs planned his demise.

His future in St. Louis evaporated. There was no future, only that moment. A point in time that seemed to stretch on forever.

He savored her.

Their lips parted as she eased away, sliding her fingertips across his cheek, grazing his skin with her nails.

"You see," she said, turning to Reginald with John still in her arms, "he doesn't like me dating other men." She grabbed the statements and interlocked fingers with John's. "Thanks, Reginald. You're the best."

A grin broke free from John, despite his daze. He caressed her thumb, playing along.

"Gotta say, Reg. This really *was* a pleasure. Thanks, buddy."

The bank manager slumped, muttering, "It's Reginald," to an empty corner.

John's heart pounded as he stepped onto the sidewalk outside the bank, Annaleigh's hand still latched onto his. He knew the kiss was a calculated dodge of Reginald's dinner invitation, but it felt natural.

He craved more.

Her hand in his was warm and steady, not a performance. Something real, something that tightened his chest.

Annaleigh glanced at him, her eyes catching the morning light, a playful smile curving her lips. That "boyfriend" line had been a ploy to fool Reginald, but after he rubbed her thumb, hers brushed back.

Her touch was electric. No one could see it, which meant no audience that needed selling. It suggested something else simmering under the surface.

He slowed, tugging her to a stop beside her cherry-red Cav, parked crooked next to the curb.

"Boyfriend, huh?" he said, voice low, teasing, but warm with a truth he couldn't hide. "And that kiss? You gotta warn me better next time."

Annaleigh leaned against the car's hood, its metal glinting, her flats scuffing the pavement. "I told you not to flinch, didn't I? Thought I'd give Reg a show, keep him off my back."

Her smirk was playful, but her eyes flickered with something deeper—nerves, maybe. He chuckled, rubbing the back of his neck.

"I can't believe *that guy* was your big promise. The one you swore you'd never break?"

"You're focusing on the wrong part, John. The words to him were fake. The... other parts? They weren't too far over the line for you, were they?"

"Too far? Hell no. In fact, we should practice some more, you know, in case we see him again and really need to sell it."

"Never know what the future holds, John Deacon Chance."

Her voice held a teasing edge. A lump formed in his throat as his smile faded. He looked away, toward the horizon where Coldwater's edges blurred into vast fields of green.

"Annaleigh, as unbelievably phenomenal as that was back there, when this is over, my plan is still up in St. Louis. That job is my only *real* shot at finding my dad."

"Come on, you know there are other ways. I could help... if you let me."

"Other ways are not the best way. I need to be able to talk to people, chase leads, and ask questions. I can't do that from here."

Her eyes narrowed briefly, like his words had stung. She tilted her head, letting out a coy laugh.

"Already leaving your girlfriend, huh? Didn't know my boyfriend was so quick to ditch me."

She winked, but her jaw also tightened, betraying the jest. A flush crept up his neck.

"Wait, no, that's not what I meant—" Her smirk stopped him, and he exhaled. "Damn, Annaleigh. Don't play me like that." His heart twisted. It hit too close. The word "girlfriend" lingered, tempting him.

"It was just a joke, John. But, yeah, all the same, I wish you weren't going."

He saw guilt. Over pulling him deeper into this, maybe over that night at Hank's Three Pump. Hell, maybe it was the fact that they weren't really acting as lawyers, but rather a pair of inexperienced vigilantes.

"No need to stand here feeling sorry," she said, her voice sharp, cutting through the quiet of Coldwater's empty street, still waking up to the early morning.

She glanced down at the bank statements clutched in her hand, her eyes scanning the pages. Her breath caught, and she froze, her finger jabbing at a series of transactions.

"Look, John. Right here. There are dozens of deposits from City Hall—thousands of dollars."

He leaned closer, squinting at the smudged ink, his faulty vision blurring the numbers. She was right. His heart leapt, a grin breaking across his face, tinged with disbelief.

"This is it, Annaleigh. A ledger was one thing, but these deposits tie Kenneth to the payoffs. Clear as day. I can't believe it was so easy to find."

"Easy? Maybe you should do the flirting next time, then." Annaleigh's eyes glinted, a sharp laugh escaping her. "I have to believe ego got the best of them. They're practically begging us to catch them."

He jumped to the side, looking up. "Why does it feel like we're about to be struck by lightning? Some things are too good to be true."

"Better lightning than fire. *Now* it's time to see the judge."

Her voice steadied, but the visible tension in her shoulders betrayed the weight of what they'd done. John felt it too, their ship, adrift in stormy waters, bobbing along with the waves. Lawyers playing crimefighters.

It was time to right the ship.

They had the evidence. But convincing a judge, with their hands this dirty, was a different kind of wager.

21

CAUGHT IN THE ACT, UNPREPARED

Coldwater's two young prosecutors stood close in the courthouse hallway, their hushed voices taut with urgency outside Judge Otto Chapel's chambers.

Floorboards creaked under John's restless paces. His stomach churned as he eyed Gamble's files, complete with their newfound financial evidence, resting in Annaleigh's hands. The implications of what they were about to do raced his pulse. With his mom's injuries fresh in mind, the time had come to take things to the next level. His throat tightened as Annaleigh knocked on the frosted glass.

"We're sure we can trust him, right?" he whispered. With Raith's shadow draped over the whole town, trusting a judge in Coldwater struck the same as betting his fledgling career on a coin toss.

"Don't worry. I've worked with him a lot. He's fair, and with what we have, no matter how we got it, there's no way he can say no."

"It's not only about being fair. How do we know whose side he's on? What if he tells Raith?"

"No way. Judges have to be impartial. Especially in small

towns, where they might have their neighbor's case in front of them."

"You sure about that? With that logic, small-town mayors are supposed to be ethical."

Otto Chapel opened the door, smiling warmly.

"Ms. Stanton, good morning. To what do I owe the pleasure?"

"Well, Judge, there's no pleasure in what we need to discuss with you." She clutched the stack of files, her eyes flicking down the empty hallway. "We'd like to present something to you in the utmost confidence. May we come in?"

"After that introduction, I'm all sorts of curious now," he said, gesturing them inside. "Let's see what you have."

* * *

"As we have shown," Annaleigh summarized, "we have evidence proving Gamble and Raith conspired to manipulate cases, in your very own court. Additionally, we've demonstrated a conspiracy at the highest levels to embezzle large sums of money from Coldwater's taxpayers. Given the circumstances, I think the *content* of the evidence stands on its own."

John shifted in the creaking leather chair, the tang of ink and old paper sharp in Chapel's prim and proper office. Their case seemed solid enough, at least for an arrest warrant, but the judge's skeptical expression suggested it wasn't as airtight as John had hoped.

"Ms. Stanton," Judge Chapel began, "Prosecutors often bend the rules. This set of cases Gamble left for you leans towards a simple case of his own judgment. We both know the power of prosecutorial discretion offers a wide latitude, something I'm sure you'll want to utilize in the future. As such, I'm not sure you want to engage in a process that might curtail that leeway. Perhaps I can see a pathway to showing that Gamble used too heavy a hand, but

I'd need more to implicate the mayor in the kind of conspiracy you are alleging."

"Fair," Annaleigh said, holding firm. "But the ledger of phantom projects matching bank activity for KRA Industries provides a direct link to City Hall. It's when they're added that we find our group of offenders. Add that to the vandalism on John's Dart, my car, and another on the walls of this very courthouse—"

"From what you've described, those would meet the bare minimum criteria to issue an arrest warrant for one"—he glanced through the files sprawled across his desk—"Kenneth Roy Atlee." Judge Chapel adjusted his reading glasses, his gaze sharp. "However, any number of people could have greenlit those projects. This isn't nearly enough for action against Mayor Raith."

John's neck stiffened, his pulse thudding inside his collar. Being denied their request, after everything was presented, came off as though the town was slipping through his fingers again.

"Understood, Your Honor," Annaleigh said. "Given Mr. Atlee's relationship with the mayor, though, we'd ask that his warrant be sealed."

"Granted. Come back if you find any credible, direct evidence of the mayor's involvement." His brows raised. "Obtained completely above board, mind you. And I'll be checking very closely, Counselor."

She drew a deep breath and gathered the files, placing the signed warrant for Kenneth on the top of the stack. "Thanks for your time, Judge." She turned to leave.

John bristled at Annaleigh's calm while the judge's denial stung. No warrant for Raith? He choked down a brewing argument, knowing it'd backfire. Instead, he leaned on the desk, eyeing Judge Chapel.

"We'll be back soon, sir. And we'll expose Raith's true colors to everyone."

He spun and followed Annaleigh towards the door.

"Judge."

"What's that?" John stopped mid-step, asking over his shoulder.

"In my chambers, you should refer to me as 'Judge', or 'Your Honor'. I know you meant no harm by it, young man, but if you do come back and present what you are so intent on digging up, it'll be best for all of us if everything is by the book. Out in the courtroom, and even here in my own office."

John's cheeks warmed from the scolding. He nodded.

"You're right, Judge. My fault. This is all a bit personal now."

Judge Chapel bobbed his head in acknowledgement.

"Give my best to your mama, okay? I was truly saddened to hear about her incident."

He then returned his focus to his desk, scribbling notes on a pad. John closed the door behind him and met Annaleigh in the hallway.

"Well, that didn't quite go as planned, now did it?"

"Not the win we wanted, but still a win. We'll make it work. We haul Kenneth in, lean on him hard, and crack him to hand Raith to us on a platter."

* * *

BACK UPSTAIRS, Annaleigh called the Sheriff's Office to provide the update on the results of their meeting with Judge Chapel.

"Thanks, Sheriff. We'll hang out here until you arrive." She slammed the phone down. "We're in business now. Parnell and Clyde are coming over to plan for Kenneth's arrest. It could get messy, so we'd better be ready for anything."

John tapped the desk, his thoughts developing quickly. Kenneth was their best shot, their *only* shot. Their aim needed to hit the target. If word made it past their trusted allies and into the ears of anyone in Raith's pocket, this whole thing could blow up, sending collateral shrapnel everywhere.

"Since it'll be a minute before they get here, do you think we could talk?" John's hand shook as he gestured to the balcony. "You know, about what you said in the hospital parking lot?"

"I wasn't sure if you were going to let that one go," she said, wrinkling her nose. "Alright, John. Let's go have a chat."

The eastern-facing balcony was cool. The morning sun warmed the rusted iron railing, flaking its rough paint under John's palms.

Annaleigh leaned next to him, close, but not quite touching his shoulder with hers. His heart thumped as her eyes met his, a flicker of hope cutting through the chaos of the investigation. She was amazing, an impossible workplace crush at first sight.

Was it crazy that he was falling for her in the middle of all this?

"It's only been a week since we've known each other," he said, voice low. "But, back at the hospital, you hinted at something more—"

"I didn't mean—" Annaleigh faltered, her cheeks flushing.

"No," he said with a comforting tone. "Don't deflect. It feels like I've known you for a lot longer than I really have."

She smiled, turned away, then back, and her eyes met his.

"But, I do know you, John. At least, I think I do. Your mother talked about you all the time. She built this perfect image of you, miles better than the idiots of this town." She drew a breath, as if to hold herself back from sharing more. "I like you being here."

"You like me being here? Like on this balcony?"

"No, that's... not... what I..."

He inched closer to her, his shoulder pressing softly against hers.

"Or, you like me being at the courthouse? Because I'm such an excellent lawyer?"

Flustered, she rolled her eyes. "John, you're not even a real—"

"Or, perhaps, you like being with me, say, at the bank? Would you like it if we were standing in front of—"

"Don't you dare say his name, Jonathon Deacon Chance."

"All that time with my mom, and she never told you it's just John, not Jonathon? Different than, Reg, which is short for—"

"If you mention Reginald's name right now—ah!" She rubbed her cheeks. "God, I wish we were downstairs in the court-room. I'm always so much better with my words there."

A cool gust mussed her hair. Thin wisps of hair veiled her eyes. John's breath hitched as he reached to brush it back. His fingers lingered at her neck, a reckless move that could unravel everything. He swallowed, not losing eye contact.

"Maybe we don't need words then."

Her grin flashed, warm and teasing, her eyes locked on his. Her tongue grazed her lips, a fleeting motion that sent a spark through John's veins.

His hand at her neck drew her closer, their lips inches apart, breaths mingling. The balcony's iron railing creaked, as if echoing his racing heart, as he closed his eyes. She placed her hands on his shoulders, squeezing.

Approaching footsteps went unnoticed as they leaned in further. A harsh voice shattered the moment as Mayor Cameron Raith appeared in the balcony doorway.

"WHAT IN THE WORLD IS GOIN' ON OUT HERE?"

The two lawyers jolted away. John spun to the side. Annaleigh fixed her hair with her fingers.

"Sorry... sir. We were just... getting some air," she said.

"Yeah, *air*. That's what you were about to get. Both of you, asses inside. Now."

John and Annaleigh shot each other a wide-eyed look. "Do you think he knows?" he whispered, close to her ear.

Her posture suddenly stiffened. A barely perceptible head shake told John the answer.

"Play it cool," she replied into her shoulder.

Raith's boots thudded on the hardwood as they stepped in, the balcony door clicking shut behind them. His voice boomed, sharp and commanding, a volume John hadn't heard since his mother's dinner calls while he was playing outside as a child.

"I gave you one task—one thing! Investigate what happened to your precious boss, keep me in the loop, and keep that untrustworthy sack of shit sheriff out of it. Clearly, you both have no idea what it means to obey."

"We've been investigating his murder all right," John said, inching forward as Annaleigh tried holding him back by his elbow.

"What he means, sir," she interjected, "is that we discovered some information that we needed to assess its credibility before we bothered you with it. The sheriff offered to help with that."

"No, little miss, you thought you could sneak around behind my back."

"We're not cops, Mayor," John said, voice rising. "We're not equipped to perform a shadow murder investigation."

Raith huffed. "Ain't that the truth. Not sure you're lawyers, either."

Annaleigh's tight squeeze on his arm couldn't stop John from continuing.

"What in the world do you need your own investigation for, anyway? Something you're trying to hide?"

"No, little man, the only ones hiding things are you two."

John had had enough. "Little man? I'm taller than you, Mayor. Look, you need to—"

Raith jabbed a finger at him, silencing him.

"No. I'm tired of your antics. This is listenin' time now. My orders for you were crystal clear. After the town hall, I see both of you chattin' it up with the deputies. Then, I see our new rookie drivin' away in the sheriff's damn car! Finally, you so rudely rejected the man I sent over here. If I were a countin' man, that'd be three strikes."

The mayor paced back and forth in the bullpen, accentuating every step with an emphatic finger point.

"And, now, look at what's happened. Your piss-poor search has gotten your dear mother caught up in it, I hear. Ended up in the hospital, all because you two lost sight of how to run my investigation. My sources say y'all don't even have a suspect."

"We haven't lost sight of anything," John spat back, the image of his mother's bandages searing his mind.

Her frail voice from the hospital bed echoed in his ears, blaming him for dragging her into this mess, though she'd never uttered those words. His thoughts were moving too fast right now, and self-doubt sank in deep. Had he pushed too hard? He shook away the thought, glaring at Raith.

"Believe me," he growled, "we absolutely have a suspect."

Annaleigh yanked his arm, urging him with wide eyes to stop. Raith smirked.

"Oh, you've got a suspect? You think you're such hot shit, huh? Let me tell you a story about a small-town nobody, fresh from law school, a dream of fightin' crime in the big city."

Raith waved in the air as if he were painting a masterpiece, his hands becoming more and more reddened.

"You see, this young nobody—an absolute, worthless, speck—wanted, so badly, to leave our little community and end up in a big prosecutor's office in the city. Let's say, in St. Louis, for example."

John's stomach dropped. St. Louis was his escape, his shot at a real career, and Raith somehow knew it. Had someone betrayed his confidence, or was Raith's reach that long? The thought made his skin crawl.

"But," Raith continued, "this *nobody* shit the bed. Screwed up. Almost got a woman killed. Because he's downright horrible at his job." He stopped drawing in the air and focused on John. "So, the mayor of that small town, well, he might feel compelled to call that big city office and let them know to stay far away from this young man. You know, really spell out how much of a liability this nobody might be to them. And, what do you know, they'd listen—of course—because a mayor always outranks a small-town nothin'."

Raith shrugged theatrically. "There's a tragic end to this story, too. Did I mention that? Sadly, this young man doesn't wind up in the big city. He doesn't live happily ever after all. In fact, he never even becomes a real lawyer. What a devastatin' end, if you ask me."

A surge of heat coursed through John, his anger coiling like a spring ready to snap. John's teeth ground together, a raw ache flaring in his jaw. The muscles in his neck and shoulders throbbed. His whole body tensed as the full implication of Raith's story sank in. How dare he suggest that his career would be ruined? That he would never become a true lawyer.

John balled his fist, cracking his knuckles. His greatest desire in that moment was to strike back with violence. Beneath the anger, a flicker of apprehension grew as his dream of a big-city career flashed before him. Could Raith really destroy it all with one call?

Raith, as the mayor, did indeed wield considerable power and influence in Coldwater. Perhaps that power extended elsewhere, too. How could he have known about St. Louis in the first place? John's fist relaxed, and he turned away, dejected and biting his lip.

Forget about this fight. He's all talk. Win the battle and find what you need to put him away for good.

"Now for you, Ms. Stanton," Raith said with sarcastic emphasis. "If there was any other competent lawyer in this damn office, I'd replace you in a heartbeat. You don't deserve this. Don't worry —I'm already workin' on findin' fresh, *loyal* blood."

He pointed menacingly at John, still scolding in her direction. "Instead of doing the job I gave you, you're galavantin' around with this fool like you're on some datin' show. Grow up, little girl!"

Annaleigh didn't flinch. She stood motionless, eyes flaring. Raith stroked his chin, his eyes glinting with smug confidence.

"I ain't got stories for you. Though I did hear some rumors that a *real* prosecutor was lookin' into your conduct back in... Cobb County, was it? That's where you come from, right? All of us Missouri mayors talk with each other. In fact, I heard that what you did rose to 'behavior that could result in disbarment', yes, I believe that's the way it was phrased. Shame, shame, Ms. Stanton." He made a snickering noise with his lips. "Pullin' a stunt like that. Then, you follow it up by fleein' the jurisdiction? Those situations end up with an arrest warrant with your name on it, don't they?"

John tried to hide any reaction to Raith mentioning arrest warrants. A glance at Annaleigh seemed to confirm she was doing the same.

Raith tilted his head downward, speaking through his eyebrows.

"You two don't know who you're dealin' with," he said, pointing at the ground. "I run this town and everyone in it. You little pukes don't deserve to breathe Coldwater air."

"You asshole!" Annaleigh shouted, lunging for him.

John reacted fast enough to catch her before her outstretched fist reached the side of Raith's jaw. He pulled her back and spun her, shielding her from any potential retaliation with his own body.

Raith laughed.

"I knew Gamble was dirty, fixin' cases and such. Hell, he bragged about overcharging that Kendrick fella you were messin' with at the Town Hall. He was almost gleeful about it. Until now, I wasn't sure if he'd roped you in, too. Better keep that emotion in check, little lady. What you say might get used against you in a court of law," he said, chuckling. "If I were you, I'd start clearing out your desks. Won't be long, now."

"Or," Raith continued, shrugging, "do nothing. Sit on your hands. I don't care. Go play kissy-face on that shit-hole balcony all day."

Raith's voice dropped, cold and final.

"From here on out, you're dead to this town."

Dead to this town.

A firing, or a darker threat? The mayor's icy tone chilled him, his smug control fueling John's hatred and a fear that Raith's power ran too deep. He'd come to Coldwater to prove himself, not to be crushed by a small-town tyrant.

Raith spun and sauntered toward the staircase, his shoulders squared in that cocky strut John recognized from his own law school debate wins. He hated being on the other end of that walk. The mayor threw one final look their way, teeth shining through a half-smile, before descending and leaving.

John plopped into his chair, the springs groaning under his weight, and drew a deep breath. Raith's exit left the room empty, as if he'd stolen its oxygen. Only the old oscillating fan's hum broke the lingering silence.

"What a load of crap," he muttered, his voice tight. "Thinks he can scare me with some tale about St. Louis? He's got no pull outside this backwater town..."

His words slowed, and his eyes darted, as his mind raced to answer his own question. He looked at Annaleigh for reassurance.

"Right?"

She hadn't been listening.

Her gaze dropped to the floor, her bottom lip trembling as if she were fighting back something heavy.

He bolted out of his chair and pulled her into his arms. "Annaleigh, don't pay any attention to what he said. He was trying to get under our skin. Everything he said was a lie."

"No, John. He wasn't lying about me."

22

THE SKELETONS OF COBB COUNTY

Annaleigh's surprise confession tore John's heart in two. Sharp, fierce, unbreakable Annaleigh had been dimmed under the weight of the mayor's threats.

His lips parted, but his throat tightened. Any potential words were caught in the courthouse's heavy, dust-laden silence. He couldn't believe this woman, whose fire he'd admired, could be tangled in anything that went against the law books stacked behind them on the shelves. At least not to the extent the mayor had implied.

Bending the rules was one thing. But, doing it for the right reasons? That was another. Did she bend them too far? What exactly happened in Cobb County?

Whatever it was, John sensed she believed it could unravel her entire career. He glanced at her, her silhouette framed by a window's dusty light. It didn't matter. He'd stand by her. It would have never occurred to him not to.

"He mentioned something criminal," he said, his voice low, testing the waters. "In Cobb County? He's making that up, right?"

Annaleigh's eyes flicked to the floor, her fingers tightening around a pencil.

"He's not wrong," she murmured. "But, it's not what you think."

"Then, tell me. I'm not here to judge."

"You say that now. Wait 'til you hear the whole mess."

"Try me."

She drew a breath, and the room seemed to hold its own, waiting for her to crack open the past.

"Last week, we were reviewing a case about a brawl outside the Wobbly Barrel, remember?"

"How could I forget? It was my first day. I messed up the details, thinking it was a simple bar fight—"

"Except you missed the description of the third individual. Do you remember what her name was?"

He shook his head, dipping it slightly. He didn't and felt guilty.

"Her name is Sarah. A twenty-two-year-old woman who wound up with scrapes and bruises on her knees. One of the bartenders was about to rape her. Only, our case wasn't a bar fight. It was a rescue. A patron stumbled out the wrong door and accidentally interrupted the act. He punched out the bartender, saving Sarah."

"I remember now," he said, still pushing down the shame he had from misreading the file and disappointing her that day. "I'm not sure I understand. What does that have to do with what Raith said about you?"

"I told you that the one thing I wanted in my career is to be known as an advocate for sexual assault victims. That's why I got a little angry when you thought it was a bar fight. It was a dark reminder for me, John." Annaleigh paused, as if weighing each word, and averted John's eyes. "I want to speak for them." Her voice hardened, catching him off guard. "Because I *was* one."

Grief surged through him, sharp as the edges of the burn marks that desecrated the trunk of the Dart. His fingers gripped the chair's armrests, the wood biting against his sweating palms, as her words stoked a fire in him to shield her from any more pain.

"No," she said, head bobbing. "I *am* one. I promised myself that the least I could do was help give others a voice. To right the wrong that happened to them. To give them... what I never got."

"Jesus, Annaleigh, whoever did this to you deserves worse than a courtroom," he said, sliding his chair closer to her. "Is he here? In town? I'll pay him a visit." He curled up a fist and pounded it on the desk.

"No need. I already took care of it." She craned her neck back and sighed. "In fact, I'm certain it's what the mayor was talking about."

"What do you mean? I mean... if you want to tell me."

"Last week, I mentioned I was offered the assistant prosecutor job in Cobb County. That was true. I also said there were strings attached to the promotion, and that's the reason I left and wound up here. That part was true, too, but it wasn't the whole story."

Her gaze fixed on the worn floorboards, as if tracing every flaw to avoid his eyes.

"One night, I was working late. The only two people in the office were me and the County Prosecutor. Everyone had gone home. He came up to my desk, saying the promotion to Assistant was mine if I wanted it. Then, he offered a handshake to congratulate me."

Her feet shifted under her, and she crossed her arms.

"I was ecstatic. It's what I'd been aiming for. St. Louis is your plan, well, that was mine. *Finally, a woman gets the recognition she deserves*, I thought. I won more cases. I showed up for the victims and got them justice. I was better than everyone else in that office. And here he was, vindicating me. I stood up to say yes and reached out to shake his hand. As soon as I did, he grabbed me by the wrist and pulled me into him. He started kissing my neck, rubbing his hands all over me."

Her shoulders shuddered, as if shaking off a memory of his uninvited hands on her skin.

"He whispered in my ear. 'The role is yours, now I want to see how grateful you are.' I told him no and tried pushing him away, but that only made him try harder. He accused me of flirting with him. Of giving him 'fuck me' eyes." Her lips snarled. "I didn't do any of that. He grabbed me tighter and locked his hands around my hips. Then," her fists clenched, "he slid them lower..."

A heat flared in John's chest. He ground his teeth. His pulse hammered in his ears. He could not let this atrocity stand. He wanted to go across the state to the Cobb courthouse and teach that prosecutor a lesson that would never be forgotten.

"I did the only thing I could. I drove my knee into him as hard as I could. He winced in pain but didn't let go of my hips. So, I did it again. And again."

She gripped the arms of the desk chair. "He fell on the ground, screaming. The kind of scream you don't want to hear guys make. That's when I noticed the blood. It was all over his pants. Let's just say, he's not quite the man he used to be."

He couldn't help but crack a smile, knowing she delivered justice right where it counted. "One of his, you know? Yikes." He crossed his legs and winced.

"Yeah." Her lips twitched into a half-smile, quickly suppressed. "I did call an ambulance for him, but as he wriggled on the ground, I quit, effective immediately. Told him, if he tried to come after me for anything, I'd tell everyone what he did."

"Holy shit, Annaleigh. You're a badass."

"Do you know what he did next? In the middle of crying, he laughed. He laughed! Said that no one would believe me. He threatened me—me!—that if I said anything to anyone, ever, he'd claim I attacked him for no reason. He'd say that I misinterpreted the promotion as making an advance. After all, he was the prose-cutor. He was the *trustworthy* one."

"Unreal."

"So, I left. Wound up here. Whatever, or however, Raith knew about it, I don't know. I have nothing to prove that he was the one who grabbed me. On the flip side, the guy is missing a, well, you know. The only proof from that night that exists goes against *me*. It proves I assaulted him. And, not simple assault, mind you. What I did was *aggravated* and carries no statute of limitations. If I'm convicted, not only do I lose the ability to practice law, but I'd wind up in jail, too. All because he tried to rape me."

She looked up from the floor and at him.

"That's why I want to throw the book at men like that. Because I know what it's like to be on the wrong side of it."

Annaleigh leaned against the desk, her fingertips tracing the top in an aimless, semicircle pattern. John watched her, his throat tight.

"When I got here," she said, her voice softer now, "I was running on fumes. Cobb County had chewed me up, and I hoped this town would be a fresh start. Your mom? She saw right through me."

"Mom? Yeah, she's got a knack for that."

Her lips quirked, a flicker of defiance breaking through her guarded expression. "She found me at the diner, alone in a booth, staring at a cold coffee like it held answers. Didn't ask what was wrong or why I was a mess, only asked to sit down. Something in her eyes made me say 'yes'. We talked for hours. Ended up sleeping on her couch that night instead of a lonely motel room."

He grinned, picturing his mother's no-nonsense squint. "Sounds like her. She's heard half the town's secrets from lounging in that place."

"Maybe," Annaleigh said, her gaze distant. "It sometimes feels like this town has a way of holding onto its own secrets. Like that burn on the wall downstairs. We were told it was a cattle brand, but I've been thinking..." Her fingers brushed the desk again.

"The Sheriff say something to you?"

She met his eyes, unflinching. "No, but I did some asking around. Brands have the farmer's initials in them for easy identification. They're not a generic handprint. There's something else going on here."

His mind wandered as Annaleigh's words sank in, heavy as the courthouse's oak doors.

He remembered being ten, standing in the town square during a sweltering May festival. Mayor Raith had been there, all smiles and handshakes, but even then, John got chills when the man's gaze landed on him. Raith's hand had clapped his shoulder, too warm, like a radiator left on too long.

"Your mama says you'll do big things, Johnny," he'd said. "Someday, you might be as important as me," he'd boasted.

That memory burned. Raith wasn't just a politician. He was a puppet master, pulling invisible strings that John was trying to discover. The mayor's threat for Annaleigh, her disbarment, her ruin, displayed the same heat.

"John?" Annaleigh's voice snapped him back. "You okay?"

He forced a grin. "Can't get Raith out of my head."

Annaleigh stood, her arms crossed tight. His chest tightened, as if her story had branded its pain into him.

"Until he replaces me, I'm going to do what's right, no matter what," she said, her voice steady now. "I'm loyal to the law, not him. The days are numbered for those who think power lets them do what they want."

"You're fighting for Gamble. And for Coldwater."

She stopped, her eyes fierce. "Am I? Maybe I'm stirring up a hornet's nest. Raith knows things, John. Things he shouldn't. Like he's got eyes in every shadow." She pointed to the scorched handprint marring the wood at the base of the stairs. "At Three Pump, Mumber told me something, and it's true. This town. It's not right. It's like it's holding its breath, waiting for something to ignite."

He rose and closed the distance. "Then we'll light the match together."

"Careful, John. With me, you might get burned."

"If I'm with you, it's worth it."

Her hand clasped his, her warmth sparking a flutter in his chest.

"If you weren't here, I'd be up against the mayor on my own," she said. "I don't want to think about how hard that would be."

"Raith isn't untouchable, no matter how much he thinks he is. We nail Kenneth first, then him. I'm with you. Every step. One thousand percent."

She pulled him in, wrapping her arms around him.

"Thank you," she said, squeezing. "I wanted you to know, but I wasn't sure how to tell you. I feel like I can tell you anything. I love holding more than just the thought of you in my arms."

He closed his eyes and let out a shuddering breath. He relished being able to feel the full warmth and comfort of her embrace.

After a reluctant release of her grip, they eased apart. As they separated, her cheek caressed against his, and her breath tickled his skin. A spark of nerves in him danced like static before a storm.

"I didn't say it before, but I should have," she said, her face hovering close in front of his. "There's no way he can ruin St. Louis for you. That town won't know what hit it after you get there."

"If I'm there, then I'm not here. What does that mean for us?"

"Us? Careful, now," she teased. "That kind of thinking just might convince you to stay."

His smile widened as he stared into her velvety brown eyes. He wasted no time in pulling her in and pressing his lips to hers.

23

HEATED ENCOUNTERS

John lingered outside City Hall, the humid late-May air clinging to his skin like a second shirt. The building's faded limestone facade cracked from decades of neglect, a relic of a town that hadn't seen a lot of change this century. His fingers twitched at his side.

Annaleigh stood beside him, her body tense, eyes scanning the empty street. No reporters, no gawkers, only the eerie quiet of a town holding its collective breath.

John swallowed, his throat dry.

Raith's hiding something, which means there's no way he'll roll over easily. But, we're ready. We've planned for this.

He glanced at an approaching Sheriff Dane Parnell, who adjusted his badge with a grim nod, ready to storm the castle. John checked his watch—noon.

Right on schedule.

Parnell burst into City Hall, yanking both doors wide, striding in like a man spoiling for a fight. John hurried after, along with Annaleigh. The swiftly closing door clipped his ankle, sending a sharp sting up his leg. This wasn't stealth. This was a showdown.

"I thought we were going in quietly," he whispered.

She replied only with a slight lift of her shoulders. "The man's on a mission, I guess."

Parnell charged down the hallway, turning left at the records room. He shouldered past Raith's secretary and flung open the mayor's office door.

"Cameron Raith," he said, voice hard, "you're coming with me."

Raith glanced up from his papers, unruffled, a smirk tugging at his lips.

"Dane, you never knock. Rude, as always."

"Judge Chapel's calling it corruptible behavior, Cameron." Parnell held up a folded paper, unflinching. "This signed warrant ends your games."

John's stomach tightened as he shot a glance at Annaleigh, who raised her chin, stoic. He forced his face blank, heart thudding.

Using Kenneth's warrant to bluff? Parnell's bold. Or insane. Either way, it's a flimsy premise. There's no way this will work.

Raith stood, pushing back his leather chair, which squeaked against the mahogany cabinets behind him.

"If you want to talk, Dane, we can do it right here. Pull up a seat and make yourself comfortable." He motioned towards John and Annaleigh. "Those two can stand."

"Sorry, Cameron. Not a social call. We're doing this by the book. Kenneth will be meeting us at the station. Separate rooms, though. I'm sure you understand."

Raith's lips curled into a cold smirk. "Your finest hour, Dane?"

His eyes narrowed, his jaw tight, fingers twitching toward the paper as if to snatch it. He leaned forward, his eyes glinting like a predator sizing up prey.

"So," Raith said, "what's this warrant really about? Some old grudge? Did that fool Gamble convince you there's a mess you need to clean up?" His voice dripped with mockery, but John caught a flicker of unease in his gaze, gone as quickly as it came.

He's fishing, testing Parnell's bluff.

John's hands clenched in his pockets, his pulse throbbing in his fingertips. He wanted to speak, to defend Gamble, maybe call out the mayor, but Annaleigh's slight head shake kept him silent. Raith's smirk widened, as if he sensed John's urge to jump in.

"You brought the misfit kids along, too. Definitely an interestin' move, Sheriff. Though, maybe not the smartest."

Parnell folded the warrant and tucked it into his shirt pocket.

"Time to go, *Mr. Mayor.*"

"Fine, let's see your little game through. I'll be back here by lunch. You three, however, will be out of a job by supper." Raith smacked his hands onto his desk, then held out his wrists.

"No cuffs today, Cameron. Lower your hands. We go back too far for that, and I don't think you're that stupid to try and run. Don't mean I trust you. I don't want the town gossiping about you in chains."

"Lead the way, Sheriff." Raith gestured wildly.

Parnell shook his head. "Not how this is going to work." He pointed with two fingers towards the door. "Ms. Stanton, Mr. Chance, out in front, please. Cameron, follow behind them. Don't get too close and no sudden movements."

John nodded and slipped past Raith's secretary, whose face had gone pale, her hands frozen on her desk. He flashed backwards glances at Raith, ensuring he followed at a safe distance. The mayor complied, but did not hide the scowl on his face.

The hallway walk was agonizingly slow. The front doors seemed farther with every step. As they passed the hallway to the side exit, John's pulse hammered in his ears as he gripped Annaleigh's arm, half guiding, half shielding her.

John's eyes darted to the framed photos lining the walls, depicting Raith shaking hands with county officials, grinning widely. Each handshake, his hand on top, the power position. In every group photo, he stood in the middle, the center of attention.

Always in control.

How many of these folks know what he's hiding?

He glanced back at Raith, whose heavy steps echoed too close for comfort. The mayor's fingers flexed, as if itching to lash out. John tightened his grip on Annaleigh.

Ahead, the front doors. Outside, through the windowed doors, Parnell's cruiser was in sight.

This long walk was almost over.

And their plan to sweep up everyone at the same time was almost complete.

At the other edge of town, Kenneth and Wesley were being ushered into custody as well. Deputy D. Clyde Brothers led that operation, and though John's objections were duly noted, Deputy Cason Foley went along to assist. Within minutes, Mayor Raith, Kenneth, and Wesley would all be in custody and, through what would surely be intense interrogations, the truth about everything —the corruption, Gamble's murder, the brands—could finally come to light.

John reached for the front door as Parnell's radio crackled to life. Clyde's voice cut through, out of breath.

"Sheriff, Kenneth's gone, gave me the slip."

John spun, wide-eyed, his gut twisting with dread.

Kenneth's loose? This just got worse. Way worse. If he escaped, we lost our leverage to get Raith talking.

Parnell's face soured as he gripped his radio, but John's eyes locked on Raith. He was grinning, a sly curve to his lips that made John's skin crawl. His grin wasn't smug. It was the look of a man who'd rigged the game.

Did he plan this? Was Kenneth's escape a ploy to throw us off balance? How did Kenneth know we were coming? Did someone rat us out?

The air in the hallway seemed to thicken, pressing against his chest. He scanned Raith's face for a tell, but those dark eyes gave nothing away, only that unnerving smile. Annaleigh's arm tensed under his grip.

Clyde's transmission was not complete.

The radio crackled again.

"We've got Wesley Raith in custody, boss. Headed your way."

Raith's grin vanished, his eyes blazing, fists clenching until his knuckles whitened. He waited for Parnell's gaze to dip and then struck.

Raith lunged, shoving Annaleigh aside and bull rushing John through the front doors. Panic flared as he fought to regain his balance, but Raith's iron grip spun him round, pinning him against the glass.

Inside, Parnell rushed to the door, using his thin frame to force the doors open. John's pinned body provided the necessary counterweight, foiling the sheriff's attempts.

"You son-of-a-bitch!" Raith shouted at Parnell. "Think you can topple me? You've got nothing on me!"

Parnell yelled back. "Then what on earth are you doing?"

Through the glass, John heard Annaleigh pounding, her voice sharp. "Let him go!"

"Annaleigh, stay back!" he managed to shout, still trying to escape Raith's country-strong grip.

"I'll make you burn like Gamble did," Raith bellowed, spittle landing onto John's cheek and shoulder.

"Cameron, don't do this!" Parnell barked. "Don't cross this line!"

Raith leaned in, his forearm digging into John's throat. John clawed at Raith's arm, gasping, his chest tight with fear.

I can't let him win. Not now.

John's vision blurred at the edges. His lungs screamed for a full breath of air. In his limited periphery, he scanned the glass behind him, catching Annaleigh's frantic pounding, her muffled shouts not registering.

In front, the cruiser sat just beyond, tauntingly close. If he could shift Raith's weight, maybe Parnell could get through. John sucked in a ragged breath, his free hand fumbling for anything on the ground nearby to distract Raith. He found nothing.

Can't get leverage. Gotta outsmart him.

"Gamble kept notes," he rasped. "A stack of folders... evidence to put you away. He's dead, and still smarter than you."

Pain shot through John's chest as Raith's fist connected, a blow like a hammer to his ribs. He scoffed, ignoring John's taunts.

"I've got your boy, Dane," he goaded. "You picked him over me? *Me?* Wrong choice, brother."

John's eyes darted to Raith's hands, the knuckles white, veins bulging, as if something unnatural pulsed beneath the skin.

Raith's snarl grew louder. "Dane! Did you hear me, Dane?"

Parnell did not respond.

John glanced over his shoulder, seeing only Annaleigh, her face tight with fear. He caught a glimpse of Parnell sprinting the opposite direction, down the dim hallway, boots pounding over creaking floorboards as he rounded the corner toward the side exit's faint glow.

He's circling. Going to flank us. Need to keep Raith focused on me.

"This... isn't helping... your case," John managed, in between breaths. "You knew Kenneth would escape... but I saw it... in your eyes... you didn't think we'd get Wesley, did you?"

Raith exhaled with a low growl, pressing John further against the glass and landing an elbow to John's chin. The cold, metal door handles dug into John's back, but he held his gaze, defiance flaring despite the pain.

"We're going to break him. Then, *Mayor*, we'll break you."

The mayor hollered, becoming more incensed. Seizing on a moment of distraction, John balled up his fist and landed a swift punch to Raith's midsection. From his cramped position, it hit weakly and accomplished little.

Raith swung back, landing another blow to John's chest and side. Raith's face boiled with rage and hate.

John struggled to break free. He shifted his balance to one foot, launching the other knee into the mayor's gut. Both men grimaced.

On his way in, John's knee scraped the side of Raith's obnoxious belt buckle. Before he could try again, Raith leaned in close.

"You could never beat me, son," he howled. "You could—"

Raith's eyes shot to his hands, widening in horror.

John's knee struck Raith's gut again, weaker this time, though, as his strength faded under the mayor's relentless grip. The air around them grew heavy, almost shimmering, like heat rising off summer asphalt. John's skin prickled, a strange warmth seeping through Raith's hands, unnatural and wrong.

What the hell is going on?

Raith's eyes narrowed, a flicker of something dangerous passing through them, like a man realizing he'd gone too far.

John's heart pounded harder, dread coiling tight as he felt it.

First, it was as if he was sitting next to a campfire on a cool, autumn night.

Then, it was as if John had stepped into the fire.

An unbearable heat seared through Raith's grip.

John gasped, terror spiking as white light flared between them. Wisps of smoke curled up, and an acrid scent stung his nostrils. Their eyes locked, Raith's face twisting in shock, John's in agony.

Then, something happened that neither man believed possible.

John's shirt had caught on fire.

24

BLAZE AND BURNOUT

Searing flames scorched John's skin as Raith's ironclad grasp fused to his chest. Terror clawed at his throat, choking his shouts as smoke surged, thick gray tendrils snaking into the Coldwater air.

Raith shoved John aside, his face contorting into painful expressions. John slumped onto the sidewalk, clawing at his torso to quell the burns, his skin stinging as if branded by a hot iron.

What the hell?

His mind reeled, searching for answers. He'd seen Raith's hands glow and felt the furnace's fire, but logic insisted it couldn't have happened.

Human hands don't burn like that. Not in Missouri, not anywhere.

Yet the agony was real. The red welts on him were proof of something unimaginable.

Had Raith's hands left these same marks on Gamble, too?

John's fingers trembled as he pressed them to his ribs, wincing. He may be a lawyer, but Coldwater's underbelly didn't care about his degree. Raith was a predator, and John became prey who'd gotten too close.

Annaleigh erupted from the lobby, her shadow falling over him.

"Oh my God, are you okay?"

Her voice was sharp, but her eyes flickered with fear. She knelt beside him, shielding him from the trembling mayor, only steps away.

"His hands... the heat..." he huffed.

Raith stood frozen, his glowing, pulsating palms hovering before his bulging eyes, like a man staring into a furnace of his own making.

Parnell tore around City Hall's corner from the side lot, gun drawn.

"Let him go!" he roared. Seeing John on the ground, he halted, stutter-stepping to a stop ten feet away. "Cameron—down on your knees! Now!"

Raith's jaw tightened, a flicker of panic crossing his face, as if this unrecognizable power had surprised him. His eyes darted between John and Parnell.

He whirled away from John and reached for the door to reenter City Hall. His fingers grazed the metal door pull, and the steel softened, sagging like wax under a flame. A hiss rose as molten droplets splattered down. He lunged for the other handle, yanking it with a grunt, and bolted inside. As the door shut, the pull warped and dangled.

John thought back to the stack of buried cases they'd found in Gamble's desk. Gamble knew Raith was dirty. But had he known about this?

What seared John's skin wasn't anger. It was something else, something impossible.

"I don't know what the hell that was, but we can't let him get away," he muttered, half to Annaleigh, half to himself. Her eyes met his, sharp with the same fire driving him.

"Then get up," she snapped, her voice cutting through his haze.

He winced as she helped him to his feet, her grip steadying him. The sting in his chest and ribs throbbed.

"You okay?" Parnell yelled at John, taking a few steps toward him.

Annaleigh raised her hand, halting the Sheriff. "He's fine! I've got him. You go get Raith!"

Parnell barked into the radio as he spun. "Hinkle, move into position! He's doubling back!"

Seconds later, screeching tires were heard in the distance, around the corner of City Hall. Parnell hustled back across the front of the building, retracing his steps towards the side entrance.

"Come on, let's go," she commanded. "We're not out of this fight."

They set off after Parnell. Rounding the corner of City Hall, the action-packed scene in the parking lot unfolded in front of John and Annaleigh.

City Hall's side exit door erupted open with a kick, the glass insert shattering. Raith shot out, shouting incoherently, palms raised, no longer glowing bright white but a dim orange, like the afterimage of a turned-off light bulb.

Seeing those hands again made John's chest ache.

With the nimbleness of someone half his age, Raith vaulted over his hood and dove inside. The Blazer roared to life.

Parnell, twenty feet away and closing, waved his arms high in the air.

"Hinkle! Hinkle!"

John quickly realized why. Deputy Amos Hinkle, Parnell's last choice for backup, had not pulled his cruiser up behind the mayor's car to pin him in, as planned. Instead, the deputy had swung his cruiser parallel to the lot's edge on the side street, merely blocking the exit.

"What on earth is he doing way over there?" John shouted.

Screaming tires filled the lot once more, this time coming from Raith. The SUV lurched into reverse and out of its parking spot. It then surged forward, tires shrieking, as the vehicle fishtailed. It came to rest pointed at the exit onto the side street—and Hinkle's patrol car.

Parnell finally caught up but only managed to lay hands on the back tailgate as Raith floored the gas pedal. The mayor's SUV shot ahead on a collision path.

Raith's next move shocked everyone.

He swerved left, running over the concrete parking block in the first spot by the exit. He rocketed into the air and crossed the sidewalk in mid-air, evading Hinkle's patrol car. The Blazer slammed onto the side street and skidded to a stop into the far curb.

Annaleigh gasped, snatched a loose chunk of asphalt from the ground, and hurled it at Raith's fleeing car. It missed and smashed into pieces.

Parnell, hands on his hips, simply shook his head. Deputy Hinkle pulled himself from his cruiser, gripping the door to steady his stance. Eyes darting to Parnell, Hinkle raised his arms in confusion.

"S-sorry, boss," he yelled.

John sensed something was off. Coldwater's loyalty ran deep, but Raith's influence ran deeper.

Was this a mistake? Had Hinkle been bought, scared, or merely too old to do the job?

Raith zoomed down the side street toward West Main Street. John cursed under his breath. They were losing him, and with him, the truth about Gamble.

Not on my watch.

He'd vowed to find answers, no matter the cost.

Parnell tore past him, bolting for his cruiser. John sprinted after him, heart pounding on the inside, pain on the outside increasing with every step. He yanked open the passenger door and dove into the front seat. The door slammed shut, but a second thud followed as Annaleigh scrambled into the back. He grimaced as he twisted, catching her fierce grin.

"You weren't planning on leaving me behind, right, boys?"

Relief surged through him. She was in this fight, too, chasing the truth for Gamble.

Parnell gripped the wheel and locked his eyes on the road.

"Buckle up."

25

CHASING THE PRIZE

The acceleration pushed John deep into his seat as Parnell's cruiser snarled to life and shot off westward in pursuit of the fleeing Mayor Raith. Annaleigh spied the scene in the City Hall parking as they tore out.

"Don't expect backup," she said, pointing as they sped by. "Hinkle's in the middle of a seventeen-point turn over there."

"Never mind that," John said. "Raith's three blocks ahead and getting away."

Parnell's hands gripped the wheel as he swerved past a pickup.

"Not if I can help it. He's hitting fifty in a thirty zone. Keep sharp." He muttered, "Dammit, Cameron, what are you doing?"

Raith zigzagged down West Main, weaving around traffic with more accuracy than John believed possible.

"Well, that plan went to crap. And now, everyone out here's in danger."

"Eyes on Raith, not my screw-ups, kid," Parnell growled.

"You mean, your deputy's mistake. He's the one who screwed up. He didn't get close to blocking him in—"

"Enough. Hinkle's mine to fix. Young man, focus on what's in front of you."

Up ahead, Raith swerved into the opposite lane and clipped

the back end of a utility trailer being towed by a slow-moving pickup truck. The short tailgate bent inward, and the impact jolted the rear of the truck to the right.

The vehicle jackknifed, exposing the truck's left front panel. Raith's Blazer plowed through it and exploded the tire, smashing the pickup onto the curb. Pieces of grill flew up and over Raith's windshield. Somehow, he maintained control and fled the scene.

Parnell slammed on his brakes to slow, but not stop, as he guided his cruiser around the incapacitated pickup.

"EMS to West Main and Marshall," he barked over the radio. His foot jammed onto the accelerator once they were in the clear. Annaleigh strained to look out the rear window as they passed the wreck, spying the motionless driver slumped against the wheel.

"Oh God, they're not moving."

"Ambulance is coming, Ms. Stanton. They'll do their job. We need to stop this chase before anyone else gets hurt."

In the entire town of Coldwater, there were only a handful of stoplights. The town simply did not require them. Mutual respect was the law of the roads in and yields were common to most folk.

The first light to be installed guarded the high school's main entrance, primarily to handle the traffic leaving the football games on Friday nights. The next came about outside the big roofing factory in the northern industrial district. After a handful of gnarly collisions with fully loaded tractor-trailers, everyone agreed that change was needed. Both signals were simple, consisting only of the standard red, yellow, and green lights, with flashing yellow as their default cycle.

The latest had been placed at the medical center on the western edge of town, where the road transitioned from suburban streets to a less restrictive two-lane road leading to the highway.

This light was special. It boasted a dedicated left-turn arrow, guiding traffic onto the side street that led to the hospital's entrance.

It was also the first light a car would encounter when entering the town, if coming from the highway. The "gateway" into the town, many called it.

Raith was leading the chase right through it. After the incident with the pickup and trailer, he weaved around the traffic more conservatively, swerving wide into the other lane to minimize further chances of collisions.

His choice was about to backfire.

Raith approached the intersection in the wrong lane, zipping past cars that had stopped for the red light. The light's dedicated left arrow flipped to green, and the lead car started his turn, unaware of Raith's approach in his blind spot. Raith jolted left, tires screaming. He barely missed colliding with the turning car and was forced to turn onto the side street.

"I'm sure he's pissed," John said, caught between a chuckle and a grimace. "He did *not* want to go that way."

"No doubt he was looking for the highway. Where he's heading, there's only houses. But, he might be trying to head out of town using back roads. Hard to set up a roadblock if we can't predict his path."

Parnell hit the intersection and skidded to follow the mayor's car, skillfully controlling the cruiser's fishtail to avoid hitting a nearby parked car.

"The list of charges I'm going to smother him with is growing with every turn," came Annaleigh's agitated voice from the back seat.

John glanced back at her. "Better start writing them down, then. Wouldn't want to shortchange the good man, now would we?"

"Hey, eyes forward. I can't see everything by myself at these speeds."

Another turn at high speed caused John to brace himself on the dashboard. They followed Raith's path and whizzed past side streets. The blur of children playing and retired men mowing lawns flashed by. Annaleigh shouted at Raith from the back seat.

"Slow down, you maniac!"

"He can't hear you, ya know?" John teased.

"Yeah, it makes me feel better, though."

Parnell skidded the cruiser through a bend in the road, trying to catch up. John's focus locked on the mayor's car. It was moving fast and nimble, steering around anything on the road that hadn't managed to move off to the side. Raith yanked his car, sliding onto South Main, just less than a mile from the courthouse.

"Oh, Jesus, he's headed for the square. So much for leaving on the back roads. We've just made one big circle," John said.

"Hinkle," Parnell barked into the radio, "swing into the square, box him in tight from the south. No messing up this time."

He dipped the microphone below his chin, as if regretting his choice of phrasing. John side-eyed the Sheriff, wondering if scolding the old deputy over the air was intentional.

Maybe he's thinking of apologizing? Trying to find the right words?

Parnell raised the mic back to his lips.

"Do *not* let him enter."

The black Sheriff's cruiser screamed onto South Main behind Raith. They'd managed to close the gap to only a few car lengths.

"We'll nail him at the square," he said, voice flat, almost forced, as if trying to convince himself. "He'll have nowhere to go."

John didn't buy it. Too many things had gone wrong today for him to get his hopes up.

"Only if Hinkle gets there in time."

A scolding sigh emanated from Parnell, but no words. They both knew this chase hinged on a deputy who'd already failed earlier at this same task. It was time. Raith was almost at the southern opening.

No Hinkle.

Raith roared in, unabated.

Hinkle's cruiser screeched in late, skidding uselessly.

John's eyes flicked to Parnell. The sheriff's knuckles whitened on the wheel, his jaw twitching like he was chewing on something bitter. Parnell's gaze lingered on Hinkle's crooked squad car a second too long, narrow and hard, like he was seeing more than a botched maneuver.

John's gut twisted. He didn't want to be right, but twice now, in succession, Hinkle had fumbled the assignment. In a town where Raith's hand seemed to grip every lever, a mistake like that spoke too loudly.

Tires shrieked, bouncing off the courthouse as the SUV looped the square, daring them to follow.

"He's playing us for fools," Parnell said, pulse hammering. He gunned the cruiser, chasing Raith's taunting arc around the square.

Hinkle reengaged and slid behind Parnell, joining the chase.

"Amos, abort and wait for me back at the station. We're gonna have a long talk when this is over."

A brief silence hung heavy. Then, Deputy Hinkle's voice broke back over the speaker, quivering with a mixture of disappointment and shame.

"Ten-four, boss. Don't think it's my day. I'll fix it tomorrow, don't you worry."

"Not now," the sheriff barked, emotionless. "Clear the channel."

John bit his lip. It was hard not to feel for Hinkle, a man past his prime, being cut down and sidelined in the middle of what was probably the most important moment in this town's history. There'd be time to reflect on that later, though.

They had a mayor to catch.

Raith had now driven three-quarters of the way around the square, hooking a right and heading back down West Main.

"Is he going back to City Hall?" Annaleigh asked. "That can't be his plan, can it? End the chase where it began?"

With one hand gripping the wheel and the other on the radio, Parnell coordinated the positions of the other deputies.

"Foley, escort young Mr. Raith to the station. Clyde, I want you with me. We're going west from the square."

Confirmation transmissions came in as Parnell slid onto West Main. Behind them, Hinkle slowed and cut his lights, taking the north exit toward the Sheriff's Office. The chase zoomed past City Hall, its parking lot, and the side street where everything had begun.

John shook his head in disbelief. "Where on earth does he think he's going?"

"Naw," Parnell muttered. "Look up ahead. Gateway light's clear now. He didn't want to turn before. I was right. No doubt he's headed for the highway."

The last time they tried to barrel through the intersection, over a half dozen cars were either stopped or crossing through it. The wail of the sirens had apparently been heard all over, as it was clear this time around.

Raith passed businesses, churches, and schools, finally leaving the more densely populated downtown area without having to weave through traffic. A few blocks later, they hit the open road. A random house or building popped up here and there, but there were fewer obstructions and more opportunities to gain speed.

Raith opened it up. Parnell countered, jamming his gas pedal down, keeping close. Annaleigh gripped the front seat's headrest, her knuckles pale. She peered around John's head.

"If he escapes, our case is dead," she said. "With Kenneth on the run, he's the only one who knows what happened to Gamble."

"Then, we don't let him get away."

"Not really our choice, is it? God, going this fast. I can't even think."

"Welcome to the fast lane, Ms. Stanton. Hang on." Parnell's eyes locked forward, hands strangling the wheel.

Out on the open country roads, they still encountered the occasional car. At these speeds, swerving was dangerous, even though there was less traffic. When Raith needed to pass someone, he darted into the oncoming lane. If another car was headed his way, he slid to the other side, onto the narrow shoulder.

On one occasion, he wandered too far and his outside tires dipped off the shoulder, digging large ruts in the neighboring grass and spitting dirt high into the air. Through either dumb luck or skill, he avoided ending up in the adjacent field and found his way back to the pavement.

Parnell tried to match Raith's speed, but the mayor managed to maintain the distance between them. The only silver lining they'd seen so far is that any car that Raith passed immediately pulled over, making it easy for Parnell to drive straight by.

"I'd hoped it didn't come to this," he said, pointing to the glove box. "Reach in there."

John popped the latch, and the compartment fell open, revealing Parnell's backup weapon—a black 9mm pistol.

"Are you serious? You want me to shoot him?"

"Not him, son. His tires. I'll get us close enough, you flatten his back tires."

"You sure I'm the one who should be doing this?"

"Well, I can't drive at these speeds and fire at the same time. So, it's either you or Ms. Stanton. I've seen you both shoot, but you're in the front seat. Pick up the gun."

Swallowing hard, John gripped the gun and pulled it out of the glove box. He ejected the magazine, checking for bullets. It was full.

Eleven chances to get this right.

He slapped it back into the handle and racked the slide, loading a round into the chamber. He rolled down the window and got immediately blasted in the face with highway winds.

"You sure about this, Sheriff?" he yelled into the turbulent gusts.

Parnell pursed his lips, his voice loud and demanding, coated in a southern drawl.

"Tires."

"You can do this, John."

Annaleigh's words of encouragement filled him with hope. He slid forward in the seat and leaned his shoulders out, bracing his arms on the side mirror. The pistol swayed off target as the barrel dipped and fluttered in the wind.

This is never going to work.

He pinned it up against the metal post and squeezed the handle tight. With this extra leverage, the barrel stayed true. He was aimed and ready.

"The next time he swerves into the other lane," Parnell shouted, "take the shot. You hear me?"

Tears streaked down John's cheek as the air howled into his eyes, making them water. He blinked and squinted, desperate to keep eye contact. He nodded. Annaleigh reached up and placed her hands on him, one on his back and the other reaching around his waist.

"I got you."

Her touch in this moment was otherworldly. His shoulders relaxed, and the stress of the situation melted away.

In the distance, the final intersection before the ramps onto the highway loomed large. There were no more traffic lights to worry about, but another potential problem sat dead ahead.

Coldwater's only roundabout. In fact, the only one within 100 miles. At their speeds, it approached in a hurry. Raith jolted himself into the opposite lane, passing a slower-moving car.

"Wait until we pass this guy," Parnell yelled.

The blur of the car whizzed by John's face. He recoiled.

Raith jumped back over the double yellow line. Parnell jammed on the accelerator. John aimed at Raith's driver's side rear tire.

"You're clear! Take the shot!"

Parnell's shouting didn't help matters, nor did the ninety-mile-per-hour wind smashing into his face. He narrowed his eyes and began to apply pressure to the trigger.

The inside of Raith's Blazer burst into light, blinding John more than the biting air. He released the trigger and slid back into the cruiser, rubbing his eyes and rolling up the window.

"What the hell is that?"

Two bright lights danced around inside the mayor's vehicle, as if waving back and forth. Within the outline of Raith's silhouette, his head twisted wildly, as if yelling.

"What in the world are those?" Annaleigh asked, squinting.

"Doesn't look like he's steering anymore. He's drifting."

"He'd better start, then. At these speeds, that roundabout is a death trap," she said. "I've prosecuted reckless teens who tried to jump that thing. Never ended well for them."

The roundabout approached rapidly. The entrance ramps to the highway, and the lifeline to Raith's freedom, sat just beyond. The interior of the cabin glowed brighter, like heat steaming off asphalt.

"He's not slowing down," John said, hands pressing onto the dashboard. "He's got to slow down to take that turn, right?"

Parnell braked hard, tires squealing. Raith continued his charge. He entered the roundabout with no brakes, the inside blazing with the light of the sun.

He struck the curb and vaulted over the median's hump, soaring into the sky.

Cameron Raith had gone airborne.

26

CRASH LANDING

Birds, airplanes, kites, and hot air balloons. There are many things in this world meant to take flight.

John knew, for certain, that a 1992 Chevrolet Blazer was not *supposed* to be on the list.

His heart raced as he watched Raith soar off the mound, twisting midair like a wounded beast, exposing its undercarriage to the glaring sun. The mysterious lights that had danced before launching now pressed downward in unison into the upside-down roof.

Parnell drifted his cruiser through the roundabout, never losing sight of the mayor's flight.

The inverted vehicle fell from the sky and slammed into the concrete, shattering the front windshield and spraying sparks in all directions. The roof screeched like nails on a chalkboard. The strange white glow that had pulsed inside the cabin vanished at the point of impact.

The Blazer skidded off the shoulder and tumbled down the embankment in a storm of metal and debris. Two dark objects shot out from one of the windows, landing some distance into the nearby grassy field.

John pointed, eyes narrowing. "Stuff's coming out. Maybe a duffel bag or backpack."

Could Raith have thrown something out to cover his tracks?

Seven rolls later, the Blazer settled on its roof, against a three-rail wooden fence in the gully below. Its wheels spun without power, eventually slowing to a stop.

Parnell's cruiser skidded on the gravel shoulder. John and Annaleigh leapt out, staring at the wrecked SUV. She crouched at the embankment's edge, her fingers digging into the scarred grass.

"No way he walked away from that."

John caught her glance, her eyes shadowed with doubt. Unease rose within him. Any other day, he would have believed her. The burns on his chest reinforced the notion that this was not your typical day in Coldwater.

Parnell snorted. "One thing we've learned today is that Cameron has some new tricks."

"Let's find out," John shouted as he scampered down the embankment.

He reached the car and dropped to his knees, and crawled low, avoiding broken glass and loose shards of metal. He peered through the shattered window.

Empty.

His pulse hammered. Raith had vanished, slipping away in the chaos.

Parnell arrived at the bottom of the hill, breathless.

"He dead?"

"No," John said through a grimace. "He's gone."

27

SEARCH... AND RESCUE?

John's loafers sank into the soft earth beside the upturned Blazer.

"What in the world do you mean, he's gone? There's no way," the sheriff said, his voice gruff. "Fan out and start looking around. He's injured. Can't be far." He motioned up to Annaleigh. "Keep an eye out up there for movement. Clyde's on his way."

She flashed a thumbs-up with one hand, the other shielding her eyes against the sun. John and Parnell split up, moving to opposite sides of the overturned vehicle. John peered around, his heart thumping in his chest. Raith's smug face, his threats, and his grip on this town were out there somewhere.

John's eyes caught only rusted scraps and shattered glass from near the dented hood of the broken Blazer. No footprints, no drag marks. No evidence whatsoever.

He neared the two-rail fence that had stopped the wreck and peered into the field of swaying grass. If Raith was crouched out there, hiding, he'd be nearly impossible to see.

John and the Sheriff fanned out, searching, each only visible in the long grass from their waists and above.

A rustle in the grass ahead caught John's acute attention.

Sweat prickled his neck as dread built. He locked his eyes on the blades, waiting for the wind or the movement to repeat itself.

Was he out there, watching, like he'd watched Gamble burn?

A cautious step forward. He stared, listening for signs. Nothing but the hum of a distant car on the interstate.

His shoulders eased as he exhaled, turning back to the wreck. As he whirled, his foot thudded against something hard. He knelt, parted the grass, and froze.

Black loafers.

Raith—caught at last.

He flailed to get Parnell's attention. "Sheriff! I've got him! Over here!"

Parnell stood motionless across the field, staring at something near his feet. His head twisted toward John, his eyes narrowing briefly before flicking back downward, then up again. A muffled shout flew.

"Look again, son. You're half right."

John shot him a look of confusion. He cautiously leaned in, moving aside more blades as he worked his way up from the pair of shoes. He lurched back when he saw it.

The legs ended in a bloody mess.

Stained with blood and intestines, a gaudy belt buckle stared back. He bent and scratched his knee, remembering where he scraped it on that same buckle back at City Hall while trying to escape Raith's grasp.

Memories of Gamble's severed arm flooded back. This looked nothing like that. No burns. Only blood and raw, jagged edges of torn flesh.

John's throat tightened, staring at the detached limbs, but no pity came for the man whose burning grip had not only seared his chest but also this town. Raith, the untouchable mayor, reduced to this. A grim satisfaction flared, sharp and cold.

Then it hit him. That duffel bag, flung from the wreck? Not a bag.

John's eyes bulged, his mind racing to piece it together, like an examination in a courtroom gone wrong.

God, it was him flying out of the window. But there was nothing left in the Blazer. Where was the rest of him?

28

RAITH'S LAST BURN

John approached Parnell across the field, staring at the upper half of Raith's mangled body. A queasy mix of relief and dread churned inside him.

Annaleigh hopped the fence and joined them, her quick steps breaking the heavy silence. He glanced at her, wondering if she shared his unease.

"Is it wrong if I'm not sad about this?" she asked.

John shook his head at her. "Same here. Does that make us bad people?"

"Y'all ain't monsters," said Parnell, adjusting his wide-brimmed hat. "Cameron didn't have to run, and now his own choices brought him here, that's for sure."

Up at the top of the embankment, a police cruiser zipped in. Deputy D. Clyde Brothers stepped out and eased himself down the decline. After a brief look at the body, he zeroed in on the sheriff.

"Boss, want me to buzz Mumber? Think we need a detective's eye on this one?" Clyde asked, bouncing on his heels.

Parnell pursed his lips, licking his upper teeth behind his trimmed mustache. "Nah. Better to let him crack the Raith kid for info, unless you think a corpse has anything to tell us."

The coroner's van from Coldwater Memorial arrived and hauled Raith's broken body up the embankment on separate backboards.

"I've seen that twice now," Annaleigh said glumly, pointing to the medical van, "and both times they've come to pick up someone that's been in multiple pieces. I hope I never have to see that thing again."

Her words hit him like a cold wind as the image of Gamble's melted remains flashed in his mind. Two bodies, defiled in ways that defied reason. He wrapped his arm around her shoulders.

"Hopefully, with him out of the picture, it'll be the last time."

Leaving John and Annaleigh near the rear of the mayor's SUV, Sheriff Parnell stepped a few feet away and briefed Clyde on the events leading up to the accident. John tilted his head toward their conversation, straining to catch the words. Annaleigh grabbed him and pulled.

"Come on," she said, dragging John closer. "No more secrets."

"...and then, he stopped swerving and drove straight into the roundabout. Thrown from the vehicle, split in two, probably dead before he hit the ground," Parnell explained to Clyde. "He knew better than to try and shortcut through the median. And, that he should have been wearing a seat belt—"

"I'm not so sure that's what happened, Sheriff." John's tone was firmer than usual.

"We were in the same car, son. Those are the facts."

"Not telling *all* the facts means not giving the whole story."

"Is our infamous boomerang saying we don't need all the facts?" A sly smile from Clyde accompanied the verbal jab.

John shot him a side-eye. "Deputy, you know that infamous means evil, right?"

"Oh," Clyde frowned. "I guess I didn't. Let's go with outstanding, then."

Eyebrows raised, John pressed on. "All I'm saying is those might be the core details, but there was something different with the way he was driving before he hit the roundabout. Something odd happened inside that caused the crash."

Annaleigh shrugged. "Likely the case of a man who gave up. He got caught. He flipped out and ran. It cost him. We all saw it. I see it in defendants all the time."

John couldn't get the memory of those unnatural flickers in Raith's Blazer out of his mind. The thoughts gnawed at him. Those weren't normal. They couldn't have been.

"Guys?" He turned to plead with Parnell. "Are we not going to talk about the lights? I noticed you left that part out. Weren't sure on how to explain those, were you?"

"Honestly, no," Parnell said, crossing his arms. "I've been trying to figure that one out myself."

"Lights?" Clyde asked. "Like... flashlights, or something? In the daytime?"

"More like a signal flare, if you ask me. But white, instead of sparkly red. And, bouncing all around," Annaleigh chimed in.

"Signal flare. Hmm..." Clyde rubbed his stubbled chin, nodding to himself.

The group fell silent, soaking in the reality of having to describe with words what they had seen. Parnell snapped his fingers.

"Fine. If what you say is true, we should find spent casings in the vehicle. If we do, this whole thing isn't as crazy as it sounds. Nothing says we can't do a little investigating, though our detective's not here." He tossed John a pair of latex gloves, a faint smirk tugging at his lips. "Suit up, counselor. Time to get your hands dirty."

"Low man on the totem pole has to earn his keep," Annaleigh said, stifling a laugh. "Bottom rung gets to crawl through the wreckage."

John caught the gloves and snapped them on, shooting her a mock glare. "All good. I know when an expert eye is required."

"An expert eye?" she asked, through a wide grin. "You sure you want to go with that one? With your history?"

He ignored her and knelt by the overturned Blazer. His heart raced as he peered through the shattered window.

I hope Raith's guts aren't hanging from the cup holders.

He lay on his back and cautiously slid halfway into the vehicle, gloved hands probing the wreckage. He searched under the seats, which now dangled above him inside the inverted vehicle.

"No spent flares," he called out, his voice echoing in the crumpled cabin. "A couple of fast food wrappers, some coins, and that's it."

"Anything else that might explain them lights? You're our detective now, son. Look between the lines."

"That's the thing, Sheriff," John said in a muffled tone. "Everything is crushed, I don't see what could have made those... wait, I don't think it's related to the lights, but part of the steering wheel is missing."

Clyde knelt and leaned in.

"Yeah, that's pretty common for it to snap off in an accident like this one, especially when the occupant is in there being thrown around."

The burns on John's shirt suddenly itched, as if Raith's hands were still gripping him.

"Snapped, sure. I could understand that. But... this looks... different. Can you check the table for it?"

Parnell walked to a pair of nearby folding tables set up to catalogue the smaller bits of debris that had been recovered. Parts were organized by size, starting with the rear bumper, which lay on a grassy mound behind the table. He reviewed the table's contents and returned with a six-inch segment of curved, strapped metal.

"Like this one?"

He handed the part down to John. Parnell and Annaleigh followed and knelt next to Clyde. Inside the Blazer, John turned the piece upside down and held it up to the steering column.

"Too small. There must be more pieces out there somewhere."

Parnell shook his head. "Only piece we found that isn't jagged metal."

"So, either another part broke off and is out there in that field, or..." John eyed the piece, then gave it back to Parnell. "Sheriff, what do those ends look like to you?"

"Well, when metal shears off or breaks, the edges are jagged. You can tell by the cross-grain," he said as he studied the part from every angle. "These don't look like I would have expected them to."

"Exactly," John said, angling his head out of the window. "The ends are smooth, like it was..." He was reluctant to say the words out loud.

"Like it was what?" Annaleigh asked. "If it didn't break off, how—"

John climbed to his feet, miming to look like he was driving. "The bottom half of the wheel's intact. That piece you're holding, Sheriff. There aren't any other pieces missing. Here," he said, nodding at her, "hold your hands in front of you, like you're driving. Ten and two."

She raised her hands, brows arched skeptically. Parnell, his face tight with curiosity, hovered the metal rod between them.

It fit perfectly.

"What's missing isn't in the field. It's where his hands were," he said, shaking his head. He paced in short, quick steps. "God, I can't believe I'm about to say this. The steering wheel, the craziness outside City Hall, my chest, it's not a brand. It's him."

"John, you're not making any sense. What happened to the steering wheel?" Her hands remained up, but her palms flipped over.

John closed his eyes and tilted his head back. He replayed the crash in his mind. Raith swerved, left, right, left, then bright white lights pulsed inside the cabin. Not flares, but something alive, unnatural. They pressed against the roof of the cabin as the car rolled in the air. He froze, his head cocking to one side and brows compressed.

"John," Annaleigh pleaded, "are you okay?"

He raised his hands to his chest to feel the scorch marks on his shirt, grimacing. Raith had grabbed him, pinned him up against the doors of City Hall, and somehow burned him. His skin still felt warm. He took in a silent breath and smelled the vaguest hint of smoke. His eyes sprang open, and he smiled.

"I've got a hunch. Watch this."

He spun around and kneeled, reaching back into the upturned vehicle. He cleared away dirt, grass, and other debris from the ceiling of the Blazer's cabin.

John peeled the lining, exposing the raw metal. A wild laugh escaped him, equal parts dread and triumph. The lights, the burns on his shirt, the melted wheel. It was Raith. It had always been Raith.

"Take a look," he said, stepping back.

The color drained from each of their faces as they leaned closer.

"What... are those?" she stammered.

Parnell's jaw tightened, speechless.

Clyde sighed. "That sure looks like the cattle brand we've been chasing, don't it?"

Etched into the underside of the car's roof were two human hands. Each finger was rendered in stark relief, a forever frozen earmark of a fleeing man's last and desperate act.

"Those," John said defiantly, "are handprints. *Raith's* prints. Burned into the metal. And, they tell us exactly what's been happening all along."

29

THE WOODS ARE AGLOW

A rush of validation washed over John. All the pieces had started to fit together, forming a complete puzzle. Something he'd suspected deep down—it had been true.

Raith was indeed Gamble's murderer.

"The prints are still warm, too," he said, brushing his fingers over the dented metal.

"Well, it did skid across the concrete for about a hundred feet before it ended up down here," Parnell said, adjusting his Sheriff's hat. "That would definitely heat the metal, maybe explain how they got there."

John caught Parnell's eyes darting around the scene, like he was searching for something to contradict the evidence. He shrugged, trying to mask the chill creeping up his spine. "That was quite a while ago, Sheriff. Feel the other spots of the roof. Only the handprints feel that way."

Parnell knelt, fingers grazing the roof's cool metal. He jerked back.

"Hell's bells, the boy's right."

The marks on the courthouse, his Dart, even Annaleigh's car, glowed in John's mind. His chest throbbed where Raith's touch had scorched him, a dull pulse under the singed fabric. He pictured those same hands, radiating heat like a furnace, melting Gamble's arm and face to bone and ash.

He could see it. He still had trouble believing it.

He glanced at the wrecked SUV, its twisted frame glinting in the late May sun. A faint smell of burnt rubber lingered, mixing with the dust of the ditch. If no one knew Raith could do this, what else might he have been hiding?

"First, it was a custom cattle brand," Annaleigh said. "Now, John, you're saying Raith's hands are magic blowtorches? I think somebody's been reading too many comic books."

"Can I tell you how it works... scientifically? No way. But Gamble's arm? Burned clean off. Cut, perhaps, with both ends seared shut. Those prints down there? Etched in, mid-crash." He tugged open his singed shirt, revealing his red chest. "And this? I felt it. It was him all along."

Annaleigh covered her mouth and closed her eyes, her face tightening as if she were picturing Gamble's attack. Seeing her flinch, he quickly closed his shirt.

"You okay?"

"Am I okay?" Her eyes snapped to him. "We've been chasing a man who burns people alive with his hands. You think that sits well with me?" She crossed her arms, her prosecutor's poise fraying. "Gamble trusted Raith. We all did. And now..." Her voice caught, and a whisper exited. "What if we're next?"

"Well, he's dead, so this whole thing. It's over. We got him."

She snorted, a bitter edge to it. "Bold words for a guy with a third-degree burn on his chest. *We* didn't get him. He got himself. And in case you forgot, we didn't get *everyone*."

"I know, but we'll find Kenneth, don't worry." John forced a grin, masking the fear crawling up his spine. Her lips twitched, but her eyes stayed hard, scanning the horizon for answers.

"Now, Sheriff, about those lights. When his hands get hot, they seem to glow. When he burnt me back at City Hall, there was a flash. The same thing happened when he was driving, they were dancing around—"

"And, in the woods?"

Parnell blinked. "Clyde, what are you talking about?"

"When Ms. Stanton mentioned the word 'flare' a bit ago, that bell rang a little close to home, I guess. Because, as it would have it, I saw lights like that in the woods chasing Kenneth."

"You saw Raith's lights all the way across town? How is that possible?" Annaleigh asked.

John's focus raced back to the first time he'd met Kenneth at the restaurant while out to lunch with Gamble. He'd been shoved hard back into his seat by Kenneth's brutish hand as he attempted to rise and shake the mayor's hand. In addition to pain, a strange heat lingered on his shoulder, something he unknowingly attributed to the strength of the man's grip.

Maybe it was more than that.

"Deputy," John said. "Tell us everything."

Clyde squared his shoulders.

"Foley and I pulled up to the Raith property. We split up. He took the main residence, and I drove further down the road, into the woods, to Kenneth's cabin. When I arrived," Clyde said, squinting as if reliving the moment, "he was on the porch, backpack in hand, like he was skipping town. Then, some kind of light —like a dang supernova—hit my windshield and blinded me. I was seeing spots."

"That would have been, like, noon, right?" John asked, eyes narrowing. "The sun would have been overhead and shouldn't have—"

"First, young man, I said *like* the sun. And second? That light was blazing straight from Kenneth's porch, Scout's honor."

"Clyde, you mean the sun was glinting off the porch?" Parnell asked. "It reflected into your eyes... from, like a window, on the porch?"

"No, boss. Wasn't the sun, that's what I'm telling ya. All of a sudden, those things started moving, running off into the woods. The porch was empty—no Kenneth. I bolted after 'em. You could say I was chasing something *bright like the sun—*", he glanced at

John, "—and hoo boy, did it have a head start. I had to shield my eyes, but I stayed as close as I could. They dipped behind some brush, and then, they went out. When they were moving, at least I had something to follow. After they went out, it was like night-time again, even though it was still daylight. My eyes didn't adjust quick enough, boss. He got away."

Parnell patted him twice on his shoulder blade. "I know you did your best, Clyde."

"To be honest, I wasn't really sure what I was running after," he said, squinting again. "With what we know now? It had to be him, right? It had to be Kenneth. And he wasn't using no flashlight."

"Yeah, that seems to be the thread that connects everything," Annaleigh said. "Every time there's been an incident or attack, there's been those flashes of light. I remember seeing one when Kenneth threatened us in our office. The stairwell lit up before we went down and saw the brand on the wall."

John's head bobbed up and down. "And, when the trunk of my car was burned, a light blinded us from identifying whoever was back there. I guess we can stop calling them brands? Now that we know what they really are?"

"Do we, though?" Parnell asked, scratching his jaw. "'Cuz I'm still racking my brain on how this is possible. If I explain this to Lily tonight, she'll think I'm crazy."

"You've been married to her for twenty-five years, Dane," Clyde joked. "She already knows it."

John paced away from the group, fists clenched. "Something doesn't add up. Why would he run? He's got this whole town on a string. Anybody who turns on him can vanish. Like, literally. He could vaporize his critics into ash if he wanted to. So, what triggered Kenneth? It doesn't really make sense."

His mind raced, piecing together the flashes of light, the burns, the cover-ups. Raith's ego was too big to flee. And yet, he did.

"Everybody thinks they'll do the smart thing when cornered. They often don't."

John spun and realized that everyone was facing him, watching and listening.

"No, Sheriff, that's not it. Well, maybe not *all* of it."

Chin strokes became hand rubs as he visualized every scene, every clue. He dipped his head, squeezing his eyes shut, blocking everything out except the problem at hand. The answers were there. He *had* to find them.

A thought materialized.

"Deputy, did you draw your gun at Kenneth's?"

"Sure did, right after those sunbeams hit me. I popped out of the car, I drew and took cover behind the door, and yelled for him to get on the ground. Couldn't see worth a darn, but he didn't know that, did he? Anyway, I expected to take fire after getting blinded like that."

Parnell's mouth opened, and he raised a finger, as if to object. No words emerged.

"And, Sheriff, when you came around the corner at City Hall, you had your gun out, too. I guess they can melt everything but bullets. Guns seem to be their kryptonite."

Annaleigh wasn't impressed.

"Not exactly a novel theory, John. Aren't guns everyone's kryptonite?"

"Depends on which end of the barrel you're looking at, Ms. Stanton," Parnell interjected. "Clyde, when we find Kenneth, and if he gets close, you've got a shoot-to-kill order. I'm done playing games. No one else is getting hurt by these two."

"Yessir, boss. I'll pass it along to the other deputies."

"The others!" John shouted, his voice cracking as the group flinched. A chill hit him.

"Sheriff, if both Raith and Kenneth can do this..."

Parnell's eyes widened. "The boy might have it, too."

"Wait," Annaleigh said. "If they all can do this, how will we ever know who *actually* killed Gamble? Especially if you two go killing all the suspects with a shoot-first mentality?"

"We might have a more pressing issue," said Clyde, whose cool drawl carried rising tension in it. "Foley took Wesley Raith into the station. I'm sure the word is getting out about the mayor's crash by now. If Mumber starts to question the kid and lets on about his father—"

Parnell was already speaking into his radio. "I need a situation update at the station."

No response.

"This is Sheriff Parnell. Anyone at the station, respond, damn it."

Silence.

"All units, give me a 10-20! Where is everyone at?"

More silence.

John met Annaleigh's wide eyes. The radio's silence screamed louder than any voice. Each unanswered appeal tightened the knot growing in his chest. He glanced at the ditch, the Blazer's wreckage glinting like a warning.

His mind flashed to the image of Detective Mumber, grizzled and stubborn, questioning Wesley alone. Not some twenty-year-old vandal, but a Raith. If he had half his father's power, there still might be no limit to the damage he could do.

John's fingers twitched, itching for something to anchor him. Beside him, Annaleigh's breath hitched, her knuckles white.

"This isn't right," she whispered. "Something's wrong."

As Clyde and Parnell bolted for the hill, ready to climb, a voice burst through the static, shattering the tense silence. They froze, heads tilted to the speaker. John, his heart pounding, noticed Annaleigh stiffen.

"Officer down... station on fire... need... hel—"

Before cutting off mid-word, Deputy Cason Foley pleaded over the airwaves for assistance.

Parnell and Clyde darted for their cruisers. Parnell dove into his, Clyde vaulted over his hood, and slid the rest of the way. John and Annaleigh were still closing their doors when Parnell's tires squealed and he fishtailed into a U-turn. They tore back into town and through the square, sirens screaming. They took the northern exit and skidded into the Sheriff's station lot.

John's mouth dropped.

The front door lay on the ground, warped with its hinges glowing red-hot. Smoke poured from the windows, flames licking the frames.

John stumbled out, the humid air hitting him like a slap. His shoes crunched on the lot, each step heavier as the heat rolled off the building in waves. A window shattered somewhere inside, glass tinkling like a broken promise.

John's eyes stung from the smoke and the dread pooling in his gut.

Was Mumber still in there? Deputy Foley? Hinkle? Wesley?

The kid's scarred face held back a powerful secret. Distortions that belittled reality, like a puzzle piece jammed in the wrong slot.

He gripped the cruiser's door, steadying himself.

The station wasn't just burning.

It was under attack.

30

HOLDING ON

J ohn watched as Parnell sprang from the cruiser, popped the trunk, and rummaged inside.

"Boss, where do you want me?" Clyde asked as he rushed over, his steady gaze cutting through the chaos.

"Take Ms. Stanton here and give her a radio. You secure all around this building and make sure no one sneaks up on us. John and I are going in."

"You want me... in there?"

John's voice cracked as he stared at the station's windows, flames curling through shattered glass. He was a lawyer, not a hero —his world was supposed to be legal briefs and arguments, not dodging fire, although it seemed like forever since he'd looked at a law book.

The weight of Gamble's death and the need for answers burned hotter than the blaze ahead. Was this what it took to find the truth? Become something he wasn't?

Annaleigh's hands clamped his shoulders, planting a fierce but brief kiss on his lips.

"You've got this. Be safe." She turned to Clyde, who handed her a radio. John watched in awe as he rattled off a set of instructions to her.

"First thing, call a three-oh-one," he said, voice fast-paced yet calm, "it's code for emergency authority delegated to a civilian. You say that, and every nearby agency will listen. Get fire and ambos here, quick. Coordinate everyone's arrival. You're in charge now, Ms. Stanton." He leaned in, locking eyes with her. "Bring the cavalry."

He vanished around the building's corner, gun raised as she slid into the cruiser's driver's seat, barking orders into the radio.

John's gaze shifted to Parnell, but inwardly, he was amazed at Annaleigh's composure. She had been assigned a high-profile case, and seconds later, without any preparation, she was giving her closing arguments, convincing the entire jury to see it her way. John's quarter-smile was interrupted by Parnell, who yanked a familiar black case from the trunk. He pointed to a compartment next to the wheel well.

"Grab that extinguisher. And, you're going to need this, too." Parnell lifted a semi-automatic pistol out of the container and handed it to John. "I trust you remember how to use it?"

"Yes, sir, I do," he said, his hands fumbling to remove his suit jacket. "Pretty sure my law degree never covered this."

"We are who the moment needs us to be, Counselor."

John's pulse quickened as he grabbed the gun and ejected the magazine. He verified it was full, jammed it back into place, and racked the slide.

It felt like it'd been years since he first held it at the Sheriff's shooting range. It still felt familiar. Perhaps it was the situation, but it seemed to weigh more, too.

"I'll go in first," Parnell said, his eyes scanning the burning station. "We'll clear it one section at a time. I want you on my six at all times. Your priority is checking on anyone we come across. Mine is to cover you. Any fires we walk past, put them out." He pointed to the gun in John's hand. "You are only to use that if I go down. Targets are one thing. Pointing that at a person is much, much different. No need for that to be on your conscience if we can help it."

"Save lives first, put out fires second. Don't shoot anyone unless I absolutely have to. Understood," he said, flicking the safety on and tucking the pistol into the back of his waistband.

Parnell twisted a knob on his radio, lowering the volume. He drew his service weapon.

"Let's go."

John followed behind Parnell as they approached the front entrance, fire extinguisher in one hand, the other on Parnell's back.

"It'll be hard to breathe, so keep low. Move quickly and smoothly."

Parnell moved over the remnants of the front door, his gun scanning with each step. John choked on the acrid smoke billowing out. The flames flickered inside, casting jagged shadows across the walls and clawing at the edges of John's vision. They crouched, trying to stay as low as possible.

The foyer was empty. No active flames and even better, no bodies, just the smoke flowing along the ceiling and out into the Coldwater air. The security door sat ajar with a pair of shoes visible in the gap.

"Body," Parnell whispered. "Once I clear the corner, you check for a pulse."

Parnell leaned against the frame, then spun through the doorway and scanned the room with a predator's focus. He waved his fingers, and John scrambled forward, his hands shaking.

"It's your clerk," he rasped. He noticed her chest rise and fall in a long, slow breath. "She's breathing. Looks like minor burns, but she's out cold." Relief surged then vanished as he imagined the condition of the others who were deeper inside.

John's fingers lingered on her wrist, her pulse faint but stubborn, a flicker of hope in this hell. He didn't really know her. He couldn't recall if they'd had a single conversation. She bustled behind the front desk, flashing warm smiles. Any semblance of a smile was gone, replaced with a pair of thin, pale lips. She lay, unmoving, scorched by the same unnatural fire that ravaged this town.

In a hushed voice, Parnell relayed the information to Annaleigh over the radio. John tapped him twice on the back, their agreed-upon signal to keep going.

"Moving," Parnell commanded.

John clung to the layout of the room despite the smoke blurring his vision. He'd only been here once, but that didn't matter. His memory was his sharpest tool, stitching together a mental map of the office—desks, chairs, back hallway—in an image clearer than the hazy reality before him. If he could hold onto that picture, one not bound by shadows, maybe he could keep them both alive.

The two men navigated their way to a fire near Detective Mumber's desk on the other side of the bullpen. Pieces of singed paper wafted into the air, and glowing ash rained down.

Parnell pointed the muzzle of his pistol towards the back hallway while John used the extinguisher to put out the fire on the desk. The burst of pressurized powder snuffed out the flames and sent the remaining papers and folders flying everywhere. As they fluttered to the ground, he crouched behind the sheriff and tapped him again. They'd only crawled a few feet when Parnell stopped.

"Body," he whispered. "My one o'clock, on the other side. Go, I'm covering."

John inched forward, his knees scraping ash-stained tile, eyes locked on a portly-shaped man, slumped on his side. He wore a tan suit jacket, still burning at the edges. John's fingers fumbled for the neck, searching for a pulse.

"It's Mumber," he choked out, voice tight. "He's alive. Can't really feel a pulse, but I can hear him breathing. Well, wheezing."

He rolled Mumber onto his back, and John gasped, a wave of nausea hitting him. The detective's face was in ruins. One side blistered and charred, the burn etched in the unmistakable shape of a hand. John leaned closer, the stench of burnt skin clawing at his throat.

"It's like someone held him down," he muttered, half to himself, picturing a faceless thug pinning Mumber to the floor. "He needs a medic, like, now."

His voice was sharper than he meant, panic creeping in. Parnell's radio crackled as he relayed the update, his tone grim.

"Mumber's down, critical burns." He locked eyes with John's. "Once we clear this place, help can get in. Let's move."

John nodded, his hands trembling as he pulled back from Mumber, the hand-shaped burn searing into his memory.

He'd been focusing on the incorrect Raith this whole time. It wasn't the mayor, but instead his son, Wesley? Or had they done everything together? What about Kenneth? How big did this conspiracy go?

John's mind looped, trying to figure it out.

They crawled towards the entrance of the back hallway. It led to the rear of the building, where the interrogation rooms and holding cell were located. The cell where Wesley would have been placed when Deputy Foley brought him back to the station.

Parnell stopped ten feet from the opening.

"I see shoes. My left side."

John edged over, his knees scraping the floor, and froze at the sight of soot-covered shoes.

"Black, like yours, Sheriff," he muttered, a shudder ripping through him. Seeing them dragged his thoughts back to the field, where Raith's severed legs sprawled in the dirt. Was he about to find another mutilated body?

He crawled forward, relief flickering as the legs connected to a torso.

The smoke parted, revealing a charred, blackened mass. Like Gamble's corpse, the skin and muscle on this person had melted into decay. White bone glinted through deep scorch marks. The smell of burnt flesh clawed at John's lungs. He waved away the haze, exposing the face of Deputy Amos Hinkle. The old man's eyes were vacant, his mouth frozen in a silent scream.

No pulse. No breath.

"It's Hinkle, Sheriff. I'm sorry," John whispered, his voice trembling. "He's gone."

The words felt hollow, inadequate against the sight of Hinkle's charred remains and the stench of burnt flesh that clawed at John's throat. He recalled the old deputy's fumbles with Raith, Parnell's sharp scolding over the radio, and the weight of the man's missteps.

Had sending him back here cost Hinkle his life?

Parnell covered the hallway, his shoulders tense, eyes scanning every shadow. John caught the Sheriff's gaze for a moment. His eyes glistened, tears cutting tracks through the soot on his cheeks.

John swallowed hard, his own eyes stinging from smoke and something deeper, a grief he couldn't name. He knew Parnell would never get to have that last chat with Hinkle—the one promised over the airwaves. Though centered around a scolding and a probable coaxing to retirement, it's a conversation he knew the sheriff would have given anything to have rather than this outcome.

"Covering the hallway," Parnell choked on his words, masking his warble with a cough. "Knock down the rest of those fires before we move on. Quickly now."

Parnell kept eyes on the back hallway as John retraced their steps, identifying the smaller fires that clung to life on shelves and filing cabinets and blasting them with the extinguisher. The flames sputtered and hissed as they surrendered to the coolant. John crept back into position behind the Sheriff.

"All fires out in the main office area," he radioed out. "Okay to retrieve two injured, but Hinkle's down." A pause. A deep swallow. "DOA." A throat clear. "We're continuing and will clear the back half."

The first doors they encountered were the two interrogation rooms. Parnell twisted the knobs and cleared the rooms with swift precision. Both were empty, as was the small observation room that sat in between. More curious, there were no flames, allowing them to rise from their crouches and breathe in clean air.

The hallway ended at a blind corner with the holding cell just beyond. John's hope vanished as he pictured the potential scenario. He knew Wesley wouldn't be there. In a sane world, none of this would have happened, and Wesley would be locked up safely with a deputy standing guard.

There's nothing sane about what's going on here.

He set the extinguisher down and tapped Parnell's shoulder twice. They rounded the corner, the sheriff's pistol steady in his outstretched hands. An odd scene materialized.

The metal door to the holding cell gaped open, its handle gleaming. The cage was empty, a void where one high-value suspect should have been. Deputy Foley lay sprawled on the ground, motionless in the dim light.

"All clear in here," Parnell radioed out. He holstered his gun, his movements slow, deliberate.

John knelt, his fingers trembling as he reached for Foley's neck. Before the touch connected, he jolted upright, coughing violently, eyes stretched wide with panic.

"What... happened?" Foley rasped, clawing at the floor.

"You tell me, deputy," Parnell snapped, his voice tight. "We've got dead and dying out there. What went on back here? Where's the Raith boy?"

Foley's coughs broke his words into fragments.

"I don't know, Sheriff. Detective Mumber brought him back... put him in the cage... door blasted open. Then, black. Just... black."

Parnell eyed the young deputy, a single eyebrow arched.

"Looks like you're good to walk. Get out there, get checked. Go."

Foley staggered to his feet, straightening his clean uniform, untouched by soot or burns. He cast a long glance at the empty cell, and after a few seconds, he lurched toward the exit.

John spied the metal cell door. Its malformed lock had oozed down, looking like melted butter.

Something is off.

Deputy Foley's spotless uniform gnawed at him. How had this dolt escaped unscathed when the clerk was scorched, Mumber's face branded, and Hinkle's chest reduced to ash?

John's mind churned. He'd once seen Deputy Foley as a foil, a fellow suitor for Annaleigh. This was no fit of jealousy. This was something deeper. Was Foley just lucky? The only other alternative was so much worse.

John and Parnell stood alone, the silence in this rear section of the building roaring louder than the chaos of the first responders in the front.

An unmistakable truth, glaring at them.

They'd gotten it all wrong.

And Wesley had escaped.

31

SMOKE CLEARS

The twisted, charred mess of the holding cell door hung open. Its metal lock drooped and warped like candle wax, as if held too long under some unholy flame. The pungent odor of the scorched steel burned John's throat, a grim reminder of Wesley's escape.

Parnell's weathered face was etched with disbelief as he traced a finger along the scarred mechanism.

"Would you look at this," Parnell muttered, as if the words could unravel what had happened.

"I'm sorry, Sheriff." John's gaze dropped to the soot-streaked floor. He knew, deep down, Parnell wasn't talking about the cell door. "I should've seen this coming. I could've put everything together sooner. I was too focused on the mayor—"

"Seen what, Counselor? Melting metal with your damn hands ain't in the playbook of things we're supposed to worry about." He exhaled sharply, rubbing his ash-smudged brow with a shaky hand. "Never lost a suspect before. Never lost a man in the line of duty, either. Both those things happened on the same damn day... c'mon, son. Let's go check on the others."

They stumbled out of the station's smoldering wreckage. The

waning sunlight was still bright to John's eyes, forcing him to squint.

The clamor of scurrying responders and syncopated sirens disoriented him after the elongated silence in the back hallway. Firefighters worked to extinguish the last remnants of the blaze, and paramedics tended to the wounded before carting them off to Coldwater Memorial.

Annaleigh stood by Parnell's patrol car, her brow furrowed, shoulders loose. She touched John's arm, her voice soft but steady.

"How are you two holding up? I was listening to every word. It sounded bad."

Parnell grimaced. "Not sure what to say, Ms. Stanton. It's a catastrophe in there. Thanks for coordinating out here. We'd've been lost without you. As for what happened, I have my theories." He fixed John with a hard stare. "But I want *yours* instead."

John's eyes widened as he pointed to himself. "Mine?"

"You played detective back there at the crash scene and did a fine job. My detective is on his way to the hospital, so I would really appreciate your perspective. Mumber and I always talked things out. Helps me process."

It was clear he was still processing the tragedies that had unfolded inside. His request bordered on a plea.

John nodded, squeezed his eyes shut, and drove his mind into Wesley's chaos.

"You bet, Sheriff. Here goes. I'm Wesley. Just found out my dad's dead. I'm gutted. My mom ran away years ago. No dad, no mom. Does that make me an orphan now? Never mind that." He shook his head and drew a deep breath, refocusing.

"Kenneth, my uncle in all but blood, has vanished. I'm alone, and I got caught. Need to bolt. But... I'm furious... at everything. At myself, for being in this cell, at the cops, blaming them for my dad's death."

Annaleigh's hand jerked upwards.

"John, you can't just invent facts—"

His eyes flicked open, brow quirking.

"It's Wesley's headspace, Annaleigh. His truth, not ours." He exhaled, sinking back into the scene.

"Mumber locks me in the cell and leaves. Foley's on guard. Rage is building. It burns through me... I need out. I heat the lock..." His fists clenched, knuckles whitening as if gripping molten steel.

"If I melted the hinges, the entire door would crash down and bring too much attention. So, just the lock. Then, I kick the door. Hard." His leg twitched, mimicking a sharp strike.

"Deputy Foley's on the other side, surprised. He staggers back, stunned. He's down now. Deputy Hinkle hears the noise, peeks down the hallway to check it out. I'm already running, so I grab him as we meet at the corner, pushing him back to the bullpen. My hands are burning him. I shove him down. His shirt and skin sizzle. He claws at me, but he's too injured to fight back. I keep pressing. Then, he just... stops moving."

John's breath hitched, his eyes snapping to Parnell's, seeing an extreme sadness growing.

"Sorry, Sheriff, we'll move on. Detective Mumber's now in the way. I push him down, pinning him down till he stops moving. Last, your clerk's in the way at the door. I shove her and she cracks her head against the floor, which knocks her out."

He opened his eyes, looking around. "That's it, I'm free."

Parnell leaned closer, eyes narrowing. "Okay, what about the fires, then? If he's free and there's no one else available to stop him, why do you think he set them? Why doesn't he just keep running?"

John's pulse quickened, eager.

"Decoys. He didn't have a lot of time, so he touched papers and folders wherever he saw them, lighting them up. He didn't get the walls or paneling, something that would have brought the whole station down. The small fires were chaos to stall everyone from chasing him right away. But, those small fires grew into larger ones, and that's why the building looks like that now." He pointed back to the station.

"Not bad, Counselor." Parnell's voice softened, his eyes lingering on the smoldering building. "The last thing I told Hinkle was to shape up over the radio. Barked at him like a damn fool. Never thought that'd be the end."

His jaw clenched, then refocused. John caught a flicker of pain in Parnell's eyes.

"Only a few crime scenes under your belt and you're already thinking like a man with a badge," Parnell continued. "There's only one piece that don't sit well with me, though."

"What'd I miss?" John's eyes darted, searching back through his story.

"You didn't miss it—you just wouldn't have known about it. It's one of our protocols. When anyone is in that holding cell, a deputy's always sitting at a corner desk, eyes on whoever's in there. Whether there was a noise or not, Foley should've seen Wesley trying to melt the cell door."

"Not to mention the blinding light, right?" Annaleigh interjected.

"Maybe," John said, head tilted. "Only if his powers work the same."

Her lips parted, hesitating. "Well, two out of three worked that way. So, if Wesley's does, too—"

John cracked his knuckles. "It means that snake Foley is in on it. It means he let Wesley out on purpose. He's responsible for everything else that happened in there." He pictured Foley's smug glance earlier and the way he'd lingered near the cell's door.

"That's a heavy accusation," Parnell whispered, tone cold. "But between Hinkle's mistakes during the chase and now with Deputy Foley's questionable actions, it appears allegiances around here are a bit murky. That young man's leash just got real short, but I'll have to handle him later. Right now, we need to hunt for the Raith boy."

John disagreed. "But if he's working with Wesley—"

"Foley!" Parnell's voice cracked like a whip, sharp enough to make Annaleigh jump. His hand shot up, palm out, silencing John as his eyes flicked to the shadow moving behind them. "Cleared for duty, I see?"

John spun, his pulse spiking as Deputy Foley loomed in the fading light, his silhouette stark against the smoldering station. A chill crawled up John's spine, the weight of Parnell's warning sinking in. With trust in short supply, suspicions needed to be kept under wraps.

"Yes, sir, boss. Got checked out and all set. Guess I ended up pretty lucky. Awaiting your orders, Sheriff," he said, straightening his belt and shirt. He flashed a proud look in Annaleigh's direction.

"Good, glad you're not hurt," Parnell said, eyes narrowing. "Others were, though, and we're stretched pretty thin. Deputy, I need you to secure the scene and our space. You're the new front door, son."

Foley's shoulders sagged, his face tightening as if stung by the assignment. He nodded curtly and trudged toward the station. Once out of earshot, John was the first to admit the obvious.

"There's no way we can trust him to help us find Wesley, right?"

"Not a chance," Parnell said, low and slow. "Ever since he admitted to stalking poor Ms. Stanton here, he's been on my special radar, but this takes it to a whole new level. Hard to believe he'd aid and abet, though, so he gets the benefit of my doubt. *For now.*"

Deputy D. Clyde Brothers joined the group, his kind eyes and smile a welcome respite.

"Sheriff, the Raith boy is nowhere on the property. I checked everywhere. I'm so sorry we weren't here to stop him."

Parnell, his face smeared with ash, spoke with a grave and resolute voice.

"It's been a long, tough day, but we're not done yet. Wesley Raith is in the wind. We need to catch him before he can cause any more ruckus or harm. Clyde, you and I are going to search every inch of this town, starting with the Raith farm. Then, we'll split up, move on to any place he might seek refuge. Businesses, restaurants, friends. Any place he could hide. No stone unturned."

Clyde adjusted his hat, transforming his eyes from kind to determined.

"Remember," Parnell added, "maintain your distance. If you see him, call for backup. And, if he advances on you? Shoot him where he stands."

Parnell's gaze shifted to Annaleigh, his brow creased with worry.

"Ms. Stanton, I want you to go with Mr. Chance and pick up his mother from the hospital. Then, I want you to hole up at their place. Bonnie's safer with you than by herself. I'll phone you at the house every half hour with updates."

"Thanks, Sheriff," Annaleigh said, hugging him. "You and Clyde be safe, too."

"Oh, we'll be fine, Ms. Stanton. You two stay together, and we'll all see each other on the other side of this."

Parnell extended his hand to John for a shake. In return, John drew the black pistol from his waistband, offering it handle-first with a quick turn. The sheriff yanked his hand back.

"John," Parnell said, his voice soft as he used John's name for the first time. "You've done more than your fair share today, but I need one last thing."

"Anything, Sheriff. Tell me what it is and consider it done."

Parnell reached back into the trunk of his cruiser. He dug around and pulled something from a leather folio, shielding it from view.

"As the Sheriff of Coldwater County, I'm duty-bound to keep Coldwater safe. From what I've seen from you, you've leaned into that same philosophy. And I know there's no one else I know that can do the job I'm about to ask of you." Parnell exposed the object in his hand, revealing a deputy's badge. "I hereby deputize you and entrust you with the responsibility and authority that comes with being a deputy sheriff."

Parnell pressed the badge into John's palm, its cold metal biting in like a blade.

Pride warred with dread. This honor was heavier than expected, its weight echoing the station's scars and Parnell's losses. Law books were useless now. This was a role for which he had no training, and failure wasn't an option.

"John, your primary mission, your only mission, is to protect one of Coldwater's remaining leaders, at least until morning," Parnell said. "With everything that's happened, we can't risk leaving her unprotected."

John understood his assignment.

Protect Annaleigh at all costs.

As his gaze drifted to her, a surge of protectiveness washed over him. As a prosecutor, working alongside her, he'd already been trying to watch out for her since the horrible views of Gamble' disfigured body stained his sight. As an official deputy, the stakes were even higher.

His hand wandered to the firearm he had tucked back in his waistband, his fingers brushing the cool metal. John swallowed hard, his mouth suddenly dry. He hoped he had what it took to live up to the trust placed in him.

Clyde enveloped John around his shoulders with a strong arm and a wide smile, drawing him out of his head.

"Welcome to the club, Deputy Chance. Wish your mama could've seen this. I'll be proud of you for her."

John smiled back, unsure of what to say. Parnell faced Annaleigh, his voice fatherly and kind.

"Ms. Stanton, with the mayor dead, the roles of Sheriff and Prosecutor are all this town's got left of its elected leadership. You may be 'Acting Prosecutor', sure," he said, mimicking air quotes for her title, "but you're the backbone of Coldwater's justice. We can't lose you."

Annaleigh's smile wavered, her fingers tightening on John's

arm. "I understand, Sheriff. And, I already have a history with the deputy you've assigned to protect me. I'll admit you've made a good choice." She dipped her head onto his shoulder.

Parnell looked back at John, his brows crooked.

"Well, deputy? What do you say? Are you with me?"

John bobbed his head up and down, despite the fatigue that weighed on his shoulders.

"I accept, Sheriff. Absolutely. I'll do whatever it takes to keep her safe. You can trust me."

Parnell clapped him on the shoulder.

"Stay vigilant, son. I'll be in touch soon."

With a final nod, John turned and locked eyes with Annaleigh. Her steady gaze met his, a silent agreement to the Sheriff's plan, her jaw set without protest.

"This way, ma'am," he said, gesturing.

"Oh, Lord, he's already got the idea he can boss me around." She smirked, then looped her arm around his. "For now, I'll allow it. *Deputy Chance.*"

They headed towards the town square, walking through the courthouse's looming shadow on their way to the parking lot. He'd nearly forgotten where he'd parked the Dart in the day's chaos.

His hand trembled as he opened the passenger door for Annaleigh, his eyes scanning the darkening lot. This wasn't chivalry or any manners his mother had taught him. John was her armed guardian now, his mind racing with plans to keep them alive.

A faint crackle snapped in the distance, like a fire sparking in the night, and his grip tightened on the pistol in his waistband.

He just needed to hold out till dawn, and surely Parnell and Clyde will have Wesley Raith in cuffs, setting everything right.

32

GUARD DUTY

John's knuckles whitened on the steering wheel as the Dart hummed along Coldwater's empty streets. The hospital's glow just ahead illuminated the dirt streaks in his windshield.

He'd been so fixated on Mayor Raith, chasing a false lead while the real killer vanished into the shadows.

What happened at the station was my fault.

Guilt clawed at him, sharper with every mile. He glanced at Annaleigh. Her profile was sharp against the fading daylight, and her silence carried a weight he couldn't read.

She didn't blame him—he hoped—but self-pity wouldn't keep Bonnie safe. He pressed the gas, urgency overriding doubt.

"Got anything to grab at your place? Once we get home, we're not leaving again until the morning, maybe longer."

"No need, Mr. Deputy, sir," she said, a sly grin flashing. "I already have a bag at Bonnie's. I mean, *your* house."

John's head snapped toward her, eyes wide.

"You're kidding, right?"

"Nope." She smirked, raising an eyebrow. "I crashed there so much, she let me stash a few things. I told you before you should've called your mom more often from law school. You would've known about all this."

"Yeah, and how I would have handled it before now is a whole other story, too."

At seven, they'd parked at the hospital and went inside to retrieve John's mother. By quarter to eight, John pulled the Dart up the long drive to his house, returning home through shadows that stretched across the lawn as the sun sank below the tree line.

"Full moon tonight," John said, easing his mother out of the Dart's passenger door. Her frailty twisted his heart—two days ago, she was completely different. And whole. But he'd missed too many moons with her, chasing a career while danger crept closer. "It's your favorite. Shame we can't sit out on the patio, but it's not safe."

"I know my son, the deputy, has bigger worries than his mama and the moon," Bonnie teased.

John draped an arm around her waist, steadying her slow steps.

"You're wrong, Mom," he said, voice thick. "I was a fool to think anything mattered more than you."

Bonnie leaned into him, her eyes twinkling as she glanced at Annaleigh.

"Seems like you might have other age-appropriate priorities these days. As well you should."

John's face warmed, caught off guard by her jab. The pea gravel crunched under his loafers as they climbed the drive and onto the porch. He took one more look at the front face of the house. As dusk settled across it, it looked more and more like a fortress, braced for battle.

A fortress with a million weaknesses.

Familiar sounds triggered new responses. The creak of the porch swing moving in the breeze sent a jolt racing through him. The groaning floorboards of the porch caused head snaps, confirming the footsteps belonged. Swaying branches and glinting moonlight conjured Wesley's shadow in the tree line, hands shining like forges.

This wasn't a house anymore. It was their last stand.

John coaxed Bonnie toward the stairs, urging her to rest upstairs in her bedroom. Instead, she planted herself on the couch, stubborn as ever.

"I'm fine right here. What if I need a glass of water in the middle of the night? I know you're not going to get and tinkle for me, either. And, who do you think will make breakfast in the morning? You, with your badge and law degree?"

Her teasing cut through the tension, but John's reddened chest tightened. She was too exposed down here, too close to the windows. He pictured Wesley's glowing hands breaching the glass, his fire licking at her.

Not on my watch.

"All right, stay put there, Mom," he said, forcing a smile. "No kitchen heroics until we're safe. I'll bring you water before bed and I promise I'll make breakfast in the morning. The other stuff is up to you, I'm afraid. In the meantime, I'm going to check outside before it gets too dark and we lock up for the night."

John rose from his chair. Annaleigh mirrored him.

"I'll join you, if you don't mind."

"As long as we make it quick and get you back in here where it's safe. Plus, two pairs of eyes are better than one, I guess."

"Wait, I'm confused. Haven't we done this already? Are we counting your eyes as one of the good pairs or not?" Annaleigh joked. "Or, perhaps your mother is coming with us, and she's the second set?"

He chuckled, reaching for the doorknob of the back door and walking out into the evening air, being sure to lock the door behind them.

John led Annaleigh through the backyard, past the wicker chairs where they'd once laughed under the stars. A million years had gone by since then, and a million things had also gone wrong. As his eyes darted around, every shadow carried signs of a threat. And he wasn't quite used to carrying a gun in his own backyard.

His pulse thrummed in his ears, eyes darting to each rustling leaf. Unlikely, but Wesley could be anywhere.

John's flashlight survey caught a ground-floor window, its pane ajar. A darkened gap stared back, like an invitation. Worry flooded him before sanity kicked in.

"Mom must've left that open before the accident. Every window needs to be locked tight. He doesn't need an easy way in. It's on the list to take care of when we get back inside."

Annaleigh nodded, helping to scan for other vulnerabilities. John continued the assessment, leading her around to the front of the house.

"The entry door is half glass, so it's a potential weak spot," he said, rattling the locked handle. "This glass could shatter easily, then he could reach in and twist the knob—"

"He escaped from a metal jail cell by melting the lock with magic fire that erupted from his hands. Is any of this really going to keep him out?"

He drooped his shoulders and reached up, rubbing his forehead and eyes.

"You're right. Sorry, I'm trying to act like a deputy, I guess."

"No need to put on an act. Just be you, John. That's why Parnell picked you."

"I know, but if we at least make it harder for him to enter, that'll buy time to defend ourselves."

"There you go. That sounded very deputy-like."

"Glorious," he said, rolling his eyes. "Let's head back in and make sure everything's locked up."

They walked around the final side of the house, noting no deficiencies. With their circle of the house complete, he stopped short of the rear kitchen door.

"Oh, one thing we've never really talked about. Do you know how to shoot a gun?"

"You're asking a country girl if she knows how to shoot a gun? Of course I do. But, in this crazy situation, do I want to be in a position to shoot *said gun*? No. The kind of justice I want for Wesley Raith is not the kind that puts bullets in him."

They entered the house, and Annaleigh went straight for the

kitchen cabinet, reaching for something under the sink. She pulled out a fire extinguisher and held it up.

"That doesn't mean I can't use defensive weapons, though," she said, a broad smile curving on her lips. "If it comes down to it, maybe I can knock some sense into him."

John locked the kitchen door and closed the curtains. His heart still raced from the perimeter sweep, but he made short, deliberate motions to keep Annaleigh from noticing. He crossed by the refrigerator, heading to the nook by the stairs, intent on closing the side window. The phone's shrill ring jolted him before he could leave the kitchen.

That's the third time tonight. Get a grip. Quit flinching. It's only a phone call.

He snatched the receiver off the wall by the counter.

"Sheriff, any news?"

"Nothing good," Parnell said, slightly out of breath. "Searched the Raith property. The main house, Kenneth's cabin, and all the outbuildings. No Wesley. Checked his usual hangouts in town, too. Nada."

John's frown deepened at Parnell's words, his head shaking slightly as he met Annaleigh's gaze, her eyes mirroring his frustration.

He motioned for Annaleigh to join him. She slid closer, and her cheek brushed his as she leaned in toward the receiver. He tilted the corded phone to share the sheriff's voice, and their breaths mingled in the tight space. The intimacy jolted him—a welcome, but fleeting distraction, from the dread pooling in his gut.

"He can't have gone far on foot, right?" she asked.

Her breath grazed John's lips, warm and distractingly close. It took every ounce of strength he had not to toss the phone aside, grab her, and pull her into a kiss.

"Oh, hello, Ms. Stanton. I didn't realize you were on the line. The problem is that he doesn't appear to be on foot," Parnell said. "A hatchback was stolen from Froggin's Diner, across the street from our station. Witnesses indicate it happened after we pulled into the station, and, from their descriptions, it was Wesley Raith. The vehicle was a pale yellow color. We're looking for it, but he's likely skipped town by now. Not sure why he would have stolen wheels, otherwise."

Her eyes widened.

"You're saying he was across the street, stealing a car while I was right there? He could have been watching me the whole time."

John's grip tightened on the receiver. Wesley had been *that* close. Close enough to harm her. His jaw clenched as he pictured Gamble's grotesque remains.

That could have been her tonight.

"You saved lives today, Ms. Stanton. It was chaos, and your focus was on us and the station. Just like I asked you to."

"Sheriff," John said, "Wesley's got nothing outside Coldwater. Why would he leave? Based on what we heard him say, he's still got a mess to clean up. He's not done with us."

"When did you hear the boy say that? First I've heard of it."

Annaleigh's eyes bulged, staring at John. They hadn't quite gotten around to sharing with Parnell how they obtained the ledger, leading to the arrest warrant that kick-started this whole fiasco.

"Another story for another day, Sheriff," she said. "We didn't take him seriously before, but we do now. Do you think he knows where John lives?"

"Listen," Parnell said. "I doubt he'll show his face tonight. He's holed up somewhere, alone and cold. We'll keep looking—all night if we have to. I want you two to meet me at the courthouse tomorrow morning, and we'll come up with a plan to sort this mess."

"Fine," Annaleigh said.

John nodded as if Parnell could see him, bouncing the receiver on both their ears.

"Sounds good, Sheriff, we'll be—"

A sharp click cut off John's words, the line dead. He froze, eyes flicking to Annaleigh, then to his mother on the couch in the other room. The air felt thick. And wrong.

Before he could speak, the room plunged into blackness along with the click sounds of appliances losing power. His heart slammed against his ribs, his mind spinning.

Not now. We're not ready. I'm not ready.

His fingers fumbled across the counter, grazing the cool metal of the nearby flashlight.

"No way this outage is a coincidence," he whispered, as his other hand found the pistol in his waistband.

He flicked on the flashlight, its beam slicing upward, casting dim, ghostly light over the kitchen. Annaleigh gripped the fire extinguisher, her knuckles white, eyes darting through the shadows. A scuffle on the hardwood snapped John's head around.

"Mom, where are you going?"

"Hurt or not, I'm going to help protect this house," Bonnie said, her voice steel despite walking with a slight limp.

John watched, jaw tight, as she crept to the cabinet by the stairs, easing it open and pulling out a long-barreled shotgun, shells clutched in her trembling, bandaged hand.

He slid to the front room's picture window and nudged the curtains apart. His mouth fell open as he spied a pale yellow hatchback parked at the far end of the drive. Its shape and color were unmistakable, even in the moonlight.

The stolen car was here.

Wesley was here.

And his power to melt lives was aimed at them.

"It's the car Parnell mentioned. He's here," John hissed. "How did I not see that earlier?"

"We can't call for help without a phone line," Annaleigh whispered. "Did he give you a police radio or anything?"

"No, just the badge. And the gun, I guess. Didn't think to ask him for a full uniform and gear. Forget that for now. Everyone, center of the room, now," he ordered. "He can't burn us if he can't reach us."

Annaleigh pressed against him, their breathing synced in the dim light. Bonnie lingered by the cabinet, half-hidden in shadow.

"Mom, get over here next to us!"

A blinding flash erupted, like the noon sun swallowing the room. John flinched, arm shielding his eyes, pistol shaking in his grip. Annaleigh gasped beside him, her shoulder brushing his.

"Mom, kill the flashlight!" he shouted.

"It's not a flashlight. Drop the gun," a venomous voice sneered.

John squinted into the glare, his vision swimming as he raised the pistol toward the voice. The light dimmed enough for shapes to emerge.

A darkened shape loomed by the cabinet, its left arm locked around his mother. Her face was drained of color, and her eyes gaped wide with terror.

Bile rose inside John's throat as the blinding light softened, revealing the figure's cruel smirk and scarred face.

Wesley Raith.

His right hand glowed white-hot, clutching the shotgun's barrel. Its steel hissed under his grip.

John's grip on the pistol faltered as he stared at his mother, trapped in the killer's hold.

No. No!

Every instinct screamed to shoot, but Wesley's burning hand was too close, too deadly.

He needed another plan—and fast.

33

FIERY STANDOFF

John adjusted his fingers around the pistol's grip as he locked
eyes with Wesley. Until this moment, John had only ever seen
the aftermath of the Raith family's powers.

While it was true he'd felt their sting at City Hall through
Mayor Raith's burning grasp, he wasn't able to quite lay eyes on it
during his struggle to get free. In that moment, what had struck
John most was the man's wide-eyed flinch, his face twisting as if
the flames erupting from his hands had caught him off guard, too.
And, as if the flames were extremely painful to him.

The look on Wesley's face told a different story.

He relished the fire.

Wesley's right hand pulsed with a searing glow, the skin from
wrist to fingertip alive with molten light, as if his bones themselves
burned with an inner sun.

Tiny white flames exited his fingers, writhing and curling like
liquid starlight. With each of his ragged breaths, they flared, their
edges shimmering with prismatic hues—gold, violet, and a blue so
deep it seemed to drink the air.

With his left hand still wrapped around Bonnie, holding her
close, Wesley squeezed the shotgun's barrel with his right. The
steel groaned, softening like wax in a furnace. The metal surface

glowed white-hot near his hold before fading outward to a pink-ish-red.

The heat was a physical force. A low hum thrummed in John's chest from across the room, like the heartbeat of something ancient and merciless. Annaleigh, beside him, stood frozen, her eyes wide with the same horrified awe, as if staring into the heart of a star about to devour them all.

The room seemed to bend under the show of power. The air shimmered with waves that warped the outlines of furniture into surreal, trembling shapes.

John's skin prickled with the heat, yet he couldn't look away. The flames were beautifully horrible, a terrible symphony of light and destruction that mesmerized as it promised death.

With a sickening lurch, he understood how Gamble's flesh and bone had been consumed. The injuries to Deputy Hinkle and Detective Mumber had no longer been caused by some invisible force. That evil had materialized into the hands of this twenty-year-old monster.

The sight of it was unreal, almost beautiful, in its raw power. That is, if it weren't a heartbeat away from incinerating his mother.

Behind Wesley, he noticed the point of entry—the window he'd identified earlier. Found ajar during his security sweep, it now stood completely open.

The damn window. I was supposed to lock that... but then I took the Sheriff's phone call. Shit.

Warm sweat prickled his neck as he cursed his oversight. Wesley held his mother because of it.

"Do you think I'm playing, cool guy? I said... drop the gun," the young man repeated, his voice sharp with command. The light from his right hand surged, a white-hot blaze flaring in time with his rising anger.

"Let her go, Wesley," Annaleigh snapped. "She's got no part in this."

"None of this was even supposed to happen!" Wesley

shouted, his breath snorting. "Kenneth said one big scare would make you all back off. I was just doing what he told me!"

John's fingers twitched on the pistol's grip, not believing the hostage taker was trying to play the victim.

"Kenneth? The guy who ran off, like a coward? You're the last man standing, which means you're responsible for it all now. You don't owe him anything. Let her go and let's talk."

"I didn't want to hurt anyone." Wesley glanced at his hands. "I just get so angry sometimes, and then they just... take over. My dad said I needed to be like Uncle Ken, learn to control it—"

"We understand," Annaleigh said, her tone softening deliberately. "We know how commanding your dad could be."

"Don't talk about my dad!" Wesley shouted as his right hand erupted further into a blinding blaze. The shotgun's barrel warped and softened like heated clay, bending above his grip and, with a sharp crack, clanging to the floor.

"Okay, let's dial this back," John said, his voice low but firm, his eyes flicking over at Annaleigh.

"We're not doing this back and forth all night, dude. All I have to do is touch her. Just one time, and horrible things happen." Wesley released the melted stump of the shotgun, its thud on the singed floorboards echoing like a gavel. "That's how it's always been. It happened with Gamble and the old deputy. That detective, too. I did it to all of them."

John's mouth dropped. Annaleigh's face paled, her eyes wide with a mix of shock and fury. Her hands clenched, as if Gamble's memory—her mentor, her guide—had been ripped open. They knew he'd killed Deputy Hinkle and critically injured Detective Mumber during his escape from the station.

But Gamble, too?

It wasn't his father that did it, but him?

And, to confess to killing him, like an afterthought?

Annaleigh's hands trembled, her gaze locked on Wesley. A stance that told John that she was having trouble keeping it together.

Across the room, Bonnie's bandages glowed in the light from Wesley's right hand. Her voice quivered as she negotiated.

"Wesley, I knew your mama. Her name is Evelyn, right? She loved you fiercely, always bragging on you. She'd hate this. Let me go, honey, and we'll figure this out."

Wesley paused. His right hand dimmed, shrouding him and Bonnie in shadows. The room fell back to being lit only by the tabletop flashlight's beam, slicing toward the ceiling.

"Good move," John said, his voice low and steady. "I don't know what you call that fire in your hands, but turning it off is a good thing."

"It's a curse, that's what it is."

"I believe you. It's a curse," John said. "And curses are bad. We agree. So, let's not have it come back, okay? Let's talk about Gamble instead. You said you didn't mean it to happen. You didn't mean to kill him. Tell us what happened."

"I talk, and you can make all this go away?"

Annaleigh's jaw tightened, her eyes flashing with a fury John caught before she masked it with a practiced smile.

"Yes, Wesley," she said, her voice smooth but edged, each word a deliberate step on broken glass. "Tell us what happened, how it wasn't your fault. Don't hurt her, and I'll see what I can do."

She flicked her eyes to John, a silent signal that her offer was as thin as paper. They both knew someone had to answer for the chaos, and Wesley's name was at the top of the list.

"Promise?"

"Swear on my law degree," Annaleigh replied, her smirk strained, desperate to hide the venom for Doyal Gamble's true killer. "Your dad made me Acting County Prosecutor, Wesley. I decide who faces the music. Let her go. Now."

He pursed his lips, shaking his head. "I'll talk, but she stays where she is until I know what kind of deal I'm getting."

John steadied his breathing with a deep inhale.

The only deal you should get is a raw one.

He adjusted his aim, eyes darting for a clear shot to end this nightmare. Each time he thought he had an opening, either Wesley shifted his weight, unintentionally closing it, or a slight wriggle from his mother removed it.

If I shoot at him and miss, he'll kill her. Need to wait this out.

"Fine," said John, teeth gritted. "No sudden moves, though. Start talking. Give Annaleigh the info she needs."

He hated to capitulate to Wesley's demands, but he needed more time to formulate a plan to free his mom.

"I killed him, I don't know what more you want," Wesley muttered as a faint flicker of white flame sparked in his palm, then died. "It was an accident. He was at my house, yelling at my dad."

"That's a start," Annaleigh said, leaning forward slightly, eyes locked on him. "What were they arguing about?"

"Gamble wanted to go public about all my dad's stuff. He was tired of having to help cover it all up."

Annaleigh's eyes widened. "So, Gamble wasn't involved in any of it?" Her shoulders slumped, and she let out a long, shaky breath.

"No, lady, are you kidding? He was in it up to his eyeballs. They fought all the time about it. Kept threatening to quit. Gamble said he was done breaking the law. Wanted to turn a cheek, or whatever. He mentioned you, man. Something about wanting to be a better role model. I thought it was stupid."

For a brief second, John dipped the pistol before reacquiring his aim.

"Me? He mentioned me?"

"Yeah, I picked him up the night before, and they screamed at each other all night. I guess Dad locked him in because the idiot was still there the next morning. Trying and trying to negotiate his way out. That's when you came up." Wesley chuckled. "Like he could ever talk his way out, the loser. Well, Dad finally had enough and stormed out. Yelled at me to get Gamble out of his sight. You know, drive him back."

"Okay, so what happened next? On the ride home?" Annaleigh asked.

"He was quiet, looking out the window. Then, he started yapping. He was trying to convince me to turn on my dad, to talk to the Sheriff. When I refused, he flipped out. He called me an idiot who couldn't think for himself. I... was just so pissed."

Wesley's right hand burst back to life. White flames danced as he waved it erratically.

"Whoa, now," John pleaded. "Easy, Wesley. Easy."

"I grabbed his arm and started shaking him, telling him to take it back. I'm not an idiot! I make my own decisions! And, then..."

As quickly as the flames rose, they receded. Wesley lowered his hand, shoulders slumping.

"He started screaming. He reached for the door handle. I squeezed harder to stop him from getting out. I... I didn't realize... his arm... it came off in my hand. I swear didn't mean to!"

Annaleigh covered her mouth. "That's what happened to his arm?"

Silent tears trickled down Wesley's face. "Yeah, it came off. I almost puked. Lost control of the car. We veered into the woods. He jumped out and ran. I couldn't let him go. Couldn't let him tell anyone it was me." He dipped his head. "I chased him down. I swear, I was going to tell him to stop. I tripped over something, I don't know, a stick maybe, we both went down. I went to brace myself, but my hands... they landed on him. On his head... it happened so fast. Then, he stopped moving. His face. It was just... gone."

John stood speechless, the gun still trained on Wesley, but his mind reeled. Visions of Gamble's dripping, melted skull flooded his thoughts, a grotesque movie playing out as Gamble limped away, clutching the bloody stump of his arm, desperate to hold the blood in.

His mother's trembling form in Wesley's grip snapped him back, her safety the only thing keeping his finger off the trigger. He swallowed hard.

"We understand, Wesley," John said, trying to calm his voice,

"You didn't mean to kill him. We get that now. I'm going to lower the gun a bit. Then, I want you to let my mom go. We'll all sit down and talk this out. Okay?"

Annaleigh sidestepped to the far edge of the couch, her movement slow and subtle. Wesley stayed locked on John, giving no sign he'd seen her shift away. Without warning, his eyebrows dropped, his eyes darkening as he processed John's words.

"Are you still trying to give me orders? My dad said you were a lawyer, but now you have a gun? Like I could ever trust you." His right hand ignited again, a scorching white blaze flaring inches from Bonnie's face. "You killed my dad! Maybe I should pay you back the same way!"

"No!"

John's heart seized as he screamed, a cold jolt spiking through him as the flames danced too close for comfort to his mother's trembling cheek. Every muscle of John's screamed to act, but he remained frozen by the risk of a missed shot. He whipped the gun back up and slid to his right, attempting to expose more of a target.

Wesley twisted to his left, obstructing John's aim. In doing so, he unknowingly presented an opening from Annaleigh's vantage point. She feigned hiding and moved three large steps away from John. She and John now had triangulated Wesley's position. John's gaze never left those fiery hands as they hovered dangerously close to Bonnie's trembling form.

"Stop, Wesley! You don't want to do this!" His pleadings fell on deaf ears, so a different tactic was necessary. "How about this? Let's swap. I'll give you the truth about your dad," John said, his voice steady despite the sweat beading on his brow. "Then, you give me my mom."

He flicked a glance at Annaleigh, catching her grip on the extinguisher tucked behind her legs. Her faint nod told him she was ready.

"What truth? You killed him, I know it!" Wesley snapped, his voice cracking. "You're why he's gone!"

"No, Mumber told you what you needed to hear, but it's not the whole truth," John said, easing a step closer. "I was there, Wesley. I saw everything. Move your hand from her, and I'll tell you what happened. You owe it to yourself to know the *real* story."

Wesley took a deep breath and eased his glowing right hand away from the front of Bonnie's face, letting it hover over her shoulder and neck.

"Talk."

34

CLOUDED IN THE TRUTH

John watched as Wesley squeezed Bonnie, jerking his left arm towards his body. She winced.

He'd seen Wesley flinch whenever his father, the now ex-mayor of Coldwater, was mentioned. To free his mother, John had to find a way to utilize Wesley's reactions against him.

"The truth is," John started, slow and deliberate, "that we went to City Hall and bluffed your dad into an arrest."

Wesley's eyes narrowed.

"Nice try. My dad couldn't be conned into anything."

"It's true," John repeated, his voice steady despite the knot in his chest as he glanced at Bonnie, still pinned. He took another small step to his right. "We walked into his office and flashed a warrant for Kenneth, holding it far enough he couldn't read the name. Your dad folded right then and there. We started walking him to Sheriff Parnell's cruiser."

"That's a lie!" Wesley's right hand erupted further into flame, flooding the room with artificial white light. The thrumming intensified.

"When he heard over the radio that the deputies had you in custody, he bolted. I think he was afraid you'd talk, that you'd turn on him, just like Gamble wanted you to."

Wesley's hand threshed in the air, as if to swat away the accusations.

"No, no, no..."

"Your dad broke free at City Hall, hopped in his Blazer, and sped away. He flew through town and headed for the highway, trying to escape. But he went too fast, Wesley. He drove straight through the roundabout and crashed on the other side. We had nothing to do with it. He basically killed himself."

The light from Wesley intensified, then darkened with spurts of gray flame. John crept forward a step.

"When we looked inside, we saw what had happened. We found out how he lost control. The steering wheel was melted, Wesley. He destroyed his only way to escape. And you know what caused it? The same thing that you can do with your hands. He could do it, too."

"No! Liar! My dad doesn't have powers... only me and Uncle Ken." Wesley screamed, fighting back tears. "But I can do more than he can. My dad said I was special."

He raised his right hand, and it glowed bright white, illuminating the area. The gray streaks in his hands disappeared as his tone slowed.

"He made me teach people lessons. He made me melt things."

He reached across his body and pushed his right hand into the door of the wooden cabinet. The wood sizzled, and wisps of smoke floated upward. The smell of campfires filled the room. He lifted his palm, leaving behind a familiar-looking scorched brand in the shape of his hand.

With a flick of his wrist, the flames moved from his palm and flickered from his fingertips. He closed his hand into a fist, capturing the fire inside.

"He made me cut through things."

He stuck out his index finger and a single, thick blaze exited the tip, like a torch. He traced it down the wall, leaving a blackened slot. The edges of the wallpaper curled and fell, setting a small rug alight.

He pulled his finger back into his fist. He relaxed, and as he shook his hand, the fire disappeared. His skin, however, still glowed, like iron removed from a forge. He looked around and reached into the side chair behind him, grabbing a pillow.

"And, he made me burn things."

He scrunched the pillow in his hand. It ignited into a ball of fire. Wesley chucked it in John's direction, who spun to avoid it. It hit the floor and rolled up against the wall.

"Wesley, I'm telling the truth. I'll show you the evidence—the steering wheel he melted." John pointed at the brand etched into the cabinet. "And he made those same marks on the roof of his car during the crash. With both hands."

Wesley shook his head back and forth. "What? He did? No, no, no," he muttered.

"Here's some more proof," John continued. "At City Hall, before he ran, he grabbed me." He opened his shirt, exposing the bandages on his chest. He ripped off the gauze, showing his reddened, burned skin.

"Look at me! He did this. He burned me. The same thing you're doing right now to my mom. I'm telling you, he could do it, too."

"No!" Wesley had started to lose control. "Why would he hide that from me? Why?"

Wesley's words spilled out in a rushed, jumbled torrent. His eyes darted around the room, wild and unsteady. He was unraveling.

Wesley's left hand, which had been holding Bonnie, began to glow, matching his right. His face expressed surprise as the fire, which had been confined to only his hands, slowly crept up his forearms until they had reached his elbow. Bonnie screamed in pain, still trapped under Wesley's beaming arm.

"Mom!" John shouted, contorting himself to find a clean shot.

Both of the boy's arms shot into the air, trembling. The muscles in his arms tensed and quivered, as if struggling to contain some unseen force. In the commotion, Bonnie hobbled over to Annaleigh, finally free of restraint.

Amidst the flickering fires that had sprung up around the room, a soft, ethereal light began to emanate from Wesley's palms, casting a haunting glow over his contorted and scarred features. The air around his hands shimmered and undulated as white-hot flames licked hungrily at the darkness that surrounded him. A pulsating hum filled everyone's ears.

Wesley's eyes widened, his face twisting as if true pain had found him for the first time. The blaze at his fingertips crackled, surging like they had a life of their own, and John tensed, unsure what was driving the reaction. He wanted to shoot, but couldn't quite understand what was unfolding.

"No!" Wesley shouted, between grunts. "I don't believe you! It can't be true!"

Wesley's breathing grew ragged and labored as the storm of emotions within him reached its peak. The energy that coursed through his veins fed on his rage, transforming into something primal and uncontrolled.

The white-hot flames that had danced at his fingertips burst into a malevolent orange blaze, solidifying into a plasma-like substance, dripping from his hands. Each shuddering breath intensified the color. Heat distorted the air around him, as if reality itself was warping under the sheer force of his anger.

Wesley's wide eyes narrowed into slits, glinting like molten gold in the orange glow. The light cast a sinister hue over the room, bathing the horrified faces of John, Annaleigh, and Bonnie in its diabolical glow.

Annaleigh's grip tightened on the fire extinguisher. Her eyes locked onto Wesley's blazing hands. John recoiled. He had approached Wesley and the flames too closely and was now paying the price. Shielding himself with his arms, he caught the tension in her stance as he locked eyes with her for a split second.

She took action.

She aimed the nozzle at Wesley and pressed her thumb on the

trigger, engulfing him and plunging the room into a cloud of white foam. Smoldering bits of rug, wallpaper, and curtains were snuffed out. The orange flames that had erupted from Wesley's hands sputtered and died, altering the room into an eerie scene. The hum vanished, and the living room fell still. Powder drifted through the air and settled onto everything. The unearthly quiet was like the eye of a hurricane.

"Mom, you okay?" John asked, pointing the barrel in sporadic directions as he lost sight of Wesley.

Before she could answer, a low rumble began, freezing everyone in place. It grew until it was as if a freight train had driven into the living room.

From within the foam, Wesley's flames reignited, surging back to life with a vengeance. His silhouette emerged from the dissipating cloud, his hands and arms once again ablaze with a blinding orange light.

Wesley advanced on Annaleigh, staggering, each step punctuated by the crackle of the flames that danced at his fingertips. The orange blaze roared up his arms, now reaching his shoulders. His face bent and shook, as if the fire itself was burning him from the inside.

John's grip tightened on the revolver, its weight heavy in his trembling hands. His finger hovered over the trigger, but his mind stalled. He'd only been a deputy for a few hours. Parnell pinned a badge on him like a rushed afterthought, only because he'd run out of employees. Law school hadn't taught him how to shoot a regular man, let alone a dragon.

At Parnell's range, targets were plywood, not flesh. What if he missed? He could hit Annaleigh or his mother.

One bullet might not stop Wesley's flames. Should he empty the clip? Parnell's only order echoed in his head.

Protect Annaleigh.

He hadn't prescribed how, though. He'd given the order for Clyde to shoot on sight. Did that extend to everybody? Was he diving into a pool of legal jeopardy even pointing this gun? The multitude of thoughts swirling around paralyzed him.

Sweat stung John's eyes as Wesley took another step, the hum of his power deafening, like a tornado roaring through the room.

The semi-automatic pistol wavered in John's grip, his heart hammering. He couldn't think, couldn't move, frozen by the thought of blood, of failure, and of losing everything.

Annaleigh threw the spent extinguisher can at Wesley. It warped mid-air, before being caught and melting like wax. It crashed into pieces on the floor. She stumbled back into Bonnie.

Wesley's white fire caused Gamble's injuries. Those terrifying, horrible, fatal injuries.

That fire was confined to his hands. These orange flames looked worse. Solid and unstoppable.

And burning from fingertip to shoulder.

It was time to end this.

Time to shoot.

But his finger wouldn't move.

His entire body locked up.

Annaleigh's voice cut through the pandemonium.

"Shoulder!"

35

EXPLOSIVE ENTRANCE

John's world slowed. Each heartbeat pounded in his ears. Sweat trickled into his eyes, stinging.

He drew a deep breath to steady himself. The pistol in his clammy hands burned against his skin from the waves of rolling heat. Annaleigh's desperate shout pierced the chaos and snapped him loose, taking him back to that hidden shooting range outside Coldwater.

Parnell had dragged him there, growling, "I don't trust a man till I see him shoot."

As ordered, John hit the targets, shot after shot. "Center mass," Parnell had shouted. "Head," he'd barked. Each command sharpened his aim, forging a bond that wound up with him being deputized and given his first mission. He had later shared the experience with Annaleigh and recounted every detail.

"So, if I call out a word, like 'kneecap,' you'll just shoot someone there? No questions asked?" she'd asked, toying with him.

"I mean, sure, I guess so," he replied, shrugging. "It's not like I'm a robot or anything, but I guess he way he shouted where to aim helped to get me out of my head and focus, you know?"

Her voice now, sharp as Parnell's, jolted him back. Adrenaline surged, steadying his grip, the revolver's weight forgotten.

Shoulder.

He aimed and squeezed the trigger. Accounting for the recoil and the swinging of the target, he pulled again.

Two hollow-point bullets ripped through the superheated air in John's living room and lodged deep into Wesley's left shoulder. The impact spun him around, and he collapsed to the floor, arms out wide, hands still ablaze. The noise stopped.

John lowered the pistol, a flicker of guilt spiking through him. He'd never shot a man before. His hands trembled as the weight of the act sank in. Had he become a protector or just another one of Coldwater's killers?

A short glance at Annaleigh's relieved face showed that he'd done the right thing. He raced to his mother and her, pulling them to their feet.

"Quick, let's go. We need to get out of here!"

"John, wait," Annaleigh said, pointing at Wesley's prone body. "Look at his hands, they're still on fire. Why wouldn't they go out?"

"Probably because he's not dead, just unconscious. That's why you yelled 'shoulder', I assume. That whole 'no bullets justice' thing?"

"Yeah, but the extinguisher put out the fire, right? I would've thought being unconscious should do that, too."

"I don't know how the math works, Annaleigh. Forget it. He's down, we need to go. Help me get her outside..."

An ear-piercing shriek shattered the air.

John's head snapped toward Wesley's crumpled form. He had begun to press up onto all fours, scorching hand-shaped marks into the wooden floor.

Wesley's flames burned brighter as he rose, his huffing screams raw with pain. Orange bursts pulsed, and blood streamed from his wounded shoulder, mixing at his wrist into a lava-like drip that hissed on impact. His gut-wrenching cries reverberated through the room as he stumbled towards John, hands out, fingers splayed, dripping flames.

John raised the gun again, ready to fire.

The front door frame splintered as Clyde kicked inward and rushed in, his face pale, eyes wide and locked on Wesley. The deputy lifted his service weapon and aimed.

"Wesley! I don't know what this is, but stop, son! Don't make me shoot!"

Wesley whipped his head, grunting and panting at the new entrant to the battle.

John eyed the aim of his weapon, his mind racing. Clyde's entrance had trapped them in a deadly line, with Wesley's flames centered between them.

John's relief at Clyde's arrival clashed with dread that a single misstep could still cost his mother and Annaleigh everything. Every lesson from law school and every promise to Parnell screamed at him to act, but his body refused. With Wesley's attention divided, he extended an arm and tried to usher the women out of the line of fire.

Wesley's face twisted with anger. In a blur, he lunged at the deputy, hands blazing.

"Clyde! Move!"

Remembering Sheriff Parnell's shoot-to-kill order, John shouted his warning and dove to the side. Shots rang out as he was mid-air. Clyde reacted quicker than he believed possible, squeezing off multiple rounds.

The first one found its mark, disappearing into Wesley's right upper pectoral, causing him to recoil and contort, twisting away from the impact. The second lodged into his gut, and he hunched over in pain. Wesley's movement caused the third shot to miss, punching into the wall inches from where John's head would have been.

On the way to the ground, John's hand banged against the

coffee table, knocking the gun out of his hands. It bounced and clattered into the kitchen, out of reach.

Panic surged. Without it, he was defenseless against Wesley's flames if Clyde's shots weren't able to stop the madness.

Wesley staggered. Blood seeped from his bullet wounds. He gritted his teeth and charged the deputy with a roar.

He slammed his hands into Clyde's chest with a powerful shove. John winced, hearing the sizzle of burning flesh and Clyde's screams. The impact hurled Clyde backwards through the door. He stumbled across the porch and down the two steps onto the gravel. As he fell, his shirt ignited, and flames devoured the fabric as he writhed, clawing at it.

Wesley stood in the doorway, his chest heaving as he watched Clyde scramble on the front lawn, trying to extinguish the fire. Seemingly content he'd reduced the threat by one, he spun back, his gaze surveying the powder-coated room.

He stumbled back into the house, his charred hands trembling, a low groan escaping his lips. He clutched at his bullet-torn shoulders as roasted blood dripped from his hands.

As he touched his own skin, the flames seared his wounds with a hiss. His face twisted, and the stench of burning flesh choked the air. His shirt ignited, and in a stroke of irony, fire now threatened to devour Wesley's chest. He tore at the tatters, revealing old burn scars crisscrossing his torso, matching his withered cheek.

Those scars screamed of past fires and held memories of Wesley's white blaze. The orange infernos burning on him blistered fiercer, as if Wesley hadn't anticipated their bite. Wesley arched back, a primal scream ripping from his throat.

A thunderous hum roared, shaking John's bones. The orange fire surged again, moving down from his elbows, consolidating solely into his hands, and erupting into a blaze of lava-red fire.

Bright red flames rippled from Wesley's fingers, melting his skin and dripping onto the floor.

He stared, unblinking.

He was beyond pain now.

John's heart seized, his empty hands useless to perform his mission.

Wesley's chin dipped, and his bloody grin taunted John.

He turned and lunged at Annaleigh.

36

EXPLOSIVE EXIT

Wesley charged, stretching out his hands as red flames dripped from his fingers like wax.

John's pulse thundered in his ears. He'd had enough of the stench of charred flesh. It was time to end this.

Skidding across the hardwood, he popped up onto one knee and caught Wesley by his forearms, bending them back to avoid being touched. John's muscles strained to hold back the searing heat.

Though Wesley's new fire had merged back into just his hands, the skin on his forearms was still scorching. It was like a living being, pressing back into John's palms, threatening to blister his grip. Face contorted with fury, Wesley shoved hard against John's hold.

"You're gonna burn! Everything's gonna burn!" he shouted, his voice raw with venom.

Lava-like flames danced inches from John's face. Blood seeped from Wesley's bullet wounds, staining his tattered shirt. Yet, his strength didn't falter, as if some primal force drove him forward.

John's shoes pressed into the floor to find leverage. Gaining a foothold, he shoved the enraged and weakened Wesley back, pinning him against the oak coffee table. The wood smoked and blackened with the drippings of Wesley's hands, forcing John to yank him away before the flames spread further.

His foot slipped, and John found himself back in the same position he'd started in. Kneeling, he pressed upwards on Wesley's forearms, balancing the downwards force Wesley exerted. John's knees wobbled, his vision blurring as the heat seared his eyes, but he locked his elbows, refusing to let Wesley's hands reach him. His palms, slick with sweat and Wesley's blood, made his grip precarious.

He tightened his hold, grinding his thumbs into Wesley's hot skin. The heat pulsed like a heartbeat, each wave hotter than the last. His lungs ached with every shallow breath as the room's air turned to ash.

Wesley surged forward with a burst of adrenaline. A jarring roar tore from his throat, and his hands inched closer. John could almost feel the skin on his cheeks tightening, shrinking from the threat of those molten fingers.

He's going to burn me alive.

The horrible thought sliced through John's mind, sharp as a blade. He shoved back, shoulders burning, wrists trembling under the strain. The room seemed to close in, the walls flickering with the growing glow of flames.

As the men struggled, another evolution occurred.

The room erupted into a maelstrom of heat and light as Wesley's hands became fiery conduits of destruction.

Flares shot upward from his outstretched fingertips, setting the ceiling, curtains, furniture, and anything else in their path, ablaze. Annaleigh smothered Bonnie with her body to avoid the onslaught. Fires sprang up around the room, casting a hellish glow.

Satan would have been proud.

John squinted, ducking under the fireworks and trying to maintain his balance. He wasn't sure how much longer he could last. If the searing heat from Wesley's hands didn't do him in, the fires springing to life behind him would.

Wesley's eyes widened, tears streaming down his cheeks, catching the fire's red glow as he glared at John.

Flashbacks of Gamble's crime scene flittered around him.

Will it hurt? Will I feel it when my face melts into my brain? Maybe it'll only hurt for a split second. At least, until my nerve endings are scorched. Or, maybe I'll feel every bit of it.

Just as John's hands started to slip, the hum abruptly stopped. Silence swallowed the room.

The momentary stillness was broken by a throaty rasp exiting Wesley's mouth. He shrieked and stumbled back from John, trembling as he stared at his hands.

A thunderous detonation tore through the air as Wesley's hands exploded, unleashing a shockwave, followed by a devastating torrent of power and debris.

Blood and bone fragments blasted into John's face as Wesley, in shock, staggered and dropped to his knees. He raised his arms in front of his face and began sobbing, revealing two stumps that spewed blood.

His wrists flashed with light, as if he were activating his power. Miniature flames spat and whistled as they cauterized his wounds. Wesley's eyes rolled back into his head, and he collapsed like a rag doll.

John fell back, momentarily blinded, as comforting hands gripped his shoulders, steadying him. Annaleigh's arms wrapped around him.

"I got you, partner." She helped John to his feet.

"Everybody out, let's go," he panted.

They exited the house over the splintered remains of the front door. His hands, helping to stabilize his mother, trembled from the burns blistering his skin. Once onto the porch, he glanced back with blood-stained eyes.

"Go, I'll be right behind you," he shouted. "I can't leave him."

She shot him a sharp glance but didn't argue, pulling Bonnie toward the cool evening air. They stumbled out against the flickering glow. He gulped a clean breath, a fleeting relief against the smoke searing his throat. He retreated into a room swallowed by flames that danced like malevolent spirits.

If I leave him, he burns. No trial. And no justice.

After everything he'd confessed to, he couldn't let Wesley escape accountability. Coughing, eyes streaming with blood and water, he grabbed Wesley by the ankles and hauled him across the scorching floor. The young man was dead weight, unconscious, his face pale as ash.

John emerged moments later, dragging Wesley's limp body onto the lawn, far from the inferno's grasp. He released his ankles, dropping them to the ground with two distinct thuds. He tilted his head back and drew a slow, deep breath.

"You owe me, you little shit," he said to Wesley's barely breathing body.

John wobbled toward Clyde, stretched out nearby, motionless. Underneath his tattered and sleeveless white undershirt, Clyde's chest sported a patchwork of raw, red burns. Smoldering pieces of his once pristine uniform lay scattered around him. John dropped to his knees, lungs burning, hands throbbing.

"Clyde, you with me?" he rasped, searching the deputy's face for signs of life.

Clyde's kind eyes fluttered, half-open, glazed with pain.

"I guess it really is summer in Coldwater, boomerang," he mumbled, voice faint. "'Cuz it's hotter than hell right now."

John managed a shaky grin.

"Cussing don't make you cool, deputy."

"I already told you, young man... call me Clyde."

John smiled, and relief washed over him as he gripped the deputy's hand in a palmy handshake. Clyde's lips twitched weakly.

"You kicked that door down and took on Wesley to save us. You said you never had a son. Well, I never had a dad. With what you did in there for us, you're part of the family now. Clyde."

"Family, huh?" he whispered, voice rough but warm. "I'll take it. Now that you're finally calling me Clyde, maybe one day I'll tell you what my first name is..." He fell back, exhaustion winning.

"One name at a time, alright? Hang in there, help's on the way," John said, his throat tight. The words were heavier than he expected.

John staggered to where Bonnie and Annaleigh sat in the grass. He collapsed between them, his arms heavy on his knees. Pain surged through his hands and wrists as the adrenaline faded, revealing angry, throbbing burns.

He surveyed the wreckage of his childhood home. A good chunk of the front was a pyre with flames reaching into the night sky. Blood caked his face, sticky and foreign, a grim mask signifying Wesley's defeat.

"We're all alive," John muttered, half to himself. "Can't believe it."

Bonnie peered at him, her bandaged face quivering.

"John, your face. It looks gruesome."

He managed a dry chuckle.

"I'm coated in someone else's blood, Mom. I'm sure it's a charming look."

"Here." She unwound a strip of her bandage, hands unsteady, and dabbed at his eyes. "Not perfect, but better." She leaned in, her embrace warm despite the shaking. "Thank you, John. Not only for tonight, but for coming back to Coldwater. I'd be lost without you."

Annaleigh leaned on him from the other side, looking at him with a soot-covered face.

"He's right, Bonnie. If John hadn't come home, we'd all be ashes. My hero, the Deputy Counselor."

John's lips twitched, a ghost of a smile. Guilt gnawed at him, heavier than the burns.

"There's still one to go, Mom. Kenneth did this to you, and he's still out there. I'm not stopping until he's in cuffs."

Bonnie's smile was faint, strained through her bandages.

"John, we'll worry about that later. But, honey, your eyes. Do they feel okay? They look... different. Lighter, like green embers. They're almost glowing."

*　*　*

SHERIFF PARNELL's black cruiser skidded to a stop on the gravel drive, kicking up dust and leading the charge of first responder vehicles. He leapt out, his eyes scanning the chaos, lingering on Wesley's unconscious form sprawled in the grass, blood pooling beneath his shattered stumps.

Paramedics swarmed, barking orders as they triaged the wounded. Wesley, after being hoisted onto a gurney, was shackled at the ankles.

Parnell checked on Clyde, then strode over to Annaleigh and Bonnie. John, who sat slumped between them, wiped at his stinging eyes. The sheriff knelt, his weathered hand patting John on the shoulder.

"Wish I'd gotten here sooner, son."

John squinted, his eyes burning as he rubbed them again.

"I know how I look, but Clyde took the worst of it. Is he gonna be all right?"

"Probably will sport a few more scars than he had yesterday, but he's tough," Parnell said. "You did good, Deputy Chance."

Annaleigh nudged John, her voice sharp but fond.

"Don't let him play humble, Sheriff. Without John, we'd be cinders in that house."

She jerked her thumb toward the blaze, where firefighters battled roaring flames. Parnell's eyes crinkled with pride.

"Of course I picked the right man. Never had a doubt. Besides a long shower to wash off that mess, need anything else?"

John blinked hard, his vision blurring, the sting in his eyes worsening.

"Know a good eye doc?"

Parnell chuckled. "We'll get you fixed up, no worries." He left to manage the scene, barking orders and sending more assistance Clyde's way.

A paramedic approached John, wiping the crusted blood from his face with a damp cloth. They bandaged John's scorched hands, giving him a set of matching wrappings similar to Bonnie's. Together, they looked like a pair of mummified survivors. The paramedic urged a hospital visit for all three, then moved on.

Annaleigh rested her head against John, her breath warm against his neck.

"You good?"

"Barely," he muttered, still pawing at his eyes. "You?"

"Same. But I swear I'll never say the 's' word again. It's too powerful."

He frowned, wincing as his eyes throbbed.

"The what word?"

She leaned closer, whispering, "Shoulder."

John snorted, a tired grin breaking through.

"With all these folks around? I'd need a damn arsenal to shoot that many. Besides, center mass is easier. Remember that for next time, okay?"

"First, I hope there isn't a next time. Second—"

"How many of these do you have?"

She slapped his arm as he winced. "Second, don't freeze, and I won't have to shout at you, anyway. Besides, no heartbeat, no justice, remember? I said 'shoulder' on purpose." Annaleigh's tease turned mock-stern. "And, for the record, this isn't a win for your first case. We're lawyers, not whatever this was. Next time, we'll settle it in court. Then, it'll count."

"Objection," John shot back, his voice dry, eyes itching. "Badgering, argumentative, and assumes facts not in evidence."

"Us being lawyers isn't a fact?"

"Nope, not until you help me study for the bar. My objection is sustained. A win's a win, courtroom or not."

"You can't sustain your own objection, John."

"I can if Judge Chapel deputized me while you weren't looking. You didn't know I'm also a judge now?"

"You hear that, Bonnie? Your son's a triple threat now."

"Too bad he still probably won't make breakfast for us, dear. Never had a judge burn my waffles, though. First time for everything."

The women shared a tired laugh.

He rubbed his eyes again. The world smeared into a haze. Annaleigh's face blurred, though her concern was clear.

"John, you're messing with your eyes a lot. Are you okay?"

His heart lurched as darkness swallowed his sight.

"No. I can't see a damn thing."

37

DUST SETTLES

A few weeks after the chaos that rocked Coldwater, Missouri, the town rallied for a special election to reclaim its future.

The new mayor, a hardware store owner with a handshake as steady as his reputation, pledged to rebuild trust in a government tarnished by the Raith family's schemes. Annaleigh Stanton was swept into the Prosecuting Attorney's office by a landslide and stood poised to carve out corruption with surgical precision. Her campaign platform honored her late boss, Doyal Gamble, by vowing to uproot the weeds he'd left behind.

Outside the courthouse, the town square exhaled.

Shopkeepers swapped tales of crop prices instead of the downfall of the prior mayor. The Raith property, home to their family since the 1890s, now sported a "For Sale" sign. Their legacy was permanently tarnished, fading across the clay hillsides like a bad dream.

Annaleigh stood next to Gamble's desk and hefted the antique lamp. Its brass base glinted as she set it onto a small table in the corner of his old office.

"Town's settling down," she said, brushing her hands. "No more Raith whispers in every diner booth."

"Except for that fire-god nonsense," John drawled, slouching in a side chair, a smirk tugging his lips. "Folks swear Wesley torched the Sheriff's Office with a single glance and that Kenneth's out there, sparking wildfires by blinking."

"We haven't had any wildfires, John."

"Oh, I know. What would it take to change the name of this place to Crazywater."

She snorted, shaking her head.

"We'll set the record straight, but gently. No sense stirring panic over fairy tales." Her voice softened, eyes distant. "Speaking of Wesley, heard he's settled in prison, awaiting trial. Somebody has to spoon-feed him meals now, apparently. It's kind of sad."

"He's lucky to be breathing," John shot back, arms crossing. "He got what he deserved, and he's where he belongs. Parnell's got half the county plastered with wanted posters for Kenneth. That manhunt's keeping him up at night." He paused, voice quieter. "Me, too."

"Anything I can do to help? If you're staying up at night, might as well be for a good reason. This town has no shortage of peach wine."

A playful wink flickered as she leaned against the desk. John's cheeks warmed, and he shifted in his seat.

He glanced at Genie, sitting just outside the doorway, and cleared his throat. He stood and hoisted the final banker's box of Gamble's belongings.

"That's it," he said, the words heavy with finality. "This office is 100% yours now, Annaleigh."

The corner office of the Prosecuting Attorney of Coldwater had been stripped bare, save for a faded Missouri map on the wall. On it, Coldwater County's borders were traced in royal blue.

No ego wall for her.

Zero framed photos with bigwigs and hollow handshakes. Not because she didn't have any. Rather, her intent was crystal clear. Her focus was the fair application of justice within her jurisdiction, not seeking fame or fortune outside of it.

"It'll take getting used to," she murmured, eyes tracing the empty desk. "Gamble sat here for a long time."

"That seat could be yours for even longer, if you wanted," He flashed a half-smile as he set the box down. "I can see that nameplate saying 'Attorney General' someday."

Her lips curved, holding back a bigger smile. "Maybe, at least until then, I get my chance to convince you to stay here. With me." She darted forward, planting a kiss on his cheek.

John froze, then grinned, adjusting his tie to mask the flush creeping up his neck.

"Well, until I leave, got plans for your old office?" he asked, nodding toward it. "It's empty now, and I'm probably due for an upgrade, you know, based on my recent performance. Instead of *all the way* across the bullpen, we could be closer neighbors."

"John, no offense, but you've been here for five minutes," she teased, laughing. "Let's wait until you can argue a case before I hand you a promotion. Unless you're trying to dodge being out here with Genie."

"Can't escape the glitter," Genie called, her voice muffled from the bullpen. "Once you've got me, I'm around forever. Can't shake me."

They stepped into the bullpen, peering around the corner where Genie Glitter sat at her desk, filing her nails with practiced efficiency. John waved his hands, surrendering.

"Genie, I would never say such a thing. You're my secret weapon."

Annaleigh handed her a small box. "Not just John's secret weapon, all of ours. This is for you, Genie."

Her eyes lit up as she tore it open, revealing a polished nameplate, etched with "Genie Glitter."

"Oh, sugar, you shouldn't have!" she crowed, tossing her old, sticky-note-crusted nameplate into a drawer with a flourish. The name 'Eugenia Johnson' occupied a proper home, upside down and behind boxes of old pens. Exactly the way Genie wanted it.

John chuckled, catching Annaleigh's amused glance. He sank

into his desk chair, rubbing his temple. Annaleigh perched on the edge, her voice softening.

"You've been seeing the eye doctor a lot lately. Any progress?"

"Tests are inconclusive," he said, reclining. "My sight's back and the shadows are still there, like always. But sometimes, I see wisps of light, like I'm seeing Wesley's hands on fire. Hard to explain. She's stumped, but she's planning a paper on me. Says I'm some kind of medical mystery."

"Better a mystery than a tragedy," Annaleigh teased, though concern flickered in her eyes.

"She also asked me to let you know that she's getting closer to finding an answer as to why all this happened."

"Other than greed and corruption by the most powerful family in Coldwater?"

"Yeah, besides that. She's talking about Wesley's blood. She's been running tests on it. Swears she can find a scientific reason someone could conjure fire. I'll believe it when I see it."

"Well, we all saw it, John. Don't know about you, but I'm not so sure I want to see it again."

He rolled his eyes. "You know what I meant, Annaleigh."

She leaned closer, voice brightening. "I know. And, speaking of knowing what I meant... I was teasing earlier, but that assistant's office *is* empty. It might be that way for a while, who knows? If you were to stay in Coldwater, make a name for yourself, it could be yours in no time. We make a hell of a team, John."

His grin widened, her words sinking in.

"You don't know how tempting that is, but St. Louis is only an hour and a half away. I'll be back every weekend, I promise. Besides, we've got five months until that happens. Plenty of time."

She raised an eyebrow, her smile sly. "Five whole months? Fine. You'll be begging to stay by then. In fact, I'm not signing off on your bar exam prep if you don't at least think about staying."

"Deal," John said, matching her grin.

Genie's nail file clattered to the floor, her sequined shirt jingling as she bent to retrieve it. "Storms make trees take deeper roots, darlin'," she said, resuming her manicure. "Maybe your roots belong here."

"Genie," John said, head tilted, "does Mr. Glitter know you're talking about another man's roots?"

Laughter rang through the bullpen, as bright as the new day dawning over Coldwater.

38

CROSSROADS CALL

A pair of loud footsteps climbed the stairs, causing all heads in the upstairs courthouse office to turn. Sheriff Dane Parnell strode in, cheeks high from a smile hidden underneath his mustache. In his hands, he carried a glass pan and spoke with his signature drawl.

"Cherry cobbler, the best dessert my wife makes, and trust me, she makes a lot of 'em. She's got a thing about baking stuff for people. Probably got it from this old bird over here," he said, thumbing in the general direction of Genie.

"Old bird, eh? Aw, Sheriff, I'd say you're sweet, but then Mr. Glitter might get mad at me for lying, you know?" Genie grinned playfully and waved him off with her hand.

"Yes, ma'am." He tipped his wide-brimmed hat at Annaleigh, then he took it off, setting it on an empty desk. His focus fell on John.

"Son, I got no updates on the search for Kenneth after his escape, but that's not why I'm here. I gotta say, you've done a damn fine job in a very short amount of time. The way you analyzed the crash scene and had my back at the station," he said, his voice filled with admiration.

"Look, I didn't see much lawyering going on, but I think

you'd make one hell of an investigator. You have some kind of way with visualizing how things happen. That thinking could do a lot of good in my line of work."

John straightened in his chair, caught off guard by the Sheriff's unexpected praise.

"To that end," Parnell continued, "I'd like to offer you a position with the Special Investigations Division. Hollis is gonna be laid up for a while. If and when he comes back, he's been talking about retiring, anyway. You'd make a fine replacement, and I'd be proud to have you as my detective."

John's mind reeled at Parnell's words. He'd never really considered a career in law enforcement, but the proposition was tantalizing.

His fascination with the law had sprouted at an early age, woven into the fabric of his childhood memories. During games of 'cops and robbers,' John, regardless of his role, would eagerly wait for the moment when the robber was apprehended. With a quiet confidence, he would approach the captured robber, a gleam of determination in his eye, and offer his services as a defense attorney in their makeshift tree house court.

Out on the front lines, deputized and carrying a weapon, he finally possessed the proactive power to protect the ones he loved. There was something familiar about it, but he couldn't quite put his finger on it.

"Sheriff, wow, thank you for saying that. I'm not sure what to say."

"Say you'll think about it, at least. You don't have to answer now. I'll bet Ms. Stanton will want to provide you with some sage advice." He winked.

The shrill tone of the phone on John's desk knifed through the office. He answered, his eyes widening in surprise as he listened to the voice on the other end.

"No, really, you're kidding?" he asked, his voice filled with disbelief. "Oh... I apologize. I mean, yes, sir, thank you so much for letting me know."

Annaleigh and the Sheriff exchanged glances, sensing the sudden shift in John's demeanor. After a few moments, he hung up, his mind racing.

"That was the St. Louis prosecutor's office," he said. "The trial that was supposed to last until the end of the year? It's over. The defendant, who swore he was innocent, confessed and took a deal. The line prosecutor on the case retired on the spot. Can you believe it?" John rubbed his lips with his hand, then shrugged. "The job. It's ready. And it's mine... if I want it. They said they want to fill it soon, though."

Annaleigh's smile faltered for a split second, her eyes flickering with something he couldn't quite place—hesitation, maybe, or something heavier.

"John, that's fantastic news," she said, her voice catching slightly, thinner than usual. "You deserve this opportunity. You've done so much for Coldwater already."

Parnell stared, shifting his glance between Annaleigh and Genie.

"He's really still thinking about leaving town?" he asked, incredulity clear in his tone. They shrugged in response. John shifted uncomfortably.

"Look, this is what I've been working toward for a long time," he admitted. "I started this job knowing it was only temporary. I think there's a lot of possibility up there for me... in a few different ways."

Parnell leaned in, giving him a gentle, fatherly pat on the back. His voice dropped to a near-whisper as he eyed Annaleigh.

"There's a lot of possibility for you here, son. I'm talking about *outside the courthouse,* if you catch my drift."

Genie's voice cut through the silence like a ray of sunshine, her southern twang bringing a smile to everyone's face.

"Now y'all, I gotta get in on this," she drawled, her tone equal parts playful and sincere. "John, I offer you my job, too. Only if it means I can retire and bake pies all day. Lord knows, I've been itching to open a little shop."

The tension eased as Annaleigh and the Sheriff chuckled, grateful for her lighthearted intervention. A wave of laughter came from all four. John spoke through a grin.

"Genie, you'd be an amazing baker. Maybe that's your true calling, who knows. I respectfully decline. There's no way I could manage a docket quite like you do."

Genie winked, her eyes twinkling with mischief.

"I like to think I've got a few callings, sugar. Right now, my calling is telling you to go with your gut. We'll be here for you, no matter what."

John leaned back, a determined look on his face.

"Sheriff, I'm truly grateful for the offer," he said, steady and sincere. "I'm honored you think so highly of me. Could I ask for a bit of time to consider it?"

"Take all the time you need, son."

* * *

LATER THAT EVENING, John sat at the scarred oak table in Bonnie's cramped kitchen, the only first-floor room in her house untouched by the chaos of their little encounter with Wesley.

New plywood patched the kicked-in front door, a combined effort of both John and Clyde. The living room's charred walls bore fresh spackle and primer, though the acrid scent of smoke lingered like a stubborn guest.

Bonnie, his mother and Coldwater's fiercest realtor, poured coffee into a chipped mug, her eyes sharp despite the late hour and the stack of repair invoices piled beside her real estate flyers.

"So, John," she said, settling across from him, "I hear you're in quite the pickle. Three paths, three different choices. Stick with Annaleigh, play detective with Parnell, or take your talents to St. Louis. I know what my answer is for you, but what's your instinct say?"

John's gaze drifted to the plastic sheeting taped by the doorway, rustling in the evening breeze.

"St. Louis has been the plan since law school. Big cases, real prestige. I never saw myself settling here. But..." He thought of Annaleigh. "Part of me feels like I belong here... with her." He shook off the thought. "Even if I did want to stay, I *have* to go, Mom. That's where I'll find dad."

Bonnie's face tightened, her usual spark dimming.

"I'd be able to dig through records, track him down. I love you, but I need to know who he is, where he went, and why he left."

She set her mug down with a deliberate clink, the sound sharp against the hum of a contractor's fan drying paint in the next room.

"Honey, I can't keep this from you anymore. Your father isn't in St. Louis."

Her voice held steady, but her eyes carried a weight John hadn't seen before.

"He's still here. In Coldwater. He never left."

39

DOORWAY DILEMMA

John approached the wooden gate with a lightness in his step, his stomach fluttering like a moth caught in a jar. On his first visit to Annaleigh's cottage, he brought with him good news. The gift he concealed was the most appropriate way he knew to celebrate it.

The bright yellow door gleamed against the evening sun as John paused halfway up the sidewalk, savoring the anticipation. His feelings for Annaleigh radiated within him.

He pressed the doorbell, tucking both arms behind him, a grin tugging at his lips. The door swung open, and she appeared, her brow creasing in confusion before softening with surprise.

"John? Fancy meeting you here. Since when do you know where I live?"

"My mom sold you this place," he said, a mischievous glint in his eyes. "I've known this whole time. Been holding onto your address, waiting for the right moment to show up."

Annaleigh pursed her lips. "Coming from anyone else, that'd sound pretty creepy."

John revealed a bouquet of wildflowers from behind his back.

"For you," he said, his grin widening. "I helped you move

offices, but never really congratulated you on the election. You're the real deal now, Counselor."

Her cheeks flushed as she took the flowers, her smile as warm as the Missouri dusk.

"Thanks, although I wouldn't have won without you. Or, maybe even be here at all."

"Coldwater's lucky to have you, Annaleigh. You're a hell of a prosecutor." He pulled his other hand forward, revealing a bottle of peach wine. "And, *this* is for what's next."

Annaleigh's laughter rang out, bright and unguarded.

"Peach wine? Does this mean you're finally spilling your decision?"

"Absolutely, and I want you to be the first to know," John said, stepping closer. "Can I come in?"

She stepped aside, her hand brushing his shoulder, a lingering touch that sent a spark through him. He followed her inside, and the yellow door clicked shut behind them.

In the soft glow of Annaleigh's living room, where lamplight coated modern furniture, John set the bottle on a side table next to a stack of crooked magazines.

"I'm staying in Coldwater," he said, eyes catching hers. "Mom dropped a bombshell. My dad's not in St. Louis. He's right here, in town. She wouldn't say who, but I've got a plan to track him down. A little detective work, you might say."

Annaleigh's eyes widened, a spark of surprise flashing across her face. She stepped forward, wrapping him in a fierce, sudden hug that stole his breath.

"John, that's huge," she said, pulling back, her voice thick with emotion. "So, you're staying? Because *he's* here?"

"No," he said, drawing her back into his arms, his hands steady on her waist. "Because you're here. I'm staying for you. It's been twenty-four years. I've got time to find him. I don't want to waste a second more not being with you."

"Well, maybe I can pitch in and help you find him."

He smiled. "Another reason why you're the best—"

"I mean, you could be walking down the sidewalk, blink, and bam! He walks right by you, and you don't even notice."

"Oh, come on, these jokes? Again?"

"I'm just saying, we make a good team. I can completely see the world around us, you shoot things indiscriminately..."

"My God, Annaleigh—"

" ...together we can be Coldwater's power couple, like Voltron."

"Like *what*?"

"Voltron. You don't know what that is? Are you not a real boy? How disappointing."

"Oh, *I* know what it is. Just not sure *you* do. You found the box of collectibles in my bedroom, didn't you?"

"A long time ago, yeah. A girl can snoop, can't she? I thought it was cute that you kept toys from your childhood."

"They're collectibles."

"Keep telling yourself that—"

"For the record," he interjected, brows raised, "you and I are not five robot lions. But, us? A couple?"

"A *power* couple."

"I like the sound of that, as long as we use our power for good, like jailing anyone who runs a stop sign."

She laughed, a soft, bubbling snicker, and wrapped her arms tighter around him. Her cheek brushed his as her whisper tickled his ear, warm and intimate.

"You may not know, but your mom's been telling me about you since I first met her. It's why I felt like I knew you already, before you even came home." She eased back, cheeks flushing a deeper pink, her gaze dipping briefly, then meeting his again. "I fell in love with you before I even met you."

John's breath caught, the shadowy rings in his vision pulsing like a heartbeat. Her words settled deep into him. He didn't have a witty reply ready. She'd captured his heart, but his head wasn't quite ready to echo. He grinned, sidestepping the weight of her confession.

"That's good, because you're stuck with me now. You and me, keeping Coldwater honest. Together."

Her smile blazed, eyes sparkling with unguarded joy.

"I can't wait to see you in the courtroom. Your only obstacle is the bar exam."

A flicker of knowing passed through her gaze, her lips softening as she caught his careful dodge of her revelation. She didn't press, her warmth undimmed, as if trusting time would bridge the gap.

"Well," John said, his tone light and teasing, a glint in his eye, "after I do pass it—and get a higher score than you, that is—there might be a slight wrinkle. My attention at work might be a bit divided from now on."

Annaleigh tilted her head, a playful challenge in her eyes as she leaned closer, her fingers tracing the edge of his collar.

"Divided? What does that mean? No more secrets between us, John," she said, soft but firm. "Not after everything."

He grinned, leaning in until his lips brushed her ear, his whisper low and warm.

"It's not a secret, just a surprise. You'll find out soon enough. And, it'll be worth the wait."

Her eyes danced with delight, a sultry smile building on her lips.

She closed the distance, pressing a long, lingering kiss to his mouth, her hands sliding to his shoulders. With a gentle tug, she led him toward the bedroom and swung the door shut.

THANK YOU

Thank you so much for reading my debut novel!

I'm beyond grateful that you took a chance on
Tunnel Vision. I truly hope it swept you into the
shadowy corners of Coldwater, Missouri.

This is the first step in the exciting journey
through Coldwater's stories.

From chilling mysteries to tender tales of love and loss,
each story will weave the charm of this
small, southern town through different eras.

Coldwater has many more tales to tell.
I can't wait to share them with you.

Stay tuned for more adventures in this anthology series!

For book and series info, updates, and more, visit
www.drywrites.com

www.ingramcontent.com/pod-product-compliance
Lightning Source LLC
Chambersburg PA
CBHW071232250626

47163CB00001B/148